Books by Will Wight

CRADLE

Unsouled

Soulsmith

Blackflame

THE TRAVELER'S GATE TRILOGY

House of Blades

The Crimson Vault

City of Light

The Traveler's Gate Chronicles

THE ELDER EMPIRE

Of Sea & Shadow

Of Dawn & Darkness

Of Kings & Killers
(forthcoming)

Of Shadow & Sea

Of Darkness & Dawn

Of Killers & Kings
(forthcoming)

UNSOULED

CRADLE : VOLUME ONE

WILL WIGHT

HIDDEN **GNOME** PUBLISHING

ISBN 978-0-9896717-6-7 (print edition)

www.WillWight.com

will@willwight.com

twitter.com/willwight

To Devin, who reads as many web novels as I do.

CHAPTER ONE

INFORMATION REQUESTED: THE SPIRITUAL ORIGIN TEST OF SACRED VALLEY.

BEGINNING REPORT...

Twice a year, the clans of Sacred Valley test the spirits of their children. Boys and girls of six, seven, even eight summers line up before their clan's elders. They wear clothes too formal for them: layered robes of muted color for the boys, intricate shadesilk wraps for the girls. Parents line the walls nearby, anxious to hear the nature of their children laid bare.

One by one, the children step before their clan's First Elder. He holds a shallow bowl, twice as wide as a dinner plate, that contains nothing more than still water. But it is not water, the parents know. It is madra, raw power of spirit, purified and distilled. The material from which souls are made.

The first girl in line dips her hand into the bowl, shocked at the cold. A trickle of something runs out of her core, something she's never felt before, and the liquid *changes*.

For her, the madra sticks to her hand, surrounding her fingers like a tight glove. The First Elder smiles, gives her a wooden badge marked with a shield, and declares the nature of her spirit. She has the soul of an Enforcer, a guardian, and will use her great strength to protect the clan. The madra returns to the bowl as the girl returns to her parents. She carries the badge with her.

The water flees from the next boy's hand, as though his presence pushes it away. He looks to the First Elder, horrified that he has somehow failed this test, but there can be no failure here. He is given a wooden badge marked with an arrow.

Each child in line sees one of four responses: the water clings, or it retreats, or it rises, or it freezes. They receive badges accordingly. Shields for Enforcers, who protect the clan from its enemies with strength of arms. Arrows for Strikers, who attack their rivals from a distance. Scepters for Rulers, who bend the powers of heaven and earth. And hammers for Forgers, whose techniques create weapons and wealth for the clan. All things in Sacred Valley can be divided in four.

And Lindon, of the Wei clan and the family Shi, knows which of the four he wants.

Hammer, he begs the heavens as he steps up for his turn at the bowl. More than anything, he wants to follow his mother as a Soulsmith, creating wondrous and magical items from madra. Molding the stuff of spirits and Remnants. *Please, give me a hammer.*

He's done his research, and he knows he needs the water to freeze. It's traditionally considered bad luck to tell children what to expect on the day of their test, but his mother considers ignorance a greater threat than misfortune.

"Wei Shi Lindon," the First Elder intones, as Lindon moves forward. The elder stands thin and straight, like a polished walking stick, with a wispy beard that stretches down to the floor. "Stretch forth your hand, and let your spirit be known."

Lindon's mother tenses behind him, but he doesn't look at her. He focuses on the bowl of madra.

Chanting *freeze, freeze, freeze* in his head, Lindon places his fingers into the bowl. It's colder than he expected, which excites him at first, because the water must already be freezing.

But the liquid doesn't grow cold, it doesn't solidify. It sits there, placid and undisturbed.

The elder's white eyebrows draw together into one solid line. He leans over the bowl, his own badge—of polished green jade, bearing the same hammer that Lindon hopes to earn—dangling over the bowl. Impatiently, he seizes Lindon's wrist and lifts it free. Natural water would have clung to Lindon's skin, but this madra only imitates water. Nothing sticks. His hand emerges clean and dry.

As though dunking laundry in a tub, the elder moves Lindon's hand in and out. A sick feeling bubbles up in Lindon's stomach as he realizes something has gone wrong.

Over to the side, his mother holds a whispered conversation with another elder. The adults are whispering now, and that never means anything good.

"There is no affinity to his spirit," the First Elder says at last. "He is empty. Unsouled."

Lindon glances to his mother, who has gone utterly pale. He's never heard this word before, Unsouled, but it doesn't sound like anything good. At seven, he's old enough to piece the core of the truth together. He won't get a badge.

But they're *right there.*

"Which badge do I get, honored elder?" he asks politely, as though he doesn't understand.

The First Elder glares at the boy. "You don't deserve these badges, Shi Lindon." No clan name. He must be angry, but Lindon knows that if you pretend to ignore an adult's anger, it often goes away.

"If you don't have one for me, I could just..." Lindon reaches out for the hammer-marked badge of a Forger, but the First Elder smacks his hand down.

"These are not *for* you!"

"Can't I pick one?" It makes perfect sense to Lindon. The bowl tells them which badge to pick, and the bowl hadn't said anything. So Lindon might as well choose.

If he had a badge, maybe his mother wouldn't look so scared. He doesn't know what it meant to go without a badge. Everybody has one.

The First Elder signals to one of his subordinates. "We will have a badge made for you, Shi Lindon. To show the world what you are."

What you are. Not *who.*

"Wei Shi Seisha, I suggest you take your son to the next testing. Perhaps the heavens will choose to have mercy on him then." Seisha, Lindon's mother, draws him to her waist protectively as the elder continues. "Until such time as they do, he will be Unsouled."

Lindon's mother sweeps him out of the hall, riding on a wave of whispered comments from relatives in the clan. She hides him with her body until they escape.

"Why didn't I get a badge?" he asked, when they were free.

"Because the heavens wish to shame us." Her voice is grim, and here Lindon learns his spirit is something shameful. Until he earns a badge, he will continue bringing shame to his clan.

So he needs a badge.

Six months later, at the next test, he smears a drop of his mother's blood on his palm. The lingering madra there makes the water stir, just for a second, before it returns to its placid stillness.

He is tested again at eight years old, and this time he comes prepared. He sneaks into the hall through the shadows, scratching a crude circle of runes on the bottom of the table in the hall. He copies it carefully out of one of his mother's books. The next morning, when his turn for the test comes, he runs a trickle of madra—the bare amount he can control, as an untrained eight-year-old—into the script.

The water in the bowl shakes, which should earn him a scepter badge. Not the hammer he hopes for, but he couldn't think of a way to freeze the water. Any badge will be fine; any soul is better than none.

In the end, it is not only the water that shakes. The bowl shakes as well, and the table with it. It takes the First Elder only a moment to glance under the tablecloth and discover the sabotage.

The elder expected this, and has brought a badge for Lindon.

It has a symbol in the middle, but not a hammer.

The badge looks the same as all the others, smooth six-sided medallions of soft wood, but there's no picture at the center. No arrow, no scepter, no shield, no hammer. Just a symbol that Lindon recognizes from his mother's lessons, a word in the old language. It means 'empty.'

Empty like Lindon is inside, the elder tells him.

As the other children grow, they leave behind their wooden badges. Their mastery over madra, their skill in the sacred arts, increases day by day. The earliest among them reaches the Copper stage at nine, upgrading his badge accordingly. The latest is thirteen.

At fifteen, Wei Shi Lindon is the only one who still has his original badge. Still wooden, still empty.

Every half a year, when the children have finished their test, Lindon slips in and judges his own spirit again. Every time, he hopes the heavens will finally have mercy on him, as his mother once said. He's tried seventeen times now.

The water has yet to move.

SUGGESTED TOPIC: CLAN CULTURE OF SACRED VALLEY. CONTINUE?

DENIED, REPORT COMPLETE.

CHAPTER TWO

Lindon looked up into the purple leaves of the orus tree. This one *felt* right—he was calmer somehow, standing in the shade of this particular tree, as though it exuded an aura of peace. Wizened white fruit waited among the leaves, far out of reach, and he sensed an ancient eternity behind the gnarled bark of the trunk.

Or maybe that was his imagination.

He raised his hammer and chisel, carving away the outer layer of bark. Then, with utmost care, he chiseled a simple rune into the soft wood.

When he finished, he compared the symbol he'd left in the tree to the tablet his mother had given him. He wasn't much of a scriptor, but he could at least copy simple scripts, and this particular circle should glow if carved into an ancestral tree. So long as he copied the runes perfectly.

There were seven runes in this script, and he carefully began chipping away at the second. This was the twenty-fifth tree he'd found and tested over the last three days, ever since his mother had found out there was a tree somewhere in the forest that was about to advance. The Fallen Leaf School kept a monopoly on most trees with any possibility to produce a spirit-fruit, but Lindon had a chance to beat them to this one. As long as he worked quickly.

Plants had to live much longer to advance than animals did. If a fox or a turtle survived their first century, they would absorb enough vital aura from the world around them to ascend into sacred beasts. These animals cycled madra, advanced in power, and left Remnants just as humans did. The oldest of them could even speak, and legends said some could take human forms.

Plants did the same, but it took several times as long. Some trees had to stay undisturbed for five hundred years or more before they absorbed enough vital aura to develop a rudimentary spirit, and they would never learn to speak. The orus tree he was looking for had lived at least three centuries, and was on the cusp of ascension.

Centuries of vital aura concentrated in the wood would nurture its fruit, giving it a potent spiritual power. Even sacred artists at the Iron or Jade stage would pay a small fortune for such an advantage. For Lindon...he only dared to imagine it. This spirit-fruit might strengthen him enough to make up for whatever his soul lacked at birth.

Before he knew it, he'd finished the script circle. With wary hope he watched his handiwork, rough symbols in pale wood.

Several breaths later, the runes remained dull and lifeless. This was always the worst part. Had the script failed because there was no madra in the wood to fuel it, or because he'd made some mistake?

With a sigh, he looped the hammer and chisel back onto his belt, picking up the bottle that was his day's supply of water. A few out-of-season orus fruits had been his only meals, but he couldn't take the time to travel all the way back to the Wei clan for more food. He'd be fine for a few days.

As he took his first step away from the tree, a flash caught his eye. Lindon scanned the depths of the forest first, looking to see where the light had come from. It might be the sun reflecting off a piece of metal, maybe a forgotten tool or coin.

The script flickered again, sending out a spark, and this time Lindon saw it clearly. The light was dim, and it guttered like a candle in the wind, but there was no mistake: his circle had worked. He'd found an ancestral tree.

Among the tree's purple leaves, a lone speck of white dangled from the highest branch: a single fruit. A normal orus fruit was like a pure white peach, and grew only in Sacred Valley. Lindon had grown up eating them in everything from pies to juice, but it seemed the outside world considered them delicacies. They had no special properties, only a unique flavor.

Fruit from an ancestral orus tree looked no different, but a bite would deliver him years' worth of purified vital aura that he could process into madra. He wanted to claw his way up the bark, but the nearest branch was far too high to reach. He should come back with his sister, or at least a ladder. If only he could find his way back here before the Fallen Leaf disciples did.

Lindon was still staring up into the tree when something shook the underbrush to his left. Seconds later, a snowfox darted out of the bush and froze, examining him.

With pure white fur and three tails waving in the air, the snowfox was as unique to Sacred Valley as the orus tree. The symbol of Lindon's Wei clan was the White Fox, in honor of this valley's snowfoxes. Or rather, one snowfox in particular.

Like Lindon, this fox was miles north of his home. It gazed at him for another breath before something larger crunched closer, and it darted off.

A young man emerged from the woods, hair mussed and skin covered in scratches. A copper badge hung pinned to the right side of his chest, and he wore a jacket lined with white fox-fur.

Lindon knew him. Wei Mon Teris, a member of his clan a year younger than Lindon. He was a threat.

"Cousin Teris," Lindon greeted him, bowing formally with two fists pressed together. "This one is honored to see you here."

"Out of the way!" Teris shouted, bowling past Lindon. Behind him, another young man and a young woman followed. Both of them were fourteen- or fifteen-year-old members of the Wei clan, and both of them Coppers.

Lindon's wooden badge hung heavy on his chest, but to hide it would be to accept his shame. He stayed bowed over his fists as they ran past him.

Deliberately casual, he backed up against the tree. If they saw the script shining, they would ask him what it was for. His only chance to take the fruit was to keep them occupied with something else.

He cursed the fate that had led three members of his clan here, so far from home. At least they had ignored him, continuing their hunt for the fox.

Which was, strictly speaking, illegal.

Just when he thought they'd left for good, he heard footsteps approaching once again.

Lindon grabbed his pack, stuffing his few belongings inside, and started running. He had hoped they would leave him alone, overlooking them according to their usual habit, but he wasn't even lucky enough for that.

Nor was he lucky enough to make it three steps before Teris caught him.

Upon reaching the Copper stage of the sacred arts, one's spirit opened. Teris could harvest the vital aura of the world, processing it into his own madra. He could use that power to fuel his body, so when he grabbed onto Lindon's elbow, there was no possibility of resistance.

Lindon came up short like a dog on the end of its leash, but he kept a smile on his face. "Cousin Teris, how can this one serve you?"

Teris wasn't tall enough to look Lindon in the eye, so he spat at his feet. "We've hunted that three-tailed snowfox for a day and a night. Thanks to *you*, we might lose it."

"Excuse my ignorance, Cousin, but has Elder Whisper blessed this hunt?"

Teris' ugly look was the only confirmation Lindon needed. Elder Whisper did occasionally allow the hunting of snowfoxes, but only under carefully controlled conditions. He most certainly would not tolerate three young Coppers running down a snowfox at the foot of Yoma Mountain.

Whisper was the reason the symbol of the Wei clan was a white fox.

But even *his* eyes couldn't see everything. Myth said the meat of a snowfox would strengthen the madra of those following the Path of the White Fox, as virtually everyone in the Wei clan did.

There was no logical reason it should be true, as far as Lindon knew, but many believed it. So Elder Whisper had therefore banned all hunting of snowfoxes without his explicit permission.

Teris formed a fist, and the air around it rippled as he gathered his power. "Are you being disrespectful, Unsouled? I don't like that look."

Lindon's heart tightened. Teris was only Copper, but the shield on his badge showed he was an Enforcer: born to focus his madra into physical strength. He *could* kill Lindon with a blow, even if he probably wouldn't. Murdering someone below your level was an unspeakable shame. If Teris killed him, and the news made it back to the clan, Teris would remain a dishonored pariah for the rest of his days.

But there was something uniquely terrifying about facing down someone capable of caving in his ribs with a punch. No one was close enough to save him.

Lindon bowed again, and spoke even more humbly. "This one begs your pardon, Copper Cousin. Please, this one has gathered a few chips together, and it would be an honor if you would take them."

He glanced up to gauge if Teris would take the bribe, but the Copper boy was looking past Lindon. Something had grabbed his attention.

And unless the snowfox had returned, there was only one thing back there. The ancestral tree.

Though it was a cool spring day, sweat gathered ran down Lindon's back.

"What is this script, Unsouled?"

"This one is practicing his scripting, Copper Cousin. At the request of this one's mother."

Hopefully invoking his mother would grant him some mercy; unlike Lindon, Wei Shi Seisha provided a valuable function to the clan. She was widely respected among all the families.

Though her reputation wasn't the only thing she'd left him.

Lindon's parents were...statuesque. They had both once been famous fighters, and he had the misfortune of inheriting their physique with none of their actual strength. He was an inch taller than anyone else his age, slightly broader across the shoulders, and some young men took that as a challenge.

Teris took a step closer, back straight as he strained for height. "Get your eyes off me. Look at the ground."

Lindon bowed even more deeply, hoping Teris would see it as a cowardly show of fear. Which it was.

Teris turned from him in disgust, which counted as a success, but unfortunately he returned his attention to the tree. "You've ruined my hunt, Unsouled. That should cost you."

Lindon took his eyes from the forest floor to see Teris drawing his fist back. "Stop!" Lindon shouted, but it wasn't soon enough.

Teris had not yet reached Iron, so his body wasn't actually any stronger than Lindon's. But Enforcers bolstered their strength with madra. When Teris drew on his Copper madra, he would be stronger than other sacred artists of his stage, tougher, and faster. His punch landed on the ancient fruit tree, shattering the bark and leaving the imprint of his fist in the wood. The impact echoed through the forest, smashing Lindon's script.

Teris stepped away. Behind him, the tree bent in the middle. Deceptively slowly, it splintered and fell apart.

Icy cold shivered through Lindon's body, and it had nothing to do with the loss of the fruit. His odds of survival had just plummeted sharply.

"You idiot," Lindon half-whispered. Teris froze.

"What did you say?"

Lindon dropped to his knees, hurriedly scratching symbols into the dirt. His tablet didn't cover this script, so he only hoped he remembered correctly. "You've killed us both. That was an *ancestral tree.*"

Teris frowned at him, then looked at the broken trunk. Precious seconds passed as he digested the news.

Lindon had almost finished the circle, scratching frantically at the dirt with his finger. "Get behind the circle!" he shouted.

Then the Remnant rose from the tree's corpse.

It was made from lines of vivid purple, like color sketched on the world by a celestial painter. The Remnant was thin and free of details like bark or leaves, as though it were the purple skeleton of the tree that once had been.

In reality, it was more like a ghost. A spirit without a vessel.

Remnants were constructions of pure madra, freed from their physical bodies. Whenever a sacred artist of enough power died, he left his soul behind him as a living force.

If Lindon died, his madra would dissipate into the vital aura in the atmosphere. The same would go for ordinary animals, or even Copper-level sacred artists. But sacred beasts and ancestral trees were on another level altogether. It would take an Iron- or Jade-stage practitioner to face one of these spirits in combat.

And before Teris could react to what he was seeing, the purple tree-Remnant clenched a branch like a massive fist and slammed it into the boy's midsection. The young Copper flipped through the air before landing facedown on the forest floor.

Wei Mon Teris' clothes were torn where the tree-Remnant had struck him, but he was on his feet and stumbling away within seconds. Even in a possibly lethal situation like this one, Lindon had time for a brief flash of jealousy. A blow like that would have killed or crippled *him*, but Teris must have been drawing on his madra. He scurried off like a roach.

The Copper ran deeper in the woods without a glance back, rushing in the direction his friends had gone. Lindon fought the urge to hurry, finishing the last rune in the circle, knowing that precision was his defense rather than speed.

It was impossible to calmly take his time as the Remnant lumbered over to him, a skeletal ghost of purple madra in the shape of a leafless tree. Its branches swayed as it lurched forward in a pathetic parody of a man's walk.

Lindon put his thumb to the final rune and closed his eyes.

He visualized his madra as a blue-white light, moving along lines like veins all through his body. He sped the flow of the energy, cycling it according to the Foundation technique he'd learned as a child. This technique was supposed to eventually become the basis for an entire Path, but Lindon had never progressed further. Any child in the Wei clan could do as much with their madra as Lindon.

But he *could* activate scripts.

The circle flared to life at the touch of his power, each rune burning with the same blue-white energy he'd seen in his mind.

When the Remnant loomed over the script, reaching out a long branch like a grasping hand, it passed through the light easily. No barrier stopped its movement. Lindon hopped backwards, out of the circle, and the Remnant stepped forward to follow him.

Lindon's limitations were many, but he knew them well. He could never empower a script to block the Remnant of an ancestral tree directly, at least not with a script as crude as this one. But he *could* draw the Remnant in. Once inside, the spirit's own madra would power the circle.

And the Remnant was much stronger than he was.

The script's light turned from blue to purple, and the tree's branches bristled into spikes. It tried to step away from the circle, to reach for Lindon, but it was forced to stop short.

Sweat soaked Lindon's clothes, and he flopped to the ground well out of the Remnant's reach. He caught his breath, shivering at the close call. If he'd been a moment slower...

Then something caught his eye that drove all thoughts of danger from his head. On the highest of the Remnant's purple branches, a single spot of white. A spirit-fruit.

As the Remnant raged, it was not silent. Its fury sounded like snapping twigs, like the crunch of splintered logs. It was at least three times Lindon's height, crowned by that single spot of white.

The fruit hung from the same place on the Remnant as it had on the tree's body. Now the fruit was forged of flawless white madra, glowing on the spirit like a crown. The physical reality was still nestled among the branches on the forest floor, shriveled and pathetic.

Still thinking, Lindon walked over to the withered material fruit and plucked it, slipping it into the cumbersome pack he carried on his back. He was no longer wary of the Remnant; if it were powerful enough to break his script, it already would have. Now he had something else to worry about.

If he could retrieve the Remnant version of this fruit, his mother could bind it back to its physical vessel. She was a Forger and a Soulsmith, a specialist in manipulating madra as a physical material. She could turn this lifeless vegetation back into a powerful spirit-fruit, good as new.

If he wanted that to work, he'd need to bring the Remnant fruit back with him. And it was attached to the head of a crazed spirit monster.

He wished he had a better plan.

With reluctance, he reached into the shadesilk pockets

of his pack and withdrew a glimmering gemstone the size of his smallest fingernail. It was hollow on the inside, like a stoppered flask carved for a doll, though this one was filled with a few drops of blue light that danced through the crystal's facets.

When there's only one road forward, take it with a smile. It had taken him weeks to fill up this crystal flask, which was capable of storing and purifying madra. He hated to waste weeks of his time here, but if he could restore the orus fruit, it would be worth more than a year of cycling. If he failed, though...

He slowed his breathing, cycling his spirit in a rhythm with his steady, even breath. Lindon placed the tiny flask, glowing blue-white, at the very edge of the Remnant's reach.

The purple tree turned to him as though it could smell the energy, silence falling over the woods. Lindon hurried to the side, but the Remnant's attention was all on the miniature crystal.

This was the main way his family used crystal flasks. The crystals had other uses, but for a Soulsmith, baiting a Remnant was by far the most practical purpose. All Remnants hungered for pure human madra, which could become virtually anything. On such a diet, a Remnant could slowly gain consciousness.

As the tree lunged, so did Lindon. He ran for the circle, leaping as soon as the tree bent down.

He might not have the strength of a true sacred artist, but Lindon still trained his body the same as the rest of his clan. He landed on the back of the Remnant, clutching its branches.

It felt more like clinging to slick, oily bone than wood, but he didn't waste time examining the sensation. He reached out, grasping for the glowing white fruit, hanging like a full moon.

A branch slammed into his arm with the force of a kicking horse, and he heard something crack.

The impact knocked him off the Remnant's back, and he had the presence of mind to roll away from the script as he fell. If he kicked one of the runes, the circle would break, and he would likely die.

But the Remnant didn't seem to have noticed him. It tossed the empty crystal flask to the ground, having finished its brief meal, and then stilled. The wind was the only sound now, and the spirit looked like nothing more than a thin purple tree planted in the earth.

Lindon saw all this through tears of pain. He clenched his jaw to keep from screaming and potentially drawing the Remnant's attention back to him. His forearm was broken, his hand dangling loosely, and it felt as though the weight of his own flesh would tear the arm apart. The pain kept him on his knees, drawing huge breaths in his lungs.

He forced a smile through his agony. In his uninjured fist, he gripped a shining white fruit.

It didn't feel like a natural orus fruit any more than its source had felt like a natural tree. Rather, it squished in his hand like jelly, but as soon as he stopped applying force it snapped back into form. He wasn't sure what aspect this madra held, or even how powerful it would be, once his mother restored it.

But he'd made it.

He tucked the Forged fruit into his pack next to its physical counterpart, plucking the transparent crystal flask and tossing it in next. Now he was only faced with the task of traveling a dozen miles through the wilderness, on foot, with a broken arm and a bulky pack.

Triumph made the journey easy.

Almost a million people called Sacred Valley home, and the Wei clan alone accounted for over a hundred thousand of those. Even so, the one resource no one lacked was space.

Each family received a generous portion of land, with a small house added on to the main complex for each member. Typically, children received their own house along with their wooden badge, as a mark of independence. Even Lindon, who could contribute nothing back to the clan, received a housing allotment inferior to no one's.

His house was made of tight-fitting orus wood, pale and smooth, roofed in purple tiles. His bed lay against the wall opposite of the hearth, in which a fire burned merrily to ward off the spring chill. He lay in his bed, broken arm splinted and tied, with a scripted ribbon wrapped around his bicep. The script twisted his madra into a basic Enforcer technique that cut off his sense of pain, but the power running through the script-circle would eventually tear the silk of the ribbon. At that point, his mother would replace it with another one.

For now, Lindon was as physically comfortable as he had ever been. He couldn't feel his arm, the fire was warm, and his bed was so soft it felt like lying on a cloud. He was used to that; his mother had packed his mattress with Forged cloud-aspect madra she'd purchased from one of her contacts. Even the Wei clan's Patriarch didn't have a better bed.

But Lindon couldn't enjoy any of it. His family was here.

The fruit now shone with the bright color of a Remnant, but it held all the wrinkles and imperfections that showed it to be real. His mother had restored it to full power in minutes. It sat on the center of Lindon's table, and the other three members of his family surrounded it like wolves circling a wounded deer.

"If I had found this years ago, I would take it," Lindon's father said. "But it's too late for me now. Kelsa will fight for us in the Seven-Year Festival, so she needs it the most."

Wei Shi Jaran had participated in the Festival before last, which had left him with a lip scarred into an eternal smirk, and a limp that required a cane. He hadn't fought since.

"It wouldn't have helped you," Lindon's mother responded. She was one of the more eye-catching figures in the Wei clan, with her long brown hair. Everyone else, including her children, had black. "This spirit-fruit only purifies energy, it won't heal you. It does nothing that months or years of regular cycling wouldn't do." Seisha scratched away at a portable slate as she spoke, her chalk pausing only rarely. Scripts wouldn't check themselves.

Her drudge hovered over her shoulder, like a rusty brown mechanical fish drifting on invisible tides. It was a Soulsmith construct, madra Forged according to a particular pattern, and it served her as a box of tools served a carpenter.

"I'm only *saying*, Seisha, that if I had gotten this early enough...who knows?"

"I do. That's not how it works."

"You know everything about the soul? All the mysteries of the sacred arts? I could have changed my Path, studied with the Fallen Leaf School, and their life techniques could have restored me. Your body is renewed when you advance to Jade."

"You're hardly more likely to advance by starting over on a different Path, even with a hypothetical elixir." She rubbed out some chalk with the heel of her hand, never looking away from her notes. Jaran's scar-enforced smirk creased into a sneer.

Lindon's sister Kelsa took over the conversation before it could devolve further, as he had known she would. "I can't do well enough for the Patriarch to notice us if I'm still a Copper. How will I fight Wei Jin Amon or Li Ten Jana without Iron strength?"

Their father snorted, crossing his arms. "That's right. There will be at least half a dozen sixteen-year-olds with iron badges already, and Kelsa should be among them. With her Path, she can give them all a surprise. I did, and I was even younger."

Kelsa nodded to her father, mostly to stop him from

drawing the story out any longer. "I'm sure I can, if fate is kind. But we still have two months, and I am already close to condensing my Iron body. It's possible I'll advance on my own before the Festival opens."

She rolled the white fruit toward herself, pulling a knife from her belt. "There's no reason I should keep it all to myself. If one of you reaches Jade, it will do more for our family than anything I can show on the Festival stage. We should split it in three."

Finally, Seisha looked up from her tablet. Her drudge whistled inquisitively, ready to be used, but she met her husband's eyes. His scowl lightened, and he nodded, eager to take part of this treasure for himself. Kelsa's blade met the skin of the fruit.

Lindon leaned forward until his bed frame creaked under him. His family turned, surprised to remember he was still there. In his own house.

"Would it be so hard to cut another piece?"

CHAPTER THREE

As Lindon sat on his bed with his numb arm in a sling, he watched his family. Around the table, they each exchanged glances.

Kelsa held up the white orus, the spirit-fruit Lindon had hunted and bled for. "Mother, can we divide it in four?"

Seisha glanced up at her drudge, but the brown shape only croaked in response. It currently looked like a toy fish floating over her shoulder, but Lindon had seen it unfold into many other forms. "We were already taking a risk with three," she said at last. "There's a limit beyond which any elixir cannot be stretched, or it is wasted."

Frustration had returned to Jaran's face. "We can't take the chance. Who knows when we'll find something like this again? Give it to Kelsa."

"No," his daughter said, cutting into the fruit. "We'll divide it as planned. It's not fair to you, Lindon, but I'll make it up to you. I'll give you my clan stipend for the next half a year, how would you like that?"

Jaran spread his hands as though presenting her idea, and Seisha returned to her slate. To them, clearly, the matter had been settled.

In fairness to his sister, Lindon had to admit that her

offer was fair. Six months of the clan's allowance to her would be a small fortune in chips for him, enough to buy lesser elixirs of his own. Maybe even a partial Path manual, so he could further his study of the sacred arts without the clan's blessing.

But those items weren't unusual. They weren't going anywhere. He could save up his own chips and buy them, if not so quickly.

This fruit was *special.* He was so far behind everyone else that he needed something out of the ordinary to catch up.

If he relied on normal means, he'd stay behind his entire life.

He nodded to her. "Gratitude. But with respect, I hunted for that on my own for three days."

"On my instruction," his mother pointed out.

"For which I am grateful. But nonetheless, the work was mine. The time was mine. I found the tree, I plucked the fruit, I fought a *Remnant* for it." He gestured to his sling. "I'll have battle scars for it! *Me!*"

Kelsa looked down at the fruit with her knife in hand, as though unsure where to cut. "I can give you eight months of chips, but any more than that, and I'm not sure I can afford to keep my garden through the winter."

"I don't want more money. I want half."

The scar at the corner of Jaran's lip made his scowl sinister instead of stern. "Think beyond *yourself.* She represents our family in the Festival. Our *clan.* The Patriarch is negotiating trade rights with the Kazan. The stronger we show ourselves, the better his position. This should be a concern for every Wei."

"But that is exactly my concern." Lindon leaned forward on the edge of his bed, radiating sincerity. "I'll be fighting among the eight-year-olds. Can you imagine the scorn if I don't take first place? Anything Kelsa accomplishes against the Irons will be overshadowed by that shame."

His father was quiet.

"Don't fight," Seisha said, reaching up and sliding her

chalk into her drudge. The floating fish absorbed it without a ripple. "The Foundation stage exhibition is a formality anyway, it's training for the real fights."

Lindon had expected this, and had prepared a counter. "And *everyone* will know why. I will forever be the Wei clan coward who ran from opponents half his age."

Jaran's frustration had become too much to hold in, and he picked up his cane, spinning it between his palms. "It doesn't matter! If I break through to Jade, or your mother does, or your sister reaches Iron, then *that* will wash away anything that happens in the children's fights." He slammed the cane down as though the matter were settled.

Gently, Kelsa shook her head. "It's a poor gamble. We're betting on possible honor against certain shame."

Those words, *certain shame*, pricked at him, but he didn't let the pain touch him. He never did. "Father, Mother, if you tell me it's likely that you will advance to the Jade stage before the Seven-Year Festival, I'll give up my claim. I don't argue that Kelsa needs to be Iron, but she's so close she doesn't need the entire thing. I have so little. To a beggar, even scraps become a feast."

His mother gave him a wry look, and Jaran's face had reddened, but neither said anything. They weren't close to Jade, as he suspected.

It was Kelsa who finally made the decision. With one clean stroke, she segmented the orus fruit in half, splitting it around the pit. "There's no honor in denying a man what he's earned. If you'd like it, Father, I'll give you my half."

Predictably, Jaran grumbled a bit but let her keep it. She walked over to hand her brother his half of the spirit-fruit.

Kelsa had gotten everything Lindon wanted in his life: the natural gifts, the favor of the clan, and the opportunity to train in sacred arts. And while she was as tall as he was, *she* didn't look like she was trying to intimidate anyone. Daily martial training left her lithe and graceful.

If she wasn't so absolutely fair about everything, Lindon might have hated her.

She handed his half of the fruit to him without malice, and even nodded to him in respect. He'd won the argument, and the Wei clan respected honorable victory.

He allowed the thrill of his prize to run through him as he took the fruit. This could be the first step of his path up. More importantly, he'd *won.*

He relished the feeling as he relished the fruit, which tingled on his tongue like a peach charged with lightning. It was gone too soon, and the shock on Kelsa's face mirrored what he was sure he showed on his own. Even in his stomach, it seemed to give off the occasional shock, sending tingling waves through his body.

"Could you describe the sensation?" their mother asked, poised to take notes.

"It definitely *feels* like it's working," Kelsa said.

Lindon put his hands to his stomach. He imagined he could feel excess energy in his fingertips. "It's like I've swallowed a thunderbolt."

Seisha had retrieved a brush and an ink jar to replace her chalk and slate, and painted notes on a scroll as fast as she could move. "Would you describe the feeling as hot or cold?"

Lindon exchanged looks with his sister. "Hot?" he said, at the same time she said, "Cold?"

"Alternating hot and cold," their mother muttered, never pausing in her writing. "Examine your core. Any changes?"

Lindon closed his eyes, visualizing his core. It sat just beneath the navel, and was where all the lines of madra connected. This was the physical location of the soul, some said, and Lindon always pictured it as a rolling ball of blue-white light.

He evened out his breathing, inhaling and exhaling in tune with the tides of his spirit. The energy flowed through his body according to his Foundation technique, the one and only sacred art he'd been allowed to learn. It allowed him to focus and purify what little madra he had, to build a foundation for...nothing at all.

He wasn't allowed to learn a Path, to harvest vital aura, so he would never advance. If he was lucky, in his later years, his innate spirit would be refined to the point that he would naturally advance to Copper. The state most people reached by age thirteen. Copper spirits were open to the vital aura of the natural world, so they could draw power from the heavens and earth to make themselves stronger. It was the true first step for any sacred arts.

"No change," he reported, the review of his lackluster destiny having dampened his excitement.

"I don't feel anything either," Kelsa confirmed. "But there's something…"

A shout came from the door. "Wei Shi Lindon, the First Elder requests your presence." It was a voice Lindon knew, but hadn't expected to hear again so soon.

He rose to his feet to answer the door, careful of his numbed arm, but Kelsa moved first. She strode over and pulled the door open.

Wei Mon Teris stood looking up at her, gawking at her presence. He was still wearing his snowfox skin, scuffed though it was, but otherwise he looked completely un-harmed by his encounter with the tree-Remnant only hours before. "Cousin Kelsa, excuse my interruption. Is your brother nearby?"

By this time, Lindon had slipped into a pair of shoes and made it to his sister's side. "Cousin Teris, I see you made it back safely."

Teris' jaw clenched. "Wei Shi Lindon. The First Elder requires your presence to review the events of the day. I'm to bring you there immediately."

"Carry our family's regrets to the First Elder," Kelsa said, "but Lindon is injured. He needs our care and attention tonight, but he would be honored to attend the First Elder at first light tomorrow."

Cradling his sling, Lindon ducked under Kelsa's arm. "How could I make the First Elder wait? My injury is noth-ing to be concerned over, just a small wound incurred in my battle against the Remnant."

Teris glared at the pointed reminder that he *hadn't* stayed and fought the monster, as honor dictated he should. In fact, as the strongest party present, Teris should have protected Lindon with his life.

Not that Lindon had ever expected as much. In his observation, honor often fled before self-preservation.

"Lead on, Cousin," Lindon said. Teris started off without another word.

The First Elder waited for them in the Clan Hall, the same place where young Wei souls were tested. Lindon had rarely seen the elder outside of it, and he seemed to have grown to fit there; his long beard matched the White Foxes on the banners, his robes jade and gold to match the pillars and tiles.

He stood in the hall as they entered, back straight, his hand on the head of a stone fox and his eyes on the golden statue of the first Wei Patriarch. He did not turn as the young men approached and dropped to their knees, bowing almost to the ground.

"Tell me what happened today, in the forest beneath Yoma."

Teris began immediately, reciting the events of the day as though he'd practiced. To Lindon's surprise, Teris stuck to an accurate retelling of events, even admitting that he and two friends had tracked a snowfox into the woods. They never actually *caught* the fox, as he hurried to clarify, and then he went on to tell how Lindon's presence spooked their game. Lindon's response angered him, and in his anger, he broke a nearby tree. He had no way of knowing the tree was sacred, and would release a Remnant.

"With my body, I took a blow that would have struck the Unsouled," Teris went on, in the furthest departure from truth so far. "When I recovered, I saw that he was defenseless, and I ran to warn my friends rather than die together with him. I do not know how he survived."

Silence fell on the Clan Hall, and still the First Elder did not turn. He stroked the fox statue's head as he thought.

"What are the words of the Wei clan?" he asked at last.

"Honor by any means," the boys recited at once. The Path of the Wei clan used madra of light and dreams to deceive their enemies...but according to the first Wei Patriarch, even deception could be used to serve honor. It was the contradiction around which the Wei clan was founded.

"There is a time when running to preserve your own life is not cowardice," the elder went on. "When the threat is so great that your death would mean nothing, then flight is no shame."

Teris let out a deep breath.

"But this was not such a threat," the First Elder said, turning around at last. His face was carved from stone harder than the statues around him. "If this Remnant failed to defeat an Unsouled at the Foundation stage, then surely a Copper sacred artist could have stood against it. Your stipend will be withheld this month, you will spend a night in isolated meditation, and at the end you will be whipped three times in front of the clan. Cowards have no place in the Valley."

Teris bowed so low that his forehead stuck to the floor, soLindon couldn't see his face, but his whispered voice was choked. "You are wise and...merciful, First Elder."

The First Elder snorted. "Report to your father, tell him what I have said, and that I allow him to add a punishment of his own if he wishes. But if I do not see you through the window of a locked room tonight, then I will make your sentence three times worse. Go now."

Teris bowed again and fled without a word.

Lindon braced himself. Part of him felt a measure of shameful glee at Teris' sentence, but he couldn't enjoy it. He knew his clan, he knew his own standing within it, and if the elder had punished an otherwise honorable Copper in front of him, it meant that there was something worse coming.

The First Elder stood over Lindon, silently judging. Weighing. Perhaps deciding which of several sentences to mete out.

If Lindon struck first, he might be able to mitigate the damage.

"This one is shamed to be here before you, Great Elder," Lindon said into the floor. "This one had no intention of interfering with the Coppers, or their hunt." Best to bring up the hunt as much as possible, to remind him that Teris and the others had been breaking Elder Whisper's rules. "This one was in search of an ancestral fruit, on behalf of his mother."

With one sharp gesture of his hand, the First Elder motioned for Lindon to get up. He scrambled gratefully to his feet.

"Did you find it?"

"Yes, First Elder."

The aura around the elder darkened, almost imperceptibly. "Did you waste it on yourself, Unsouled? I know you were tempted."

Lindon's stomach was still buzzing with trapped lightning. It was all he could do not to swallow, afraid the First Elder would take that as a sign of guilt. "It went to my older sister. I mean...this one's older sister."

The intimidating aura dispersed like clouds before the sun, and the First Elder waved irritably. "Speak freely, Shi Lindon. I've seen you in here often enough."

Lindon fought back a smile. "Yes, First Elder, but I have little to add. Cousin Teris told the story accurately."

The First Elder had the longest eyebrows of anyone Lindon had ever seen, and they shot halfway up his forehead at this. "You know what you've done wrong, then?"

That was a trap if Lindon had ever heard one. Sweat trickled down his back, and the lightning in his stomach boiled up. It would be worse luck than he deserved if the fruit made itself known *now.*

"I...was...too far from clan territory, First Elder. I know

it now. In the future, I will travel in the company of my sister. Thank you for instructing me."

The elder sighed, rubbing at his eyes with two fingers. "You found yourself in the way of three Coppers, Lindon. That was your sin."

Lindon hesitated. "I am sorry for it, Elder. But I could not have known they would run past this one tree in the forest. Can I predict where lightning will strike in a storm?"

The First Elder slapped his hand down on the statue of the white fox, sending a sharp *crack* through the air and leaving a fissure in the fox's skull. In a blinding flash of madra, he repaired it instantly. "You could not have *known?* If a party of Kazan dogs had stumbled on you instead, or the honorable disciples of the Fallen Leaf, they could have killed you as easily as Teris broke that tree. Only honor might restrain them, and honor is a poor hook on which to hang a man's life. And if they did choose to kill you, *our* clan would have to apologize. For inconveniencing them."

Lindon started to respond, but he had nothing to say. Shame blotted out his thoughts, shame that burned worse than the fruit's lightning, shame that crawled along every inch of his bones and ate him from the inside like a colony of ants.

The First Elder's tone softened, but his words didn't. "If a sacred artist with an iron badge burned down your home with you inside, at most I could give him a punishment like I gave Teris. For the dishonor of picking on the weak. He could not be executed, or maimed, or even fined, because in taking your life he cost the clan nothing."

Lindon squeezed his eyes shut and bowed, hoping that would cover the tears he fought down. Weeping like a child would only shame him. He shifted his injured arm in its sling, pretending his wince came from sudden pain.

"I do not say this to wound you further, Lindon. The heavens can show great cruelty in a man's birth. But the foundation of any Path is learning to accept the world as it is, not as you wish or even observe it to be. Every slight, every insult, every injustice in your future will be *your fault.* Your fate is not fair, but it is true. What should you have done today?"

"I should have returned home as soon as I saw Wei Mon Teris," Lindon whispered.

"Wrong! You should *never have left."* The First Elder stabbed a finger at him, and it skewered him as thoroughly as a sword. "You have a place in the clan archives. Let that be your turtle's shell. Help your mother with her work, or stay in the archives, and fade into the background. Humility and anonymity are your protection." The elder sighed, his shoulders slumping. "They are the only armor I can give you."

Tucked away in the corner, on a stand designed for the purpose, waited the testing bowl. Seventeen times, he'd placed his hand in that bowl. Seventeen failures, in a test no one failed.

He returned his gaze to the floor.

"Yes, First Elder."

The elder sighed again. His slippers moved as he paced back and forth, in a greater display of emotion than Lindon had seen from him before. "I won't punish you. Your fate, and the injury to your arm, are punishment enough. But if I am seen to do nothing, the Mon family will hold you responsible for Teris. As such, I would like you to feed Elder Whisper tonight."

Lindon looked up sharply, a strange hope filling him along with the storm in his belly. "Gratitude, First Elder."

The First Elder shook his head. "Maybe he can give you the help that I cannot."

●

Most buildings in the Wei clan were purple and white, reflecting the purple leaves of the orus tree and the white fur of the snowfox. From a distance, the clan was a collage of those two colors. Only one tower stood out: a needle of white, so tall that it seemed thin, rising above the purple-roofed sea like the mast of a great ship. It had been made of white stone in the age of the clan's founders, and it was one of the most prominent landmarks in all of Sacred Valley.

It was filled with stairs.

There were only two rooms in Whisper's tower: one at the bottom, and one at the top. In between was nothing more than a spiraling staircase, thousands of steps that represented a monotonous journey to the clan's oldest ally.

Lindon took a deep breath as he faced the first step. The founders had obviously designed this tower with sacred artists in mind. And why shouldn't they? Everyone practiced sacred arts, so everyone had a madra-reinforced constitution greater than their bodies would normally allow.

Except for Lindon, who had to face this staircase with little more than the strength in his legs. He could cycle his madra to prevent exhaustion, to restore some stamina when his feet began to flag, but he would run out halfway through if he didn't ration his spiritual strength. A Copper would have the madra to climb these stairs in half the time and arrive in perfect condition.

Without further hesitation, Lindon began the long march up the stairs. He carried a bucket filled with jade-scaled river carp: Elder Whisper's twice-daily meal.

Normally Lindon would never have been chosen for this task. It was easier to ask any Copper-stage artist, and they would finish faster with less effort. Today, Lindon's eagerness carried him through the hour it took him to reach the top. The First Elder's words had left him feeling trapped, doomed, cursed to a lifetime of insignificance and weakness.

If anyone could tell him how to break free, Whisper could.

Elder Whisper had joined the clan founders to create the Wei clan, dominating the native Remnants to carve out a section of wilderness in Sacred Valley. He had created the Path of the White Fox, the most common Path in the entire clan, and used its powers to control and assimilate several lesser clans. Not even the current Wei Patriarch was as honored as Elder Whisper.

So when Lindon finally reached the door at the top of the stairs, he set his heavy bucket down and took a moment to catch his breath. He couldn't appear before Elder Whisper panting like a dog.

To open the lock, he had to brace it in the crook of his sling-wrapped arm and twist with his free hand. Both the lock and the key were heavy bronze, each bigger than his head. Why they had to use such giant devices to secure Whisper's door, he couldn't imagine. They didn't appear scripted, only heavy. Surely a normal lock and key would work just as well.

Once he finally wrestled the lock open, he had to lean his shoulder against the slab of a door, forcing a way inside with his whole strength.

He pulled the bucket inside and let the door slam shut once again. The inside of the door was covered by a scripted mirror—part of a spirit-trap, designed to keep Remnants and sacred beasts imprisoned by their own madra. While the door was open, the circle was incomplete, and Whisper could sneak out.

If he did, he would find himself stuck on the stairs, unable to cross the closed circle at the tower's base. As far as Lindon knew, Whisper had never even tried to escape. He enjoyed a respected position, intervened in clan affairs as much as he wanted, and the elders released him from the tower on formal occasions. As a boy, Lindon had wondered why Whisper was trapped in the first place, but it was simply one more part of the way things were.

Lindon had heard several myths about Whisper's imprisonment, but never one he believed. The truth was likely beyond his comprehension.

Elder Whisper sat on his haunches, watching the clan below through an open floor-to-ceiling archway. A line of script engraved in the floor prevented him from simply leaping out and running down the side of the tower.

Cold wind, crisp with the scents of a spring night, ruffled his white fur. Five bushy tails lashed behind him, tracing arcane patterns in the air that reminded Lindon of a script.

"You have eaten of a wonderful fruit," said the sacred fox. "Tell me the story."

Lindon dropped to his knees next to the bucket of fish, bowing respectfully. He was more conscious than ever of the flickering lightning in his core. "This one found an ancestral orus tree, Elder. This one was fortunate enough to obtain its fruit after it was destroyed."

Whisper turned slightly, fixing Lindon with one jet-black eye. "There is more."

CHAPTER FOUR

Naturally, Lindon concealed nothing before Elder Whisper. "This one engaged in a small conflict with a Copper practitioner from the clan. In the battle, the tree was broken, and a Remnant released. This one was able to protect himself."

The Wei clan's signature Path of the White Fox had been created by—and named for—the very sacred beast that stood before him now. They produced madra that deceived the senses, that created illusions, that twisted light and sound. And Elder Whisper was the Path's original master.

A second five-tailed snowfox stepped out from the first, like an image walking away from a mirror. This second body dipped its muzzle into the bucket of fish even as the first continued speaking. "The Foundation stage defends himself from a Remnant, and leaves with its prize. Commendable."

Lindon bowed deeply. "This one is unworthy of such praise."

Neither Whisper responded. One continued devouring the fish, while the other examined Lindon with eyes of opaque darkness. On any other day, Lindon would take his leave now.

But the First Elder had thought that Whisper might be able to help him. "This one humbly begs a question of you, Elder."

A fuzzy snout slid over his shoulder, cold lips brushing past his cheek. He focused his entire body on remaining still, on *not* trembling, as a third Elder Whisper rested his head on Lindon's shoulder.

"Speak," the third sacred beast said quietly.

"This one is not allowed to follow a Path of the sacred arts."

"Why should the Wei clan water a tree that will never bear fruit?" Elder Whisper asked, simultaneously watching Lindon from three directions.

"An Unsouled may never have a family of his own, for fear of passing on his deformity to a new generation." Lindon couldn't keep bitterness from his voice. "He cannot practice sacred arts, and so cannot travel or engage in battle. This one cannot rise if he does not bring honor to the clan, but he is not permitted to do so."

Elder Whisper and his two reflections began to pace around him, three five-tailed snowfoxes each bigger than a man. Lindon shivered as the fox's head slid back away from his shoulder, but kept himself in place out of discipline. The elder was still an ancient sacred beast, mysterious and feral, and if he devoured Lindon no one in the clan would make a sound of protest.

"What are the sacred arts?" the elder asked, his murmur coming from three directions at once.

"The path of refining a spirit and pursuing connection to all of creation," Lindon recited. There were many correct answers to Elder Whisper's question, and any child of Sacred Valley could recount them on command.

"When does that path reach its end?"

This answer was more vague, but Lindon answered as best he could. "When an artist's spirit is as pure as gold." Gold was the final stage of any sacred artist's Path.

A tail whipped the back of Lindon's skull, leaving a sharp sting. "Is a Gold practitioner one with heaven and earth? Does he control everything in creation? Can he create worlds and break them at will?"

The obvious answer was 'no,' but Elder Whisper would not be satisfied by the obvious. In humility, Lindon fell to his knees and pressed his face to the floor, despite the groan of pain from his broken arm. "This one is unworthy to even guess at such profound answers, Elder."

The fox's chuckle softly filled the room as his three bodies continued to circle. "There is no profound answer here, young human. The answer is 'no.'"

Hesitantly, Lindon raised his head. "Pardon this one's ignorance, but...does the Path not end with Gold?"

"The spirit has no limit, nor does the sky. How could a true Path have an ending? If you studied until the end of the universe, you would still have not touched true comprehension. The Path of the White Fox is but one among countless others, and none reach the end."

"This one thanks you for the enlightenment, Elder Whisper," Lindon said, though he still didn't fully understand what the sacred beast meant to teach him.

All three foxes paused, side by side, regarding Lindon. "When a traveler cannot find a path, sometimes he must *make his own.*"

Understanding washed over Lindon, and he bowed again out of gratitude. The shame that had been exposed by the First Elder's words ignited like tinder until determination blazed alongside the lightning in his belly.

One of the Whispers blinked out of reality, leaving one staring Lindon in the eye and one feasting on fish. "Remember. Cutting a road through a forest is always harder than following one already cut."

Lindon straightened. "If all it takes is work, Elder Whisper, this one will not fail you."

"Fate is not fair, but it is just. Hard work is never in vain...even when it does not achieve what you wished." With those words, the five-tailed fox faded away, leaving only the real Elder Whisper enjoying his meal.

Though the elder had clearly dismissed him, Lindon had to show his respect before leaving. He bowed deeply three times to Elder Whisper's back, taking the empty bucket from the elder's last feeding and returning down the stairs.

The trip down was no easier on Lindon's legs than the trip up, and his broken arm had begun to ache even through his mother's script, but he spent the time in contemplation. The First Elder had spoken of Lindon's situation as though he should give up and accept his fate, but Whisper had given him the opposite advice.

Lindon knew which he preferred. The First Elder would have him wait at home, safe and relatively content, but he would die having accomplished nothing. The fruit's power tingled in his core, begging him to process it, urging him to take the first step on a Path of his own devising.

When he returned home, his family was gone. He sat cross-legged in the center of his house, focused entirely inward, cycling his madra with a greater intensity than ever before.

He felt as though he should make some breakthrough tonight, as though Elder Whisper's words should trigger some understanding that would take him to a higher level and allow him to comprehend some deep truth. Or perhaps the spirit-fruit would show more of an effect than it had so far, allowing him to unexpectedly advance to Copper.

Nothing happened beyond the ordinary. The storm in his core subsided somewhat as he continued digesting the fruit's pure madra, and his legs eased somewhat as they received fresh power after their exertion earlier. Even his broken arm felt better, though he could just as easily attribute that to the fresh pain-suppressing script his mother had left for him.

He quickly bathed and slept.

The mirrored door to Elder Whisper's chamber swung shut, leaving the ancient fox staring at a reflection of himself. He tilted his muzzled back, snapping up a fish and letting it slide down his throat.

He had spent most of the past five decades in this room, where every day was much like another. Compared to the excitement of his younger days, this was a perfectly satisfying way to spend a few years.

But now the Unsouled had visited of his own volition. *That* was interesting.

He left the remainder of his meal, pacing circles around his chamber. In the mirror, his sleek white reflection followed him.

Whisper harvested both light and dreams into his core, blending them so that he could blind any eyes, stifle any ears. The humans understood light to some limited degree, but they had great difficulty with dreams. Whisper, however, had spent a hundred years meditating on the nature of dreams.

For the most part, a dream was nothing more than a mind deceiving itself. Only rarely did dreams tap into greater forces...but when they did, they could reveal pieces of fate.

Over the years, Elder Whisper had developed a sense for that fate. It was distant, imperfect, but he could dimly see the shapes of impending events.

"The Unsouled is connected," his reflection said.

"He *could* be," Whisper corrected himself.

The reflected snowfox whipped its five tails in irritation. "A drowning man will seize any branch, no matter how thin."

For centuries, the shape looming in his dreams has been dark and impossibly vast. It would crush them all beneath its ponderous weight, and there was no stopping it. Sacred Valley's past was coming back and bringing death with it. But there was something strange about his premonition this time.

Somehow, he felt as though the titanic threat were years distant and months close at the same time. One and then the other, like fate had yet to decide.

Now, he saw the familiar shape of fate's touch on the Unsouled: the resolve in his eyes, the agony of a difficult decision in the set of his shoulders, the timing of his appearance in the tower. The boy's future was in flux.

However it turned out, Whisper had done what he could. Now he would wait...and watch.

Every morning, the entire Wei clan turned out to meditate and cycle. The more distant families followed this tradition in their homes, but the core members of the clan all gathered together. It became the time where clan business was conducted, and a center for gossip and competition.

Ordinarily, Lindon arrived in the central courtyard outside the Hall of Elders to find fifty or sixty people already in conversation. The number would grow as the sun approached, and by daybreak the two hundred or so most honored members of the Wei clan would be united in cycling their madra. Even Lindon, an Unsouled, was no exception.

Today, the courtyard buzzed with excitement. Under the gray light before dawn, over two hundred people gathered in the courtyard of the Elder's Hall, and none were meditating. News of Wei Mon Teris' punishment had spread, and they were here to witness the penalty for cowardice.

Public punishments weren't unheard of, but the most recent one was over a year past. They were always an occasion for the families of the Wei clan to snipe at one another, to witness a rival falling down a step on the endless ladder of position. The Patriarch hadn't shown himself, but the First Elder stood atop the steps of the hall, his long eyebrows hanging down to his white beard.

Wei Mon Teris knelt before him, no ropes binding him. Honor would keep him in place. The rest of the Mon family stood behind him, his immediate family in the front, with aunts and uncles and cousins behind.

Teris' father, Wei Mon Keth, stood like a mountain over his son. With his arms crossed, his face set, and a sword on his back, he looked like the statue of an ancient guardian.

As dawn broke, the First Elder addressed the crowd. "Yesterday, the young Copper Enforcer called Wei Mon Teris failed our clan. Faced with a Remnant on the slopes of Mount Yoma, he fled for his life, abandoning a child of the Foundation stage to danger. For this punishment, I will deliver three lashes from my own hand. Let this serve as a warning to cowards." From his belt, the First Elder produced a thin stick of supple orus wood.

More than pain, these lashes were meant to deliver humiliation. The clan didn't want to injure a sacred artist with a future, but they had to curb any potential embarrassments. A public lashing would show the Mon family as weak, and would undermine their position in the Wei clan.

If they fell low enough, eager relatives would seize their assets, leaving them weakened in truth. Weakness and the appearance of weakness were the same, and only strength had a place in Sacred Valley.

For his part, Lindon would take no pleasure in watching Teris beaten. He had never expected the Copper to defend him in the first place, and this whole process was a grim reminder of what could happen to him at any time. He was reliant on the honor and goodwill of others to protect him, and those were thin walls.

But if he could walk his own Path...then strength would be his defense.

As the First Elder raised his hand for the initial blow, Wei Mon Keth stepped forward. Teris' father was also the head of the Mon family, and it was expected that he should defend his son. But the glance he sent toward the Shi family, toward Lindon, carried an impending threat.

"One moment, Elder," Keth said, stepping in front of his son. "There is one matter we must resolve first."

The First Elder's switch blurred through the air, halting to point at Keth's face with the threatening air of a sword. "It is not your place to guard your son from punishment."

Teris' father scowled even deeper. "I beat Teris myself when he came home a coward. But he was not the only one to run." Keth turned to Lindon. "Let the Unsouled be punished with him."

Lindon froze when the crowd turned its attention to him. Keth was only trying to save face by pulling the Shi family down together; it was a common enough tactic in scenes like this, and the elders would see through it. Lindon was patiently waiting for the First Elder to rebuff Keth when he caught sight of someone pushing his way through the gathering.

Wei Shi Jaran had to lean on a cane, but he still shouldered other families aside. His scarred face turned from Lindon to the Mon family, but in the end, he addressed the First Elder. "First Elder, why do you allow this dog to bark?"

Lindon's stomach dropped, and he could see his sister over the crowd. She paled when she heard her father's words.

Mon Keth loomed over Shi Jaran, glaring down at the cripple. "Men do not fight with words alone. Will you face me on the stage?"

Jaran acted as though he hadn't heard the challenge, keeping his attention fixed on the First Elder. "By what right does Wei Mon Keth accuse my son? Surely it is not lack of courage that keeps a Foundation child from defending a Copper fighter."

"Of course your son could not have protected mine," Keth responded, before the elder could open his mouth. "But he is a coward nonetheless. What bravery has he shown before the clan? What courage? Surely he should work twice as hard to prove his worth, but what has he brought to the clan?"

Jaran's scarred lips twisted further into a sneer. "Once, you would not have said such things to my face. If not for these injuries, I would teach you a lesson here."

"First prove that you have taught your own son *his* lessons." Keth looked around and found his daughter, a ten-year-old girl with an arrow on her wooden badge. She ran to him eagerly, and he placed his hands on her shoulders. "Your son is at the Foundation stage. If he is not a coward, he will accept a fight from someone his own level."

The little girl looked Lindon straight in the eyes. "I, Wei Mon Eri, challenge Wei Shi Lindon to a duel of honor before the entire clan."

The words echoed in the courtyard, accompanied by shocked silence.

They planned this, Lindon realized, hearing the girl's recited challenge. *They needed to distract the other families from their dishonor.*

Perhaps the First Elder would have prevented Wei Mon Keth from speaking further, had he been given a chance. He'd surely seen more complex gambits from subtle opponents. But Lindon's father had opened his mouth, and thereby opened a crack in his son's armor. Now, Lindon was feeling the sting of the blade.

When a child first passed their test of spirit and received a Foundation-level badge, they were taught a rudimentary Foundation technique. This technique was the same for everyone in the clan, and was designed to acclimate children to feeling and cycling their own madra. When the child was ready, they would learn a more advanced cycling technique, one suited for their future Path. Unless the child was Unsouled.

Lindon would never learn a Path, so there was no point in preparing his soul for one. Even eight years after reaching Foundation, Lindon practiced the same basic cycling technique. Asking him to fight was like asking a soldier to step onto a battlefield armed only with a training sword.

Even the ten-year-old daughter of the Mon family would be better off than he was. She was a Striker on the Path of the White Fox, and surely her family would have taught her a better Foundation technique. Lindon had the advantage of size and weight, but she had the advantage of superior madra control.

He had no certainty in being able to defeat a girl five years his junior. He should have been used to shame by now, but that realization still hurt.

"Well?" Mon Eri demanded, when Lindon hadn't responded to her challenge. The entire courtyard, packed with the heart of the Wei clan, stood waiting for his response. "Do you accept or not?"

"He has no reason to fight," Jaran said, with a glance back at his son. "Only the Mon family has something to prove. Besides, you can see his injury for yourself."

Wei Mon Keth crossed his arms and gave a harsh laugh. "If he is not a coward, he will answer."

Hundreds of the Wei clan were gathered, including the First Elder. The weight of the combined attention pressed into him on every side, like a tightening fist.

The pressure seemed to push his shame deeper, rubbing it in like salt into a wound. He was useless, he was crippled, and now everyone was staring at him. The pain that leaked through his sling-bound arm was nothing compared to this. Lindon looked up to Whisper's tower, imagining he could feel eyes on him even from the room at the top.

"When a traveler cannot find a path, sometimes he must make his own."

Eri stepped forward when Lindon didn't answer immediately, rubbing her fist like she couldn't wait to drive it into Lindon's face. Her father held her back, looking somewhat surprised.

When Lindon's voice finally came out, even he was somewhat surprised. "In the Wei clan, there is only one family that produces cowards," he said to Keth, the head of the Mon family.

Laughter and whispers traveled quietly around the gathered families, and Keth's face turned red with anger. He forced out a few words: "Then you accept?"

It was up to the challenged party to set the terms, so he did. "Seven dawns from now," Lindon said. "To surrender."

For Lindon, there was no winning this fight. Either he defeated Eri, in which case he had beaten a ten-year-old girl, or he wouldn't. No matter the outcome, he would lose face for his family.

He could only salvage a little by putting up a brave front, bowing to Wei Mon Eri with his fists pressed together. After a moment in which she looked like she would attack him, she returned the salute.

"If this distraction is over, I will get on with the business at hand," the First Elder said. He flourished his smooth orus branch, looking down on Teris.

As the first strike cracked across Teris' back, leading to a cry of pain, his family paid no heed. They were still watching Lindon.

When he wasn't carrying out a special task for his Soulsmith mother, Lindon spent the second half of every day in the clan archive. The building was scarcely more noticeable than any ordinary house, with faded white walls and a wide purple-tiled roof. If Lindon had never seen it before, he might have mistaken it for the home of one of the Wei clan's smaller families.

As the sun passed noon, he arrived in the archive. He first retrieved a broom to sweep the front step, which took twice as long as normal since he was forced to work one-handed, then re-organized the Path manuals that a few young Coppers had disturbed the previous evening. His fingers itched when he worked on this shelf, and he had to fight the temptation to sneak a glimpse, though the minimum penalty for an Unsouled studying sacred arts was a private beating. He'd survived such punishments before, and he would again. If he had to discover his own Path, he would eventually need an example.

For now, he'd settle for a shortcut.

The Eighth Elder was supposed to monitor the archive, but Lindon could never tell when the man was doing his job properly or not. As a Forger on the Path of the White Fox, the man was a master of the Fox Mirror technique; he could craft illusions as precise as a mirror's reflection. More than once, Lindon had dared to sneak a glimpse into a simple Path manual, and the elder had appeared out of nowhere to punish him. Other times, Lindon had left the archives to spot the elder passed out on the roof.

For his purposes, so long as he didn't open a Path, he had the archive to himself. Once he'd finished his chores, which took him only an hour or two, he began to gather the scrolls, folders, tablets, and books he needed for research.

Following a Path of the sacred arts was often likened to a journey, and he would never embark on a journey without a plan.

Shortcuts of advancement were common legends in Sacred Valley, and while many were proven to be effective—like the fruit of an ancestral orus tree—most were too rare, expensive, or dangerous for ordinary sacred artists. Lindon needed to hunt for a loophole, which meant poring over every option one by one.

Fortunately, the archive was not the clan's most popular building. He had plenty of time to himself.

One scroll contained a personal letter from an explorer who had visited the four peaks of Sacred Valley in search of exotic madra aspects. She wrote of Greatfather's tears, a spring that bubbled at the top of the mountain known as the Greatfather.

"One handful of water restored my aching body and flagging spirit. Two sent me into a cycling trance from which I would not emerge for three nights and days, having imparted to my spirit a density and potency that I had never before known. As I had not bathed in all that time, I dipped myself briefly into the spring, only to find the water anything but gentle. It scoured my arm like a frozen blade, and when I removed my hand, I found my skin more youthful and supple than ever before, in great contrast to the rest of my body. I advise any artist of the Jade to visit Greatfather's peak as soon as they are able, provided they can withstand the storms and the pain of the pool itself."

Lindon held down the scroll with his broken arm and copied the passage with his own brush, though the spring was not a possibility for him. Not yet. The Holy Wind School, which claimed the Greatfather as their territory, would never allow anyone less prestigious than a clan elder to visit their spring. And then only if they brought generous gifts.

The next possibility came in the form of a recipe pressed onto a wax tablet:

Bloodmaker Pill

Four feathers of a downy shrike
The spring branch of a marauder root, shaved clean
Three small leaves from any life-aspected herb
Blood essence from one Remnant of at least the fire aspect
Blood essence from one Remnant of at least the water aspect
Refine all ingredients in a refinery of twelfth grade or higher, arranging them according to the Six-Pointed Star method. Combine into a state of balance, then weigh and blend. Shape into pill form, and allow to stabilize for three days. A successful pill should have the sheen of polished gold and the color of new blood.

Carries the blood aspect, but improves the basic spiritual foundation. Most effective when taken before Copper.

Lindon copied it down, and a quick perusal of the clan's herb stores—located in the back of the archive—suggested that they should have all the necessary ingredients in storage. His excitement grew until he realized that the only refiner with enough skill to prepare such a pill was gone, on a pilgrimage to the Heaven's Glory School. Lindon couldn't even begin to understand what the "Six-Pointed Star method" was, much less imitate it himself. And he had no idea where he would get a refinery of any grade.

The disappointment was a blow, but not enough to stop him. He had a time limit now, and if he couldn't figure out a solution before his duel with Eri, he might as well not show up. His next possibility came from an offhand mention in a funeral document, chronicling the possessions of a traveler who had died in Wei clan territory. *"He carried with him a parasite ring, of braided halfsilver etched with intricate script, which went into the keeping of the Patriarch to award to a promising practitioner of the Sacred Arts."*

That one bore investigation for later. A parasite ring would slow the cycling process, making it more difficult but also more rewarding. He'd heard it likened to weight training for the soul. He would keep watch for a way to earn or steal this ring from the Patriarch, or possibly earn one for himself if he could find a craftsman from the Golden Sword School. The only drawback was time; it would take time to acquire such a ring, and longer for it to show any effect. He marked his notes on the parasite ring, indicating that he should consider it once the duel was over.

Other books held fanciful legends for young sacred artists, their imaginations full of the wonders and powers out there in the world. It spoke of ancestral orus trees and their fruits—a story that was true, per Lindon's experience, but exaggerated—and the Jester Twins, who would alternately hand out miraculous gifts or crippling curses. It told of the heavenly guardian within Mount Samara, and how enterprising disciples of the Heaven's Glory School might earn a mark of its favor, and of the mythical "true badges" that amplified the power of human madra. Of the Oblivion Wine, which the Fallen Leaf elders always sold a year after the opening of the Nethergate. And it spoke of the Torchyard, an apocryphal location that Elder Whisper was said to have visited in his youth.

The Torchyard was supposedly a field of condensed fiery energy where, if you survived, you could harvest enough vital aura to fuel your advancement even to the legendary Gold stage. According to clan rumors, though, even Elder Whisper hadn't managed to bear the torments of the Torchyard *that* long.

The story of the sacred fruit lent credibility to the other tales, but none of them were real possibilities. One could only meet the Jester Twins by chance, and their gifts were as likely to harm as help. He wasn't a disciple of Heaven's Glory, the true badges were no more than stories, and the Torchyard was far beyond his power. Even if he could endure the trip and make it back in less than a week, he didn't know how to harvest natural fire aura, so he would simply burn to death.

His notes became shorter and shorter, his brush-strokes weighted by disappointment. He had combed through piles of likely manuscripts all day, and while he hadn't exactly expected to stumble across a miracle, he had at least hoped for a possible lead. He'd only started with six full days between him and his deadline, and now the first was gone.

The sun had completely set, and he stood to light a candle. Once it burned down to the next mark, the archive would be closed, and he could leave. He would use this last hour to clean up, returning his texts to their places.

As he did, the Path manuals caught his eye once again. There were eight copies of *The Path of the White Fox,* two for each specialized technique. If he could borrow the one for Strikers, he could at least familiarize himself with the Foundation Mon Eri would use. Maybe he could find some weakness, something to exploit.

But he would never be able to read the manual long

enough, and besides, Paths were meant to be studied for years. The White Fox was not the only Path on the shelf, though. There were two scrolls and a thick tome as well, all of them bearing Paths that the Wei clan had acquired from outside. No one practiced them, as far as Lindon knew, because they required madra of different aspects than the Wei clan cultivated. Those called to Lindon, but ultimately he turned from those as well. They may allow him to win the duel, but the First Elder would recognize what he had done and punish him afterwards.

He reached down and shelved a tablet, and in doing so, caught a glimpse of another shelf he hadn't considered. Technique manuals described skills that could be cultivated in addition to a primary Path, and they were much shorter than Path manuals, often a single plaque or a finger-thin scroll.

Lindon knelt for a closer look. The section for technique manuals took up two shelves, divided according to the aspect the techniques required. Strips of white jade labeled the sections: here the character for fire, there the symbol for purification. His gaze skipped from section to section, from cloud to lightning to light to dreams. The last two had by far the largest selection, dealing as they did with madra of the White Fox.

But there was a section at the end of the bottom shelf with only one entry. An old book, it was little more than a sheaf of yellowed papers, bound together by string on one side. The jade strip declaring its requirements said, simply, "None."

Carefully, Lindon withdrew the book, examining the name of this technique: *Heart of Twin Stars.*

CHAPTER FIVE

While it violated clan decree for Lindon to follow a Path, it was technically allowed for him to study technique manuals. After all, he couldn't actually *use* the techniques without madra of a compatible aspect, which he couldn't harvest. Learning a technique outside of a Path was like tearing a branch off a tree and expecting it to bear fruit.

But this one didn't need any particular aspect, nor did it require him to be of Copper level. He turned the first yellowing page, expectation transforming into a hopeful excitement.

I leave this manual out of obligation. Any technique deserves to be studied and remembered, in the hope that it may someday spark greater inspiration. Even such a dim spark as this one may one day strike a great flame.

The impetus for this technique comes from a longtime rival of mine, a deceitful and cowardly man whose name I will not honor by repeating it here. I bear the great shame of sharing a clan with this man, and thus we have challenged each other many times since our youth. They say that a good rival sharpens a warrior as a stone sharpens iron, but not my deficient opponent. I defeated him handily each time, and had no reason to grow in strength or skill. He was a pathetic match.

But some scrap of talent must have remained in him, for he developed an underhanded technique that he christened the "Empty Palm." I will not lower myself to attempt the technique on my own, but as I understand the theory, he focuses neutral madra into a simple palm thrust. How he cancels out the aspects of his spirit, I have not yet deduced, but the result is undeniable.

When his Empty Palm makes contact with my core, his madra disrupts my own. For a few seconds, I am as powerless as a wretched Unsouled. Even more so, perhaps, as I can hardly muster the energy to control my own limbs.

I tried a series of techniques to defeat him, but each time he managed to land a single Empty Palm upon my core. Even such as he, with his lack of talent, can lean upon a technique as a crutch.

It is thus in desperation that I have developed this defense, and at last rightfully triumphed over him. Should he pass down this Empty Palm, I can rest at ease, knowing that my future disciples reading this manual may oppose his legacy.

Heart of Twin Stars is utterly simple in its concept: you must divide your core in two. Thus, even when one core is disabled through some device such as my rival's, you have a second to rely upon.

The observant reader will notice that this does not increase the power available to you. Splitting one's core is a painful process prone to many risks, though it is mercifully quick. If attacks such as the Empty Palm ever become commonplace, I wish to leave behind this defense.

Here at last, I leave a record of my journey to split my core, in exacting detail. Be sure to follow my path to the very step, lest you suffer a crippling injury from which you cannot recover.

Useless. Heart of Twin Stars was an utterly useless technique, which doubtless explained why no one practiced it. Even if he wanted to split his core in two, Wei Mon Eri wouldn't have any techniques like this Empty Palm. He would be just as defenseless as before.

The book did include a cycling technique, which would at least work better than his own pathetic Foundation method, but he wouldn't see any benefit before the duel. Besides, the cycling technique was designed to prepare him to split his core, which he never intended to do. The Heart of Twin Stars wouldn't even make up for his broken arm, which—even with his mother's scripts—could never heal before he had to fight.

His enthusiasm had dimmed, but not died entirely. The technique manual had given him a few other ideas he could try, and maybe a new search tomorrow would reveal more promising results. After locking up the archive—leaving the Eighth Elder drunk on the roof again, perfectly visible—he returned home,
cycling his madra according to his new technique. His nerves kept him at it until dawn, and he would have continued except for a brutal hammering on his door.

"Get ready," Kelsa told him, dressed in the orange shadesilk training clothes of a Copper Ruler. Her copper badge, marked with a scepter, hung proudly in the center of her chest. "You're training with me today."

Lindon brought his pack to the Shi family gardens, surrounded by blue mountain roses and tiny clusters of cloudbell, and knelt across from his sister. They faced each other over a stretch of grass.

Ordinarily, they would have joined the rest of their family in the main courtyard for daily cycling, but Kelsa seemed to have something else on her mind. She started off studying him, her hair pulled back and face severe.

"You seem tired," she said at last. "You didn't sleep well, which will slow your arm's recovery. What were you doing?"

Over the years, he'd found that the fastest way to deal with his sister was to respond immediately and honestly. "Cycling. I was trying to process the rest of the fruit."

"And have you?"

"Not fully." The foreign madra still crackled like lightning in his core, but less than it had the day before. He couldn't tell how much less, or if digesting it had made any difference at all. This was not the effect he'd ever imagined from a legendary natural treasure.

Kelsa cupped her chin in her hand, pondering for a moment. "We'll come back to that. For the moment, we should discuss our strategy in getting you through the duel."

Only five days left. "Can we?" he asked.

Her answering glare was as firm as a strike to the chest. "This is our family's honor. If I can't get you to acquit yourself well, I don't deserve my badge."

Lindon straightened his spine, adjusting for the increased pressure on his shoulders. "Then where do we begin?"

"Obviously, there's no good outcome if you fight the girl. You're shamed if you win, and shamed if you lose."

He didn't need a reminder of that, but he remained quiet, waiting for her to continue.

"Your only honorable option is to challenge someone of greater standing in the Mon family, like perhaps Wei Mon Teris. This has the disadvantage of getting you killed."

That was a slight exaggeration; the Mon family wasn't likely to kill a relative in front of the whole clan. But they could. And honor would require them to injure Lindon severely, which was another consequence he'd prefer to avoid.

"I suggest you fight the girl for a while and then concede. You could say that an Unsouled is not worthy to fight someone of the Mon family, which gives them face. They'll accept, you'll be embarrassed for a while, but in the end your reputation will improve. You will have handled the duel with grace and accepted defeat with dignity."

"At the price of telling the Mon family that I'm worth less than they are."

She nodded once. "Yes." Kelsa never shied away from the truth.

Lindon didn't think of himself as overly prideful, but he burned at the thought of humbling himself in front of all the other Wei families. For one thing, his Shi family would be seen as vulnerable if he publicly demonstrated his weakness. Their rivals would push them, seeking to exploit a perceived opening.

After watching his expression for a few seconds, Kelsa folded both hands on her knees. "But I'm sure you didn't waste the day yesterday. What's your plan?"

Sheepishly, Lindon reached into his sling, where he'd tucked the technique manual. "I found this technique in the archives. It's not directly useful, but it might have given me an idea."

She snatched the manual from his hand and glanced over the first page. "You want to split your *core?*" Her tone made it clear exactly what she thought of that idea.

"No, of course not." While cycling according to the method described in the *Heart of Twin Stars* manual, he'd spent the night thinking. He suspected there were other uses for a split core rather than just defending against one specific technique, but they were too risky or difficult to test. "There's a second technique in there."

Kelsa looked back down at the book. "The Empty Palm."

"It would be easier if I was Copper, I know, but in theory it's just injecting your madra into a certain spot. It could be enough."

She flipped through each page in the thin manual, paying special attention to the back. "It doesn't describe the timing, or the energy flow, or the Foundation you'd need to pull it off. Only how to defend against it." Kelsa snapped the pages shut. "But ultimately yes, I think there's enough information here that we could develop a version of the Empty Palm. It's simple enough anyway."

Lindon leaned forward, eager. "Can you teach me?"

In the Wei clan, most sacred artists reached the Iron stage in their twenty-first or twenty-second year. For Kelsa to have reached the barrier between Copper and Iron at the age of sixteen meant that she was more than merely talented; she had the discipline and skill to match.

Abruptly, Kelsa rose to her feet. "That's up to you. I have some ideas, but I need a living target with a functioning core if I want to try them out. That means you."

"You can disable my spirit, but it won't do much. I can hardly defend myself to begin with."

Kelsa stretched first one arm, then the other. "That's not what I mean. The manual mentions that he had to achieve purity for the technique to work. We don't have time for that, so I'll be pushing my madra into your core until I get a feel for the technique."

As a sacred artist on the Path of the White Fox, Kelsa cultivated aspects of dreams and light, bent toward the purposes of deceiving enemies. Accepting it directly into his core meant...

"I have another idea," Lindon said, with a half-step back. "I could try on *you* first, and we could work from there."

"I need to understand the theory myself," Kelsa said, dropping into a balanced stance on the balls of her feet. Her left hand was extended, her right held back, her whole body angled sideways. "First trial."

Lindon tried to protest again, but Kelsa unfolded in a deceptively quick movement that left the heel of her palm against his core, just below the navel. She'd used hardly any force, and the strike came with no pain; it felt like a light slap, if anything.

But the world went mad.

The soft blue cloudbell flowers at his feet took flight, flapping around his eyes. Shadows in the bushes flickered and giggled, while the clouds zoomed around like zealous fish in the ocean of the sky. Grass tickled his feet through his shoes, and he tiptoed around to avoid it. The ground must not have liked that, because it finally had enough and slapped him in the back of the head.

He came to in a wrench of returning sensation, lying flat on his back in the garden and staring up into the sky. His arm had begun to ache again.

Over him, Kelsa was flexing her palm. "Too slow. The motion has to carry the madra, you can't rely on transmission through contact. Stand up, I need to try again."

Lindon crawled to his feet, still dizzy. "Wait. I think it's worse on me, because I can't—"

She hit him again.

After the garden stopped partying without him, he spoke from the ground. "I'm not standing up again. I'm not."

Kelsa was moving at half-speed, stepping forward into a slow palm thrust. She repeated the first step a few times, working something out in her head. "Then you'll be worthless for the rest of your life," she said casually, but the words were like a spear to the ribs. "You don't want to shame the family? Stand up." She didn't so much as glance at him, as though she didn't care whether he stood or not. "I've almost worked it out...it has to transmit all at once. Not like a stream, but a gust of wind."

Lindon stood up again. And again.

Eleven more times.

By the end, the earth never stopped spinning, even when the effects wore off. He tried to rise again, but *up* and *sideways* seemed to have swapped places, and he stumbled into the cloudbells. Their stalks were sharper than they looked.

Kelsa reached in and hauled him out with ease, steadying him with a grip on his shoulder. Ten breaths passed before he could take a step without swaying.

"Rally yourself," she said. "Step forward and shove in one motion, focusing madra in your palm. Release it in one breath like a gust of wind, being sure to exhale and cycle to the rest of your body for stability. Understood?"

Lindon was trying to determine if his senses were back under control. Was that flickering shadow a sign of lingering madness, or a leaf blowing in the wind? "Please, I need...I need a moment."

Kelsa rarely had the patience to wait around, and though she allowed him his rest, she did so reluctantly. She paced in the garden, studying *Heart of Twin Stars* as she did. "Let's return to an earlier subject," she said, without looking up from the book. "The fruit. Have you finished cycling it?"

"Almost all," he said, sensing the tingling sparks that lingered in his core. "I haven't noticed much of a change."

She squinted at the page. "I can't see clearly. Bring out your light."

Lindon looked around at the bright morning light. "Do you need me to find a healer?"

She used the manual to point at his robes. "You're my disciple for the day. Pull out your light."

To his sister, Lindon would have protested. To his master, Lindon would have obeyed without a word. He spent a few seconds deciding which she was, and eventually reached into his pack to produce a palm-sized board.

The board was covered with an intricate three-layered script circle, and when he fed his madra into it, it burst into white light. The runelight was much stronger than from an ordinary script, and remarkably steady. That was this script's only purpose: to produce light on command. It would last as long as the user's spirit did.

Lindon held the board over the book with the shining script down, though it made no discernible difference among the bright sunlight.

Kelsa didn't thank him, but spoke as she read. "I finished processing the orus last night. It was quite the experience. Did it feel as though you'd swallowed a thunderbolt? Mine did. But as I continued cycling, I didn't feel much else. It was as though the fruit vanished. I wondered if Mother was mistaken, and this wasn't the miraculous spirit-fruit she thought."

She looked at him but kept her book open, so he didn't remove the light. "It wasn't until early this morning that I noticed the changes. Tell me, does your light seem brighter than usual to you?"

Lindon flipped the light over and examined it himself. It was almost impossible to tell how bright it was, especially compared to a memory. "Perhaps a little?"

"Keep watching until you can see a difference."

Lindon knew his sister was headed somewhere with this, and he would exhaust himself eventually. He kept the light ignited, staring into it, looking for the slightest difference in illumination. He noticed nothing.

Finally, she told him he could stop. "How do you feel?" she asked him.

"Absolutely ordinary."

"Yet you burned the light for fifty-two seconds, and you could have kept going. How long could you do it before?"

Unlike the brightness question, he could answer this one. "Thirty seconds, at most." He had used this board to light his way while diving in the river, so he knew exactly how long he could keep it lit. But he must be wrong. When he sensed his core, he didn't *feel* any stronger. "Are you sure you counted properly?"

She snapped the technique manual closed, wearing a pleased look. "The fruit's madra integrates so smoothly with our own that we don't notice. Yesterday I was Copper, and today I'm on the verge of condensing Iron, but I don't feel any different. And yesterday, you wouldn't be able to use the Empty Palm more than once without passing out."

Lindon's breaths were coming more quickly, and the flowers in the garden suddenly smelled almost painfully sweet. "What about now?"

She adopted a low stance, balanced and firmly planted, prepared to be hit. "How should I know? Now, disciple, Empty Palm!"

This time, Lindon snapped into action as he would for

a real sacred arts master. He stepped forward and pivoted at the hips, launching a palm strike at his sister's stomach. Synced with his madra, it should have driven energy through her core like a steel spike, but it splashed like a cup of water instead.

"One gust, not a breeze!" Kelsa barked. "Again!"

His head was already light and his limbs weak, but he tried until he passed out. When he woke, he tried again.

Four days later, the most prominent families of the Wei clan gathered once more before the Hall of Elders at the break of dawn. A few industrious sacred artists sat cross-legged in the courtyard, cycling in the first light of dawn. Everyone else stood, eager to watch the show. If something went wrong, an honored family might fall from grace today.

The Mon family waited on one side of a cleared space, Eri in front. She hopped in place, practicing attacks on an invisible opponent. Her scowl said she was looking to kill. Keth stood over his daughter, arms folded, scanning the crowd for the Shi family. Which was why Lindon had shown up together with his family. Kelsa and his father walked beside him, while his mother kept up as best she could while taking notes.

The First Elder stood on the stairs of the Hall, as he had before, but this time his brow was furrowed in a frown that seemed carved into his wrinkled face. "This is a duel for honor, and so it may continue. But any wounds to the young are wounds to our clan, so I must ask if there is any other way for the offended parties to resolve this."

Eri executed a series of punches that veered ominously low. "No other way!" she declared.

Before his training with Kelsa, Lindon would have agreed with her. He'd seen no other way out. But while practicing the Empty Palm, he'd been struck by an idea.

A terrible idea.

He bowed toward the Mon family, bending over his wounded arm. "Honorable head of the Mon family, this one has a request."

Keth straightened his back, responding to Lindon's humble speech. "I will not release you from the duel."

Lindon could probably appeal to the First Elder on the basis of his injury, and at least ensure a little more time. But there was an opportunity here, and if he let his own crippling weakness get in the way of opportunity, he'd never achieve anything. "This one would dare not ask so much. Instead, this one wishes to challenge another member of your family."

Eri's mouth dropped open in a comic show of disappointment, and she turned to her father as though to ask if he could *possibly* allow this. Keth, for his part, worked his jaw as though chewing the idea over. His eyes roamed to his fur-clad son, Teris, who still sat gingerly after his whipping. "Which would you challenge?" Keth finally asked.

Lindon met the eyes of this grown man more than twice his age, this fighter legendary for his unflinching courage in combat. "I challenge Wei Mon Keth."

He had somewhat expected gasps from the surrounding families, or at least derisive laughter, but the crowd reacted with utter silence. A Foundation artist challenging an Iron wasn't interesting gossip, it was like an infant trying to bite a tiger.

Copper souls could process vital aura, giving them a supply of madra that was both more expansive and more effective. But a quick or clever Foundation child could overcome that disadvantage. An Iron body was a qualitative difference; compared to Copper or below, Irons were superhuman.

Wei Mon Keth looked as though he'd lost what little respect he might once have had for Lindon, but he didn't dismiss the idea out of hand. "Explain."

"This one must prove his courage, as must your son,

Teris." A dark cloud passed across Teris' face at even the indirect mention of his cowardice, but Lindon plowed ahead. "However, the opponent Teris faced was many levels higher than he. It seems only fair that this one should face an adversary as exalted."

This time, a quiet murmur did ripple through the crowd. Lindon and his sister had spent two days making sure their argument was sensible enough that those gathered would have no choice but to take it seriously.

Within his sleeves, Lindon clenched his fists. He was close to the outcome he wanted, but he needed Keth to agree.

The head of the Mon family rubbed his short beard with two fingers. "This is a better way to demonstrate courage. What terms would you accept?"

Traditionally, the challenged would set the terms, which meant Keth would have been within his rights to set a fight with no restrictions and then knock Lindon onto the peak of the nearest mountain. But the other families would have looked down on him for abusing his power against a junior, so he took the honorable course and allowed Lindon to define the fight.

Which was Lindon's only hope.

"One strike each, if it pleases you. First, you take one strike from this one without defense or resistance. Then you strike me in turn. The first to lose his footing is defeated."

Keth's brow furrowed. "You would be wise to set different terms."

There was precedent for a duel like this, if not one so hilariously out of balance. Jade elders had once exchanged pointers one blow at a time, with the more confident party agreeing to take the first hit.

But this was supposed to look like Lindon was throwing himself on Keth's mercy, and he had to hope that the Mon family head would see that. "This one hopes you might hold back when you strike, but at least this one may show that he is not afraid to take a blow."

At last, Keth's face lightened as he understood. Lindon was giving him a chance to administer a punishment equal to Teris', humiliate Lindon publicly, and remind people of his own strength in one blow. As long as he didn't kill Lindon, he would be seen as both strong and merciful, and he would only gain in reputation.

"You're clever," Keth said with a nod. "You show courage. I agree."

That was it. The rules of the game were set, all his cards played. He almost couldn't believe that it had gone so easily. He moved away from his family as though he drifted forward in a dream, opposing Wei Mon Keth across the open space in the center of the courtyard. He kept expecting someone from the Mon family to object, but none made a sound.

As the First Elder ordered them to face one another, Lindon's heart pounded on the inside of his ribs. This was his chance. His first real chance since he was seven years old. It had been a long time coming.

So why did it feel too soon?

"If none object..." the elder said, almost hopefully. No one did, and the dawn air froze. The First Elder straightened his back, sweeping his hand to present the challengers. "Then may this duel begin!"

Lindon faced Wei Mon Keth, who stood taller even than he was, and twice as wide. The man seemed to take up more of the horizon than Yoma Mountain, looming over Lindon and blotting out the rising sun.

The older man's arms fell to his sides, leaving his slate-gray robes completely undefended. "The first blow is yours," he said. He didn't even brace himself, as Kelsa had done. And why should he? With all of Lindon's strength, he wouldn't be able to tip over an Iron balanced on one foot.

Lindon stepped in, preparing his attack, cycling energy through his limbs to keep them under his control. He felt as though they would shake away from his body.

He cocked his upper body, drawing back for a palm strike. As he did, he focused his madra at the base of his palm, as he'd practiced. One pulse, like a gust of wind, but focused like an iron spike.

At the Copper level, this part of the process would be quick and simpler than breathing. His madra would have been dense and powerful. As it was, Lindon had to focus his entire strength on his palm for three breaths of time as he prepared. It was slow, it was clumsy, and it would never work against a prepared opponent.

But he wasn't facing a prepared opponent.

The Empty Palm landed accurately, just below Keth's navel, along with an invisible thorn that he drove like a hammer driving a nail. Lindon felt his own madra snapping into the man's core, sensed the shiver of feedback that ran through the spiritual lines that crossed his body like veins.

Keth trembled and looked at Lindon in shock, but he didn't stagger backwards as Lindon had hoped. He hadn't taken a single step.

Panic shook Lindon even more than the Empty Palm shook Keth. His Empty Palm had been *perfect...* but if Keth didn't lose his footing, it wouldn't matter. Lindon would have to take a blow from an Iron Striker who knew that he'd been tricked. If Wei Mon Keth caved in Lindon's rib cage with a fist, he would face no more than a fine.

"What have you—" Keth began, but Lindon followed up with a second attack driven by all the raw-nerved terrified desperation in his soul. This one wasn't guided by any technique or sacred art; it was nothing more than an ordinary punch to the gut. Every observer in the crowd would know how useless it was. He would have a better chance punching an iron plate than an Iron practitioner.

Pain echoed up Lindon's knuckles and reached his shoulder as though he really had punched a metal plate, but Keth's breath whooshed out of his lungs. He clutched his stomach and took two steps backward, his legs shaking as he tried to stop himself from going to his knees.

Except for Kelsa and Lindon, every single other person present drew in a sharp gasp. It sounded like a ghost passing over the crowd.

Before anyone could speak, Lindon bowed to his still-staggering opponent.

"This one thanks you for your instruction," he rushed out. "You are the victor."

Then he scurried back to his family.

He didn't need to win, after all. He only needed to save face. And while he may have been able to endure an attack from an Iron sacred artist who adhered to the honorable rules of a duel, he would never survive a blow from an enraged Iron with blood in his heart.

"Stand where you are, Unsouled!" Keth roared, and the shout was driven with all the force of his madra and fury. He straightened, which meant he'd recovered his spirit from the disruption of the Empty Palm. During Lindon's tests with Kelsa, it only took her four or five breaths to recover, so it wasn't surprising that someone at the Iron stage would be even faster.

Power gathered around Keth's fist until it was visible, warping the air in a haze that reminded Lindon of the attack Teris had used to fell the ancestral tree. "I owe you a strike."

His imagination provided him with an image of his body cracking in half as easily as that tree had, his bones snapping like dry branches. He was relying on someone to intervene on his behalf. His life was in the hands of the crowd, and for a long second, they were all silent. Even his father, Jaran, stared at him in confusion, still too shocked by the events of the duel to do anything to help.

To Lindon's relief, the First Elder stepped between him and the Mon family head, his long eyebrows and wispy beard flowing in the morning wind. "Wei Shi Lindon has surrendered. The duel is over, and you are the victor. Congratulations."

Lindon let out a heavy breath, and the sudden rush of

relief stole his strength. He half-expected to collapse onto the stone at that instant.

Even the First Elder's harshest critic could not have found a trace of mockery in his words, but Keth turned to him in a fury. "He cheated! He violated the terms of the duel by striking *twice,* in a deliberate attempt to humiliate me!"

"For which he deserved to lose," the elder reminded him. "As he admitted his loss."

Keth drew up in absolute rage, swelling to seemingly twice his size. "He conspired to ruin my dignity as an Iron!"

Jaran's laughter was high and scornful as he hobbled his way forward, leaning on his cane. He'd finally overcome his confusion to side with his son...or at least against an old rival. "Whatever trick a mouse uses, it cannot defeat a lion. If Lindon decided to charge you with a spear, what is that to you? His strength should never have been able to harm you, no matter how he cheated. A *true* warrior of the Iron stage would not be shaken by a child's punch."

Lindon winced and pushed back further into the crowd. He had more or less expected Keth's reaction, but he hadn't anticipated his father making everything worse.

His sister caught him by the shoulder as he tried to sneak by. "Well done," she whispered. She moved in front of him, ready to defend him at need.

The madra around Keth's fist condensed into spinning balls of purple-edged white fire. Foxfire was only an illusion of flame; it produced no actual heat, but if it touched flesh, it would burn with the agony of real fire.

"I see how the Shi family addresses members of the same clan," Keth shouted, trying to drum up support from the audience. "With shame and dishonor! Grant me a contest against Shi Jaran, the one responsible for the Unsouled, or I will find my own satisfaction here."

The First Elder raised a hand. "Keth, Jaran, I have seen enough. Return to your families. This duel has concluded, and the Mon family is victorious."

A few laughs from the surrounding gallery. No one present believed that the Mon family had won, least of all Mon Keth. By afternoon, there would be a new Mon family myth: the Unsouled who had struck down an Iron.

Lindon couldn't deny his pride at the thought.

When the First Elder turned his head, thinking the matter settled, Keth flowed forward. He must have used some movement technique, because one step brought him before Jaran, his fist cocked back to deliver a blow that shone purple with foxfire. Lindon's father raised his hands to defend, but even Lindon could tell he'd been caught off guard. His cane fell to the ground as he lifted both hands, his scarred face tightening into a grimace.

The scene flickered.

Jaran and the First Elder had switched places, and now Mon's flame-wreathed fist was crashing down on the *elder*, not the head of the Shi family. Jaran's hands were still raised to defend himself from nothing. For an instant, Lindon's mind refused to accept what he was seeing. Had the First Elder switched places with his father in that breath?

In a move that seemed slow and clear—but must have taken half a second at most—the elder held up two fingers. He placed them to the side of Keth's wrist, gently guiding the strike down and to the side. Foxfire *swished* through the air as illusory purple-white fireballs struck the stone, dealing absolutely no damage whatsoever.

Jaran lowered his hands, stunned.

The First Elder continued his movement, moving his two fingers to Mon Keth's shoulder and pushing down. He didn't appear to exert any effort, but the much bigger man collapsed to his knees, his hands behind his back. The elder flicked his sleeve, and intricate stone manacles appeared around his wrists.

Keth shouted, trying to force his way to his feet, but the First Elder had already placed a hand on the man's hair. A ripple of force disturbed the air as it passed through Mon Keth's body, flattening his clothes and sending a pulse of dirt blasting out.

His knees slammed back into the ground, and he resisted no further.

"Wei Mon Keth will be in isolation training for the next month," the First Elder mentioned. "No doubt he wishes to meditate and learn from today's events. During this time, the Mon family will be responsible for him. You are all dismissed."

Lindon froze, replaying the scene in his mind.

The First Elder was a Forger on the Path of the White Fox. He couldn't switch bodies, he could only Forge deceptions: copies of reality made of dreams and light with no real substance. White Fox illusions had no structure and could not resist the weakest attack; they relied entirely on crafting a perfect appearance. Forgers had to craft their pictures detail by detail. Even the First Elder could never have created an illusion so layered, so complex, as the scene Lindon had just witnessed.

Could he?

Suddenly Lindon found himself unable to tear his gaze away from the First Elder, the man who had directed the entire scene and maintained absolute control the entire time. Even now, as he instructed the Mon family to carry Keth away, he looked no more concerned than a man ordering his breakfast.

This was what a real sacred artist looked like. This was the sort of power Lindon wanted.

The power he would gain on his Path.

CHAPTER SIX

Jaran slammed his clay mug down on the table, sending orus wine sloshing over his wrist. "That was *stupid.* A warrior fights with his mind first. With strategy! You don't risk your life on a *fool's* plan that will leave you even weaker than you already are! When I was younger, I would never have..."

Lindon's father went on, talking about the glorious days when he'd been one of the most promising sacred artists in the entire clan. They were alone in Lindon's house, with no one to listen in, so Lindon nodded along and kept the mug filled. He already knew he'd been foolish.

He should have told his father and mother first. He was only blessed that they had been too confused to intervene, or they could have ruined everything in trying to save him.

How fortunate that they had left him alone.

"...don't know what you were thinking," Jaran continued, raising the mug to his lips. "So stupid." With one hand, he roughly reached out and grabbed his son around the shoulders, pulling him into a one-armed hug. Lindon almost knocked over the bottle of wine.

"But it's the best kind of stupid," Jaran said, staring into his mug. "Only an idiot accepts a battle he's sure to lose, but bravery and idiocy share a border. The son of a cripple might be a cripple, but the son of tigers won't be a dog."

Jaran coughed out a laugh, raising his wine as though for a toast. "They'll soon see what a couple of cripples can do, son! A three-legged tiger's still got a bite!" He downed the rest of his wine.

A golden rush filled Lindon from his core to his fingertips, like a pulse of fresh madra. His father *approved* of him. He hadn't heard open praise from his father since he'd learned to walk. Certainly not since he'd first received his Unsouled badge.

Before Lindon could think of an appropriate response, Jaran upended his cup on the table, leaving it upside-down. That was even more of a shock; there was still half a bottle left. But his father leaned forward on the table, his expression turning as grave as his scarred lips would allow.

"You and your sister did well with the plan today, but I can't be left out again. What do you intend for the Festival?"

Lindon had been more concerned about surviving the week with his honor intact, but he *had* given the upcoming Seven-Year Festival some thought. "The children at my stage will have better foundation techniques, but the Empty Palm gives me an edge in combat. I should be able to take first."

"Empty Palm..." Jaran muttered. "Is that what you call it? Disrupts the enemy's spirit with an injection into the core?"

He should have known his parents would see through it immediately. "Yes, Father."

"You're lucky. If you had cultivated any aspects at all, it wouldn't have worked so well."

Lindon rubbed his temple, memories of dream-like visions swimming in his head. "Kelsa put me on the ground with the same technique every time. I couldn't trust my own eyes."

"Of course she did. She's a Copper, and you're Unsouled. You can't defend against her any more than an ant can stop a boot. If she had tried the same thing you did on Wei Mon Keth today, he wouldn't have even noticed."

That violated everything Lindon knew about the sacred arts, but his father wouldn't be mistaken about something like this. "Surely when Mon Keth left himself undefended, Kelsa's Empty Palm would have done far more damage than mine."

Jaran's fists tightened on the table. "Son, if that's what you think, you came close to a harsh lesson today. A weapon held in ignorance only wounds its bearer."

Lindon sat up straighter, a chill running down his spine. He thought he'd prepared for the morning's duel as well as he could, but if he'd made a mistake...he really could have died.

"If it worked as you imagine, why doesn't every sacred artist in the Wei clan use this Empty Palm? We could disable any opponent with one strike!"

"Because it's difficult to strike the core," Lindon said, knowing he was playing the fool. "The enemy would be on guard against it. I know it only worked against Mon Keth because he didn't defend himself, and who would do that in battle?"

"You're missing the most fundamental reason. It's because your madra is *pure*." He raised his hand, palm-up, where a hazy purple-white impression danced on his palm. His own power. "Our White Fox is formed from aura of light and dreams, and it will act according to its nature. Even unformed, you see."

Lindon peered closer. As the energy danced in his father's palm, it gathered in the shape of a running rabbit, of a flag snapping in the breeze, of his mother's face. He thought he heard sounds, impossibly distant: the cry of a wolf, the panting of a man running for his life, the steady drip of water. The White Fox, unrestrained, tricked the senses by its very nature.

Jaran closed his fist, and the images vanished. "Untrained madra, that of a child or an Unsouled, is still pure.

It has no form, and so it affects only the spirit...but it does so more naturally than anything else. There's very little defense against it. A strike from me would not have affected Mon Keth's core; if anything, it would have confused him for a moment before his own spirit rejected my influence. But yours influences the core directly."

Lindon remembered a line from the *Heart of Twin Stars* manual, a note he hadn't given much thought: *"How he cancels out the aspects of his madra, I have not yet deduced, but the result is undeniable."* The developer of the Empty Palm had come up with a way to purify himself in spite of his previous training.

Only a moment ago, he had worried that his ignorance may have taken him too close to death, but now he couldn't deny a measure of excitement. Of all the sacred artists in the Wei clan, only *he* had yet to absorb any vital aura. That meant he had capabilities no one else did.

His father saw his thoughts, and held up a hand. "Unfortunately, pure madra has only two uses. It can activate scripts, just as anyone can, and it shakes the spirit. That's all. For anything else, you may as well have no power at all. It's also incredibly difficult to strengthen your spirit without harvesting aspects from the world, and it typically requires elixirs or natural treasures. Like the fruit you found.

"If you cultivate aspects that exist in heaven and earth, you can soak vital aura from the environment as you cycle. That's how I do it, that's how your mother does it, that's how everyone does it. To keep yourself pure, you'd have to give up the easiest and most reliable way of getting stronger. Worse, you'd sacrifice your most dependable means of self-defense. A fire artist could burn arrows out of the air mid-flight, and a sword artist could strike them out of the air. An artist of pure madra would be helpless to affect the flight of an arrow. He would die as helpless as a bird."

Lindon nodded seriously along with Jaran's words, but his enthusiasm didn't dim. It wasn't as though he meant to cultivate pure madra *forever*; he would start on a Path as soon as he was allowed. But this was an advantage he had now, an advantage that had gone to waste. Even an Unsouled wasn't entirely useless after all.

Having firmly driven his point home, Jaran drummed his knuckles on the table. "Your sister knew all this, so you were safe this time. But carelessness is a short path to death in the sacred arts, remember that. It's why a good plan is so important. Which brings me back to the Festival."

Lindon thought for a moment before speaking, choosing his words carefully. "I plan to use the Empty Palm on my opponents. At the Foundation stage, they should have no defense, and I'll take first place easily."

Jaran leaned forward, rapping him on the top of the head. It hurt more than he'd expected. "You said that before, but I was hoping you'd think this time. Acting without thinking is bad, but it's worse to think like a coward."

Jibes and backhanded insults from his father were far more familiar than compliments. "Excuse my foolishness, Father, but I don't see the error in my words."

"After the first strike, you *always* follow up with a second." He laughed suddenly. "Like Mon Keth this morning, right? First hit lands, in comes your second one. You landed a hit today with your plan, with your sister's help and heaven's own luck. People see you as the Unsouled who beat an Iron. That's an advantage to you, which means you've got to strike again *now*. What can you get out of this?"

Lindon's body thrummed with hunger. The same appetite that Elder Whisper had woken by speaking of a new Path rose up in him now, a yawning void that demanded to be filled. *This* was his chance to snatch another piece for himself, to climb another step closer to everything he ever wanted.

He'd forgotten about his father, his mind racing from option to option. Could he leverage this notoriety into a request for training materials? He could borrow the parasite ring from the Patriarch, with the excuse that he needed it to prepare for the Festival.

No, he would have to appeal to the Patriarch directly, who wouldn't be able to show him favoritism. Lindon had fought with another member of the Wei clan, and thus not brought any honor to the clan as a whole, so the Patriarch wouldn't be able to reward him.

Maybe he could go to the Eighth Elder in the archive, and request a few minutes with the Path manuals. Not to take one, just to study and learn. But given the Eighth Elder's personality, he wouldn't be swayed by anything Lindon had done.

So it came down to one question: who had enough power in the clan to give him a gift *and* the motivation to do so?

A figure appeared in his mind, and he abruptly stood up. He froze when he remembered his father; even though this was Lindon's home, Jaran was both father and guest. If Lindon left, it would be disrespectful.

Jaran saw his dilemma and laughed again, flipping his cup over. "Go, wherever you're going. That's not the face of a coward, so my work is done here. And I have your wine to keep me company."

Grateful, Lindon bowed his way out.

Lindon used the morning's duel as an excuse to enter the First Elder's home, which was readily accepted by the elder's niece. She congratulated him on the way in. As soon as he passed through the door, he understood why the First Elder of the Wei clan would live here. It was the perfect place to cultivate White Fox madra.

Inside the hallway, mirrors shone to his left and right, reflecting his image in an endless chain stretching off to eternity. Foxfire flickered in the lamps, purple and white, casting phantom images on one mirror that weren't reflected in the other. The effect, even one step inside the doorway, was like swimming in a sea of dreams.

The hall was perfectly straight, but Lindon still slid forward one careful step at a time, not daring to trust his senses. Since he'd trained the Empty Palm with Kelsa, he had gained a new appreciation for just how disorienting the Path of the White Fox could be.

As he moved deeper in the house, he passed more oddities intended to focus dream aura. One painting of abstract shapes reminded him of a stern face one second and a tight flock of crows the next. A snowfox statue seemed to follow him with its eyes as he passed. Clusters of chimes on the ceiling were interspersed with ribbons of paper, trailing his entry with soft whispers and fragile music. As sticks of incense burned, they produced conflicting scents; sweet like mint, acrid as charred paper, savory like a haunch of roasting meat.

The senses bent and warped in the house, and Lindon's head ached after only a minute or two inside. He couldn't imagine living under these conditions, but then again, he didn't follow the Path of the White Fox. Maybe the First Elder was more comfortable here.

"Lisha?" the First Elder called from the other room. "What are you doing out there?"

A human voice gave Lindon something to anchor to, and he stumbled in that direction, running his good hand over the wall searching for a door. He found one, sliding it open.

The elder was inside, kneeling beside a low table, brush poised over a scroll. "I didn't expect to see you again today, Shi Lindon," he said, without looking up.

Lindon bowed over his broken arm. "This one begs your indulgence, honored elder."

The First Elder waved his hand irritably. "Wait there quietly. I must reply to one of the esteemed Schools, who *insist* that we honor them by intervening in a problem that does not concern us."

He had been ordered to silence, but Lindon took a risk. "A problem, First Elder?"

The elder rubbed a spot on his temple, glaring at the scroll as though it contained a death threat. "The honorable Heaven's Glory School has lost no less than four disciples to abduction, it seems. Apparently an outsider is torturing and killing them for the secrets of their sacred arts."

Despite the grim news, Lindon was somewhat excited. Torturing a rival disciple for secret arts only happened in legends. "Do they suspect the Wei clan?"

"No, no, don't worry. This has nothing to do with us, and this certainly isn't the full story, but they *still* want 'assurances of our immediate and absolute compliance.' The clans have enough to deal with without taking on the burdens of the Schools as well."

"We'll show the other clans our power at the Seven-Year Festival," Lindon said, angling the conversation around to his point.

"As the Li and Kazan clans will seek to show us," the First Elder pointed out. "The Kazan in particular are maneuvering aggressively for one of our farms by the river. They either know something about that farm, or they have some secret that allows them to act arrogantly. But the roaring tiger loses its prey to the tiger hidden in the brush. The Li clan has made no motion to improve its strength before the Festival, and that worries me most of all."

The elder placed his brush down and straightened. "I forgot myself. These are not matters for an Unsouled. What brings you here, Shi Lindon?"

"This one has a request, honored elder," Lindon said, bowing again. Then he dropped the humble speech and met the First Elder's eye. "Today, I've shown that my ability reaches beyond my level of advancement."

"You've shown that you can use tricks to embarrass a man more skilled and powerful than you are."

"Honor by any means," Lindon said, and the First Elder conceded the point with a nod. "I have every confidence in my ability to sweep the Foundation stage competition at the Festival."

"As you should," the elder pointed out. "You'll be the oldest one competing by at least two years. That will win us no honor among the other clans."

This was the very point Lindon had come to address. "The elder speaks truly. But this one wonders if the First Elder has considered the exhibition match."

The victor of each stage won the right to challenge one competitor of higher advancement to an exhibition round. The Foundation winner could challenge a Copper, the Copper winner could challenge an Iron, and so on. It wasn't a true contest, but rather a display of skill. Against a more advanced opponent, one could display one's true ability.

The elder ran fingers through his long white beard as he thought. "It would improve our standing...*if* the Foundation champion from our clan could fight evenly with a Copper from another clan. If you could pull a trick like you did today, embarrassing another clan, then you would have earned a reward. What is your request?"

"A Path," Lindon said simply.

"Out of the question," the First Elder responded without hesitation. "Do you understand why we forbid Unsouled to practice the sacred arts? It's for your own protection. You're as likely to maim your own soul as to advance to Copper. Elixirs and training would be wasted on you. You would forever be the weakest one on the Path."

Lindon was prepared to negotiate for a lower prize, but he sensed an opening here. As long as the elder was using reason to convince rather than making absolute statements, that left room for discussion. "The resources of the clan should obviously go to more promising disciples than I, but if I have defeated a Copper from another clan, then surely I've proven that I have as much ability as they do. If that's true, then why should I be forbidden from practicing a path?"

Foxfire flickered in the corner of his eyes, showing him phantom motion that was as much in his mind, tempting him to turn his head. But he watched the First Elder as the old man thought. Hope grew with every second of the elder's silence, and finally he opened his mouth to say, "You'll be entirely on your own, you know."

"If I may say so, being on my own has never stopped me before."

The First Elder considered a moment longer, and then slowly nodded. "You'll have access to the Path of the White Fox. I'll have a copy made for you, so you don't take resources away from other students. But, Shi Lindon, heed me: you must *win*."

●

ITERATION 110: CRADLE

Suriel lurched from the Way into reality in a flash of blue light, floating at the high edge of atmosphere. A planet spread out beneath her like a childhood blanket, blue and green and familiar.

[Successfully arrived in Iteration One-one-zero,] said the ghostly Presence on her shoulder. It had come with the job, because no lone mind could control all the powers at Suriel's disposal. [Local time is +5.2 deviations from standard.] She would lose time here, and communication with Sanctum would be delayed, so her journey would take longer.

But then, that was the point.

[What is the purpose of your visit?] the Presence inquired. It was an innocent question, as the Presence was innocent, but Suriel wondered at the answer herself.

[Recovery?] the Presence asked, and all over the planet, displays lit up in Suriel's vision with diagrams and glowing ribbons of text. They marked artifacts of the Abidan, lost over the millennia, matching them to last known locations and possible uses. With a thought, Suriel declined.

[Education?] Places of historical and cultural significance lit like beacons, from the Arches of Dairan to the Twelve Rivers.

[Entertainment?] Sky dancers, spinning on clouds of wind madra, trailed Remnants like glowing streamers. An arrow pointed to a performance in progress on the other side of the planet. A play moved through the audience, actors in painted masks carrying prop daggers, sneaking around as though the viewers didn't exist. A duel between two experts; one riding a stag with lightning for antlers, another carrying a spear of solid flame. The life and death of a nation rode on this contest, but she could watch from safety like an interdimensional voyeur.

[Business?] the Presence asked, and though it was equally innocent, Suriel imagined an accusatory tinge to the construct's voice. Before she could stop it, details of Ozriel's life spooled out on the spectral display, locations of interest blinking into being all over the planet.

The mountain under which *he* had been born in a dark chamber of stone.

The ruins of the library where *he* had once developed his own Path.

The pillars where *he* debated the ten greatest scholars of the day, leading three to commit suicide soon after.

The City of Anvils, sealed now, where *he'd* forged his first weapon.

The labyrinth where *he* died and returned to life.

The country home, buried beneath a meadow now, where *his* fury had first touched the Way.

Suriel wiped the display with a thought. She'd been a fool to come here in the first place. She was the Phoenix, not the Hound. The healer, not the detective. She didn't need to find Ozriel—she needed to find his aftermath. The billions of people affected by his refusal to *do his job.*

Someone had to bring them back to life.

But here she was, shirking her duties in the safest world of all creation. Even Sanctum was more likely to fall to corruption than this place.

Cradle was the birthplace of the Abidan, and theoretically Ozriel could cripple their organization for millennia by destroying it, but crippling them was never his goal. Makiel didn't understand that, though Suriel did. He would never return here, and he would not allow it to fall through his inaction. Of all the worlds she oversaw, this was the most secure.

[Then why are you here?] the Presence asked, sensing that Suriel needed another voice. From anyone else, the question would have been damning. She was a healer, the greatest in existence, and she was dallying on the way to a war zone. Thousands died in every second that passed here. If they remained dead long enough, even she couldn't bring them back.

But he might be right.

Ozriel had done unconscionable things in the service of the Abidan Court. They were all in the name of order among the worlds, but anyone else would have been indicted for war crimes. Though she understood his rationale, she had never felt comfortable with Ozriel on the job.

Then he quit. Ozriel, the celestial executioner, had refused to demolish condemned worlds. The Reaper had hung up his scythe. The other Judges were out for blood, and they expected the same of her. But how could she blame him for *not* murdering billions?

[The corruption spread from his inactivity will affect trillions,] her Presence said, responding to her unspoken question. [If it is not curtailed, then it will soon spread to tens of trillions, until the Court is forced to implement quarantine procedures.]

That was why Suriel delayed. Not because she didn't want to heal the dead and dying, but because the other six Judges would have gathered together. They would want her to vote on a world-spanning quarantine that would leave dozens of worlds without the protection of the Abidan.

It was the exact attitude that had driven Ozriel to leave.

She needed a moment to think, here in a world outside of it all. A world that, though it was torn in an eternal thousand-sided war, existed in isolation. For her, that meant peace. Time to consider. Maybe she could solve some small problems, as a break from the cares of an entire universe.

[Problems,] her Presence acknowledged, and constellations of dots and lines spread all over the planet. Spooling text and images showed Suriel all the wounds she could heal, all the small problems she could fix while ignoring the larger troubles that overwhelmed her.

Here, a monstrous eel undulated through the ocean, spreading clouds of poison over an underwater city. Ten thousand kilometers away, a plague devastated a spire full of white-clad pacifists. On another hemisphere, a kilometers-long azure dragon flew on a violent storm, moving like a hurricane toward a small kingdom.

The text showed her ten million people she could save: from rape, murder, genocide, slavery, starvation, ignorance, disease. Ozriel would try to save them all, and would fail, but the world would be better for his efforts. Makiel would leave those problems to mortals and focus on the bigger picture.

As Suriel stared at the web of information spread out over the planet, trying to decide, another star flared to life. It was red rather than blue, representing a crime that was fated to happen. She focused on it.

[Imminent spatial violation,] her Presence reported. [Domination of local inhabitants by an outside power is predetermined to follow.]

Someone who had grown beyond this world was trying to return to Cradle, using outside power to set up their own fiefdom in this relatively simple plane of existence. That was a grade three violation, something that the local

Sector Control Abidan would address, but they'd take their time about it. This level of crime was far beneath her notice, but both Ozriel and Makiel would have agreed it was worth stopping.

It was perfect.

She took a quick stock of her appearance, to make sure that she wouldn't start any myths by descending. Transparent gray ghostlines ran from the back of her head, twisting down her right arm to terminate in her fingers. Those would be strange, but not alarming. The Mantle of Suriel ran behind her like she'd tied a river of burning light around her neck, and she made that vanish. Her white uniform was seamless, a layer of inch-thick liquid armor that coated her from her neck down to her toes. It would be obviously unnatural, but shouldn't alarm anyone. They would assume it was Forged madra, which was close enough to the truth. She left it.

She couldn't bring her weapon, though it pained her. The meter-long shaft of blue steel hung at her hip, innocuous enough, but she couldn't take the one-in-a-billion chance that she might somehow leave it in Cradle. With an effort of will, she banished it back to Sanctum.

Her long hair drifted around her, luminescent green and shining against the darkness of space. She toned it down to a deep shade of jade barely distinguishable from black, then focused on her eyes. Her irises had expanded to take up most of the sclera, marked with a ring of symbols that a few people on the planet below might recognize as script. They were tools to help her see the flow of fate, but they might advance the development of Cradle scripting beyond acceptable limits. Her eyes burned as though she'd pressed them against red-hot iron, but she endured, altering them to a roughly natural shape in a matter of seconds. They were still large and purple, but they looked human enough.

Suriel's will flickered to the Presence, which acknowledged her command. [Plotting course to the fated violation. Destination: the Sacred Valley. Distance: one hundred sixty-two thousand kilometers. Engaging route].

In a streak of blue, Suriel took off.

CHAPTER SEVEN

Once the sling came off Lindon's broken arm, he re-doubled his training. The Seven-Year Festival raced closer, looming over him, and he resented every minute of rest that might cost him his chance to read a Path manual.

He still intended to find his own way in the sacred arts, as Elder Whisper had told him, but he didn't know enough yet. He needed to research the Path of the White Fox, and once he did...well, maybe he would find that it fit him. Maybe he wouldn't need to explore a new Path at all.

He spent the mornings in the Shi family courtyard with Kelsa, where her beating him counted as training. After-noons belonged to the archive, and he spent that time studying the other technique manuals to which he was allowed access. He never found anything else as perfectly suited for him as the Empty Palm, but he studied the theo-ries. In the evening, he cycled.

The cycling technique in the Heart manual was intend-ed to prepare him for splitting his core, which he never expected to need. Still, it was also a technique meant to improve pure madra manipulation, and thus a better match for him than the Wei clan's Foundation technique. So he continued to use it.

The orus fruit treasure had long vanished, its power incorporated into his own, and he no longer felt the tingling lightning in his core. He felt no stronger, but his results spoke for themselves: he could practice with Kelsa for hours, using the Empty Palm ten or twelve times, before he gave in to fatigue. And that was due to his sister's relentless beatings more than spiritual exhaustion.

Three days before the Festival, only a few hours before noon, Lindon spotted an opening in his sister's stance. He took it, driving an Empty Palm at her belly.

She knocked his wrist wide, stepping in to put a fist into his side...and froze, her elbow cocked back, loose strands of hair drifting in front of her face. Her eyes were fixed on something behind him, beyond him, and he knew at once something was wrong.

"Kelsa?" he asked, taking a careful step back. She didn't respond, and if he couldn't hear her breaths, he wouldn't have known whether she was still alive. In fact, she was still breathing in rhythm according to her Foundation technique.

Her eyes still glazed over, she folded up and sat on the grass. Her hands rested on her lap, her breathing deepened, and tiny balls of foxfire began to dance in the air around her.

When Lindon realized what was happening, he ran for his parents.

He found them together, outside their house, his father cleaning a boar as his mother did something similar to a Remnant. A bucket of bloody guts sat next to a scripted basin containing loops of light and color. Claws of Forged madra slowly fizzed into nonexistence next to slabs of meat leaking blood.

Lindon skidded to a halt in the yard. "Kelsa's advancing to Iron," he announced, then he ran back the other direction.

His mother overtook him in seconds and his father wasn't far behind her, hobbling on his cane faster than Lindon could run. They both reached Kelsa before he did.

Sweat already soaked her training robes, plastering her hair to her neck. Her breath came in labored gasps, and each exhale was tinged with White Fox madra. Phantom images danced in the vital aura around her, complete with sounds; half-formed, unrecognizable ghosts that screamed, laughed, growled, and muttered as they were born of dreams and light.

White Fox madra swirled around her in a cyclone of illusion and color. Purple and white predominated, but every color flickered through, like bright-scaled fish flitting in and out of the light. Purple sparks twisted in the air, cast off Kelsa as though from a bonfire.

Nearby, the underbrush rustled, and a snowfox peeked its snout out to watch. It was young—only one tail trailed behind it in the bushes—but it was still drawn to the madra it sensed was so similar to its own. According to legend, the first Wei Patriarch's ascension to Jade had drawn snow-foxes from all over Sacred Valley in a pilgrimage that lasted three days.

Kelsa's eyes drifted closed and then snapped open, blazing with purple-edged light. All around her, vague dreams bloomed from the earth like squirming flowers.

"Second stage," his mother noted, scribbling as she watched.

"She might be as fast as I was," Jaran said, a proud smile on his twisted lips. "Copper to Iron in less than an hour, and no worse for it."

"Then we should prepare for the third stage," Seisha said.

"Prepare?"

"Not us," she said, with a significant glance at Lindon. "You should leave, son."

Lindon rarely defied his parents, but this was an exceptional chance. He'd never seen anyone advance to Iron before, and this was his sister. "I'd learn more if I stayed to the end."

"Too dangerous," Jaran said, hobbling over to take him by the arm.

Then a ripple of purple-white madra pulsed out from Kelsa, and Lindon learned what his father meant.

White Fox Forgers used the Fox Mirror technique to create illusionary copies of exact appearance but no real substance; some built false walls, or hid in fake trees, or adopted the clothes of their enemies. Legend said the Patriarch could create a twin of himself as indistinguishable as his own reflection.

Enforcers kept their madra close, even inside, and White Fox Enforcers deceived their opponents by hiding their steps or subtle movements in a skill called the Foxtail. Their punches looked slightly longer than they were, their steps shorter, their motions faster, their reactions slower. In battle, where victory or defeat could ride on the accuracy of split-second judgments, Enforcers of the Wei clan could be the most frustrating enemies.

Strikers cast their madra out to use on others, and White Fox Strikers learned to manipulate foxfire. They could make a target feel like he was burning to death, or illuminate a target with a spark only they could see, or cloud an enemy's vision with phantom lights. The Striker technique was considered the weakest in the Path of the White Fox, but nonetheless it had certain advantages. Foxfire did no real damage, but it did inflict pain, and its purple-and-white flames could not be extinguished.

Rulers worked differently. Rather than manipulating their own madra, they used their madra as a catalyst to control vital aura. As for Rulers on the Path of the White Fox, they directed aura of light and dreams to trap their enemies in a Fox Dream.

As Kelsa's power flew out of control, Lindon's vision fuzzed as though every surface crawled with ants. One of the nearby bushes seized the ground with one branch and hauled itself out of the earth, its exposed roots trailing dirt. It scooted toward him, pale blue cloudbells bobbing. Shadows giggled and whispered, flinching away when his gaze moved to them. They scuttled away in shy groups to spy on him from another angle.

One of the clouds dipped down from the sky to look him in the eye, until his vision was filled with cottony white. Once it was pleased with whatever it saw in him, the cloud left on its merry journey.

He recoiled after a single glance at his parents' faces. The scar at the side of his father's lip expanded until the man's face was only one giant mass of tissue, pale and puckered. His mother's eyes glowed, and every word dropped from her lips with the weight of heaven's decree. The earth shook as she spoke, and Lindon clapped his hands over his ears.

When the earth righted itself, he found that he was curled up fifty feet away from where he'd started, and his hands weren't over his ears at all. They were contorted into claws, and his wrists were firmly pinned against his chest by his father.

"You won't tear your eyes out now, will you?" Jaran asked.

Lindon shook his head, too afraid to say anything. He had hated the times when Kelsa injected her madra into him, but she hadn't ignited any vital aura then. His delusions had been much more detailed this time, like an utterly convincing dream. Last time, shapes and colors had lurched around until he couldn't tell where anything was, but this time...he had seen a plant uproot itself in full color, and now the cloudbell bush sat planted as solidly as ever.

"Even you can develop a defense against this sort of thing," Seisha said, though most of her attention was on her daughter. "Your spirit has supreme control inside your own body."

Lindon was very interested in learning more about that, but for now, one thing mattered more. "How is she?"

It wasn't common, but there was always the possibility of disaster during advancement. When someone was interrupted while advancing, or tried to advance during a fight, or used elixirs to force an advancement early, they could end up facing a backlash. Their madra could turn against them, killing them or removing their ability to practice the sacred arts.

In that case, Kelsa might be no better than an Unsouled.

Seisha leaned over her daughter, brown hair falling into the girl's face, and cast a clinical eye over her body. Kelsa was now lying in a heap on the grass, sweat-soaked but breathing evenly. She was streaked with grit like black mud, which gave off a stench that burned Lindon's nose from yards away. Advancing to Iron refined the body, expelling impurities. Seisha pressed two fingers to the girl's throat, and then to her core.

Kelsa groaned, stirring.

"Did you do it?" Jaran asked, leaning over her.

In response, Kelsa reached out and gripped a young sapling with one hand. In one simple movement of her thumb, she snapped it in half.

"Call the elders and break out the wine," Seisha said. "The Wei clan has a new Iron."

The same night, the clan turned out for a celebration in honor of Wei Shi Kelsa. Even some guests from the other two clans and four Schools were in attendance, having arrived early for the Festival. The Patriarch presented her with her new badge in front of all the gathered families, and the First Elder gave her a polished case containing a trio of valuable elixirs. They represented a significant expense for the clan, but the wise gambler bet on the fastest horse. Resources went to strengthen those who were already strong, not to bring up the weak.

It was the way life worked, and Lindon had no cause to complain. He might as well complain that the heavens hadn't given him a stronger soul. Instead, he looked forward. His sister was ready for the Seven-Year Festival, and now it was his turn.

That night, Lindon stuffed a shovel into his pack and prepared to cheat.

The Wei hosted the Festival this year, an honor and a responsibility that increased the pressure on their families to perform well. As a result, the clan's Enforcers had been working for over a year to construct a brand-new arena in which to display the contests.

The arena was circular and made almost entirely of orus wood, with one huge script etched around the inside to prevent power from spilling over into the audience. The seats were tiered in layers and separated by clan colors— purple and white for the Wei clan, green and gray for the Li clan, and brown and red for the Kazan. One higher box would contain guests from the four Schools, separating them from the common rabble outside.

The stage itself was a square of pure white stone a hundred yards to a side, divided in eight sections by lines in the floor. The Foundation children would use all the sections at once, with eight fights simultaneously until the number of participants was reduced. The Coppers would use a quarter of the stage each, the Irons half, and any pair of Jades who decided to settle a grudge or demonstrate their skill for the younger generation would have the whole stage to themselves.

Outside the arena were four polished wooden columns, each ringed in script and topped by Forged snowfoxes. These five-tailed white foxes, each an almost exact copy of Elder Whisper, paced on their columns or yawned or licked their paws just as live sacred beasts would have. They would be indistinguishable from life to every sense except touch, which explained why they were elevated so far above the ground.

If not quite famous in the Wei clan, Lindon was at least known, and the guards allowed him inside on the pretext that he was checking a script for his mother. She had led the work on the four foxes, for which she was expecting a reward from the Patriarch.

Under the protection of his mother's name, Lindon had a thorough look around, inspecting the stage, the columns, the seats, and especially the ground inside the arena.

Then he walked into the woods.

He carried a spirit-map with him—his mother's analysis of the local Remnants—and there were a few around here that might cooperate. When he reached a likely spot, he knelt down and scratched a script circle in the dirt around him. His skill as a scriptor had improved since he was a child, but only to the point where he wouldn't embarrass his mother by laying a simple layer of protection. At least, not while he was copying it from a book.

Mount Samara loomed over the Wei clan to the east, lit by the massive halo of white light that they called Samara's ring. It glowed brighter than the moon, casting all of Sacred Valley in white, but the depths of the forest were still bathed in shadow. He had expected to use Samara's ring for enough light to read, but he had come prepared nonetheless, pulling a candle and a striker out of his pack.

Seconds later, he squinted at his mother's scripting guide by candlelight. He could have used the scripted light in his pack, but he wanted his madra fresh to deal with the Remnant. He smoothed out one symbol, correcting another, brushing pebbles and twigs aside to keep each rune as close to the guide as possible. After satisfying himself that the circle was at least as secure as he could make it, he sat cross-legged at the center, book on one side and candle on the other.

Then he threw a rock at the hornet's nest.

Hornets buzzed out an instant later, furious and seeking vengeance...but not *living* hornets. Remnants. They were made of bright emerald color, as though some artist had dipped her brush in a jar of green ink and painted them onto the world. But not in full detail. Rather than accurate depictions of the hornets they'd been in life, these Remnants were mere sketches. Outlines, swirls of lines and shape that somehow *suggested* hornets.

The swarm flitted around Lindon's circle, stingers at the ready. Script wasn't some magic language of the heavens, as old mythology suggested. Each rune was a shape that guided vital aura in the air, reshaping it to a new purpose. This particular circle was the reverse of the one he'd used on the Remnant of the ancestral tree; it would catch and eject any madra that attempted to cross the line.

And Remnants, while strange and powerful, were made entirely of madra.

The hornets could fly high enough that the script circle would lose its effect, but they didn't. They stayed, either unaware that they could fly over, or intrigued enough to hear what the human had to say.

Lindon hoped it was the latter. For one thing, that suggested that these Remnants were intelligent enough to hear him out. Which meant they'd be less likely to flock through and sting him to death as soon as the circle dropped.

The only way to judge a Remnant's intelligence was through experience. The tree-Remnant, the newborn spirit of a plant, had displayed little intelligence at all. If this swarm was smart enough to wait on him, he could take a little risk.

Lindon held up the other object he'd brought inside the circle with him: a clay jar with a wide mouth and a tight-fitting lid. He opened the lid, showing the hornet Remnants the shining blue crystal—barely the size of a child's fingernail—that lay within.

At the sight of the crystal flask, the hornets buzzing increased to a frantic pace.

"Honored sacred beasts, this one comes to you in humility," Lindon began. They weren't sacred beasts any longer, but more respect was always better than less when it came to Remnants. Or people, he supposed. "In exchange for this offering of spirit, this one begs you to wait inside this vessel for only three days' time."

Sacred artists typically filled flasks this size by the handful, but this one had taken him almost a week. It was the best he could do, considering how little strength he started with, and how exhausted his spirit was after a day of training with Kelsa.

The bright hornets buzzed frantically, pushing as close to the circle as they dared, hungering for the bare human power they sensed within. A few of the green-sketched shapes got a little too close, and their own energy activated the script. Runes shone weakly, and an invisible force pushed them backwards.

This circle could be overwhelmed, and would do precisely nothing against Remnants with bodies bigger or more solid than these insects, but tonight it held.

Can they understand me? Lindon wondered. He cleared his throat and tried again.

"Honorable...cousins of the hive, this one wonders if you would agree to rest inside this jar. In return, this one gives you an offering of his spirit. In only three days—"

A buzzing interrupted him, forming a voice, harsh and monotone. "WHY?"

Lindon's breath caught. He had hoped they were intelligent enough to accept a crude barter. It had never occurred to him that they might *speak*.

He bowed forward so deeply that his forehead pressed against dirt, just shy of the script. He almost shivered, knowing that their emerald stingers were only inches from his scalp, but it would be disrespectful to show fear in front of this strange Remnant. Not to mention unwise.

"This one wishes to call upon your might before the sun sets three days hence. This one will break the jar, whereupon you will attack another human of my direction. Not this one, if it pleases you. One other."

The buzzing dipped and rose, as though the hive were trying to find the right pitch for the words. "WE...TAKE. SPIRIT. ROCK."

The flask. "Of course, sacred ones! Take it. Drain it dry. It is yours."

The hornets spun around in a dance, conferring with

one another. Human madra was more than mere food and water to Remnants; they could advance with it. Evolve. Gain in wisdom, power, and concentration.

He didn't care if they ascended to the heavens, so long as they helped him.

"AGREE," the hive responded.

Lindon hastily scuffed the nearest symbol with the heel of his foot, but fear punched him in the gut as soon as he did. In his eagerness to close, he hadn't specified anything about his current safety. They had agreed not to attack him once he released them, but nothing stopped them from plunging their stingers into him *tonight.*

Abandoning dignity, he curled up into a ball as they swarmed past him and into the jar. He held arms over his face for a full minute or two, sweating, before he realized that the buzzing had quieted.

He glanced into the jar. A cluster of hornet Remnants, like sketches of green paint, climbed all over each other at the bottom. The tiny flask was only visible as a faint twinkling of light, and as he watched, that light dimmed. A few of the closest Remnants brightened visibly, gaining new details: here a new joint on a leg, there a segment of carapace, as though they somehow grew more real before his eyes.

He bowed once more to the open jar before carefully placing the lid on. As soon as they couldn't see him, he wiped sweat from his brow and sagged down in relief.

Remnants weren't likely to kill him, not as long as he dealt with them in good faith, but they could very well have taught him a painful lesson. This had been a gamble—not a huge one, but one with a potentially uncomfortable downside.

The wise gambler bets on the fastest horse. The Wei clan had taught him well. Eagerly, he wrapped a line of weighted shadesilk around the jar. When tied, this held the lid, ensuring that an awkward misstep on his part wouldn't spill hornets everywhere.

The Remnants could fly straight through the jar, if they

wished. A ring of script around the sides discouraged that, but it was even weaker than the circle he'd used to protect himself earlier. They could push through as easily as a man pushing through a screen. What really held them was their word.

It wasn't as though Remnants couldn't lie, but rather that they acted exactly according to their nature. For most, they simply wouldn't accept an unfavorable deal. It would never occur to them to accept and then break it.

Lindon erased all evidence of the night's work in minutes, packing his gear up in his worn brown pack. The jar of Remnants went in last of all, carefully secured.

It was most of two hour's hike back to the clan, but he hardly noticed the time. His chances had just doubled.

He walked past the street that led to his rooms, instead heading back to the arena. The guards allowed him back in without further questions, leaving no one to watch him. They were his family, if only distantly; they knew him. So no one saw as Lindon took a shovel to the soft earth, digging straight down until he bared the sides of the stone blocks that made up the stage floor.

When he got beneath them, he adjusted his angle, hollowing out a space under the block. A space just big enough for a sealed clay jar.

He was sliding the jar into the opened earth when his mother's voice sounded from behind him.

"Still practicing?"

CHAPTER EIGHT

Lindon turned to face his mother, hiding the hole and the sealed jar behind him. "Your son is honored to see you here, Mother. But why...I mean, if I may ask why you..."

Seisha saved him the effort of explaining by walking forward and leaning over the hole he'd dug. Her drudge gurgled as it floated over her shoulder, no doubt detecting the Remnant sealed within.

"While the arena is under construction, the staff answer to me," Seisha said, kneeling to run a finger along his scripted jar. "I asked them to report anyone entering tonight, but I never thought it would be you."

Lindon was afraid to move, lest it somehow push his mother over the edge from calm to furious. "I'm sorry to have disturbed you, then."

Seisha stood, flipping brown hair over one shoulder. "You can think of nothing else you've done that might warrant an apology?"

Despite the cool of the night, he broke out in a sudden sweat. He had thought of cover stories depending on who caught him, but none of them would pass his mother.

She looked into the hole with brown eyes, lighter than anyone else in the clan. "Back home, we had a saying. 'The disciple follows the master, but the genius blazes their own trail.' You should cover this up before someone else sees it."

Lindon wasted a second on astonishment before grabbing his shovel and setting to work. He piled the dirt back in hastily, hoping she wouldn't change her mind. "Mother, are you calling me a genius?"

"Obviously not. It's just a saying." He couldn't deny a moment of disappointment before his mother continued. "Nonetheless, I'm proud of you."

The shovel felt light in his hands as his mother's words danced through his mind, so it wasn't until he'd worked in silence for minutes more that he thought to ask a question. "Who were you expecting?"

She gave him a wry glance. Because he knew her, he knew what it meant: she had hoped he wouldn't ask that question. But Wei Shi Seisha would answer it anyway, because she believed that curiosity should always be rewarded. "Have you heard any rumors about the Li clan recently?"

The First Elder had said they were too quiet, suspiciously so, but Lindon suspected he wasn't supposed to have that information. He shook his head.

"Three months ago, they purchased an unusual item from an auction. A fragment of a stone tablet dating back thousands of years, supposedly found at the base of the Nethergate. It was covered in runes that may have had some...unique properties. But no one could ever prove it."

"What sort of properties?" Lindon asked, leaning on his shovel.

"It looked like half of a script intended for direct spatial transportation. The stuff of myths. Walk into one circle and emerge in another one a world away, stories like that. I examined the tablet myself, before the Li clan bought it, and I could not confirm it."

Still, Lindon's imagination burned with the possibilities. That really was the stuff of legends.

"Since they bought the tablet, we haven't heard much

from them at all, but we've started to receive reports that they've been hunting specific Remnants. A rabbit that crosses yards in the blink of an eye. A bat that can vanish into nothing. A mole that burrows through thin air. We believe they're trying to condense spatial madra."

Spatial madra. It sounded ridiculous. "Apologies, Mother, but how could that be? How could madra take on the form of *space*?"

She pointed at him, and he knew he'd struck the heart of the matter. "It can't. Madra can imitate anything from fire to dreams, and we call those forms 'aspects.' Obviously, to speak of space having a form is absurd. They are actually seeking to pierce and control space *using* madra, which should be impossible."

But there had to be more to the story, or his mother wouldn't be so uneasy. "Then the Li clan is wasting their time. And their money."

"I've worked with some of the Li Soulsmiths, who would be leading any project involving Remnants. They're underhanded and some of their theories are suspect, but they wouldn't commit clan resources to a project unless they had reason to believe it could succeed. *That* is what scares me. Everything I've heard leads me to believe that they're investing everything into a fool's dream, so they've either gone insane...or they know something we don't."

Lindon shivered even as he finished filling in the hole he'd dug beneath the stage, patting the soil down so that it fell flush with the stone block. If the Li clan did try something during the Festival, it reassured him that he at least had one hidden weapon.

Seisha held a glowing blue stick of Forged madra up for her drudge's inspection, and it ran segmented legs over the stick before whistling in response. She noted something down on her notepad. After only a few minutes, she'd already moved on to her next project. "If you've finished, we should leave the arena. It won't be long before someone asks what we've been doing here, and the shovel will be hard to explain."

On their way out, Lindon asked a question that had unnerved him as soon as he'd thought of it. "Will the Li clan try something during the Festival?"

"Undoubtedly they will," she said, deep in her notebook. When he responded with uneasy silence, she elaborated. "The clans always try something during the Seven-Year Festival, because it's the best time to strive against one another. They'll propose 'sure' bets, or try to rig trading agreements. Nothing unusual. As for our earlier discussion—" They were walking past a guard, who nodded to them as they left. "—I suspect it will take them years before they have anything functional. Real research takes generations to perfect."

"Then why were you expecting them tonight?"

She gave him a wry smile. "Because I try to expect the worst."

INFORMATION REQUESTED: THE SEVEN-YEAR FESTIVAL. BEGINNING REPORT...

Every seven years, the clans of Sacred Valley hold a festival.

While the original purpose of this gathering was to promote unity, it has become the primary stage on which they compete. The children of the clan are taught to identify the others by their clothes—armor and a red sash for the Kazan, with their banners bearing three stone dogs; a white fox with five tails for the Wei, who always match white with purple; and the Li, who wear too much jewelry and carry banners bearing the Snake and the Tree.

These are your enemies, the children are told. *One day, our clan will be strong, and we will crush the other two under our heels.*

It has been this way for a hundred generations.

The Wei clan hosts the Festival this year, so outside craftsmen have inhabited clan grounds for months. They build booths of orus wood, dig trenches, paint houses, smooth roads, and generally prepare the clan for an influx of rivals. The Wei are never so clean, organized, and well-presented as in the days leading up to the Seven-Year Festival.

The outsider craftsmen are confined to temporary housing around their projects, and are kept to a strict curfew. Most don't mind. Beyond clan territory, Sacred Valley is still wild, and they are accustomed to the ravages of weather and wild Remnants. Living in the security of a community is a luxury most cannot afford for long.

When the booths are arranged, the White Fox banners flying from the tallest homes, and the arena prepared, the clan is ready. The outsiders are paid and sent away as the other clans begin to arrive.

The Kazan announce their arrival with a host of trumpets when they are still miles away, and the ground rumbles under the impact of their advancing army. When banners flying the Stone Dogs are visible in the distance, streams of red flowing in the wind, the least dignified of the Wei gather to catch a glimpse of their visiting enemies. Most only see a Kazan clansman every seven years.

Every man, woman, and child of the Kazan wears armor, even where it could not possibly grant any protection. Women wear shadesilk dresses with a sleeve of delicately wrought mail, or plates sewn into the bodice. Men wear helmets over red robes, or wrap themselves in loose-fitting cloth with thick belts of iron and leather. Children carry shields, or run around in tiny breastplates.

All of the Kazan wear badges, of course, but these are seemingly crafted with perfection in mind as well; they are four or five times bigger than those of the Wei clan, so that the adults wear plates of copper or iron over their entire chests.

Even the mounts they ride, for those rich or important enough to afford mounts, are armored. They are stone dogs the size of horses, Forged constructs created by Soulsmiths, and every step of every paw strikes the earth like a drumstick. The bulkiest of these craghounds, as they are called, drag wagons behind them—wagons laden with the goods of Mount Venture. Halfsilver ingots, sky-iron statuettes, and goldsteel blades flash in the sun, delighting the eyes of the Wei children.

The families of the White Fox mock the incoming Kazan for their blunt ways, for their lack of subtlety, for their obvious stupidity. The Wei clan will rule their lands soon, as it once was, and as it is meant to be again.

The Li clan is too sophisticated for trumpets. They unleash Remnants to fly around their heads as they approach, swift jade hawks and shining silver butterflies and twin-headed crimson eagles, all trailing lines of vivid color behind them in the sky. The display is a delicate tapestry woven among the clouds, accompanied by music from the most accomplished Li performers. Flutes and stringed instruments drift in sweet tones around the Remnants' dance, leading some Wei children to laugh in delight. They will be reprimanded by their parents later.

There are no wagons visible among the Li at first, as their mounts and cargo will be taking up the rear. They will present nothing unsightly to their enemies. Those of the Jade stage march in the first rank, their badges displayed proudly among necklaces of gold and silver. Those most honored in the Li clan are also the most bedecked in jewels, with Jade elders wearing five rings in each ear and two on each finger.

The ranks of Iron and Copper follow Jade, though only the best of each stage are represented here. Those who have stagnated at their level for too long are miles behind, with the pack animals and the children, to arrive with no fanfare and no apparent connection to those who have gone before.

Each Copper carries a tall wooden branch, unpolished and uncarved. At the height of this branch is a green banner. When the Coppers raise their branches together, it is as though they march in the center of a forest, with leaves blowing over their heads. A few of the most outstanding Coppers have snakes carved into their branches, as the Tree and the Serpent are the symbols of the Li clan.

Mothers and fathers of the Wei families lean over their children, pointing out the ostentatious jewelry, which flash in the gleaming Remnant rainbow overhead. This is vanity, pride, and arrogance. Only the truly strong deserve to be arrogant, and the Li clansmen think too much of themselves. With such displays, they will someday provoke a power much greater than their own, and that will be their downfall.

At the same time and in the same voices, the Li and the Kazan mock the Wei in their own ways, and for their own reasons. Such is as it has been for a hundred generations.

For all its talk of humility, the Wei clan will not lose to its guests. And masters of illusion are, after all, masters of presentation.

The gates of the Wei clan—newly constructed for the occasion, and carved with purple flowers and white foxes—peel open under the strength of invisible chains. The Li display is put to shame when the sky explodes in sound and color, foxfire popping in purple flares and raining down among the visitors in a million harmless sparks. A legion of phantom snowfoxes wait on their haunches, lined up along the street of the clan as the Li and the Kazan enter. The eyes of the foxes follow each stranger, even as illusionary cheers fill the atmosphere. Flower petals of pink and white and purple spin on the wind, and sweet scents fall from the sky as though the air itself has been perfumed.

The Wei swell with pride as they watch this coordinated masterpiece of White Fox madra, and the elders—their conductors—nod to each other in satisfaction. They have outdone their rivals in hospitality, welcoming them in a fashion appropriate for receiving an imperial procession.

In their minds, this is more than their enemies deserve.

Suggested topic: the fate of the current Seven-Year Festival. Continue?

Denied, report complete.

CHAPTER NINE

All the important events of the Seven-Year Festival were to take place later, once the esteemed guests had settled in. It would take several days for everyone to arrive from all over Sacred Valley, and the Wei clan wanted as broad an audience as possible.

But the Foundation fights were scheduled for the first day.

Lindon understood why. These were children, after all; while each clan would still try to make sure *its* children were the best trained in the sacred arts, there was nothing at stake beyond pride. When a clan revealed a new talent at the Iron level, then they were displaying a new military power. Likewise, Coppers were the future of the clan. Showing weakness before rivals could be a clan's death sentence.

As for the Foundation stage, unless a boy or girl revealed a truly extraordinary genius talent, these fights existed only to give the children experience. A victory would gain face for the clan, but nothing remarkable.

Lindon reminded himself of this to keep from vomiting all over his white training robes. His wooden badge seemed to burn on his chest as he waited on the bench with the other Foundation-level Wei fighters. The seats that he'd seen empty a few nights before now roared with life as sacred artists from all over the Valley gathered.

Besides him, the oldest person on the bench was a twelve-year-old girl from the Chen family. Three years younger than he was, and already on the verge of breaking through to Copper.

The arena spread before him, a huge square of pale stone, but now it looked as vast as a field of snow. If he failed, everyone would see it. Not just those in the Wei clan, who already knew about their Unsouled, but the Li and the Kazan as well. They would see what a shame the Wei had produced.

He looked up to the corner of the arena, where a five-tailed snowfox curled up on a pillar. It opened its eyes as though sensing his attention, staring at him with a gaze of absolute black.

Elder Whisper and his mother had both told him to move forward. He couldn't be a coward now.

Even if he felt like one.

A powerfully built man in elaborate purple-and-gold shadesilk glided past the bench, his thick beard blending in with his wild hair until he looked like a silver lion. He winked at the children, ignoring Lindon, his jade scepter badge hanging over the White Fox emblem on his chest.

Wei Jin Sairus, the Wei Patriarch, rarely involved himself in the day-to-day workings of the clan. The elders handled such mundane matters. He was the idol for the younger generations to follow, the sacred artist fixated entirely on his Path, seeking power to the exclusion of all else. When he did emerge from seclusion, it was usually to battle a powerful Remnant, seek out rumors of a newfound treasure, or directly threaten a rival clan. He personally represented a significant fraction of the Wei clan's strength.

Wei Jin Amon, the Patriarch's blood grandson, followed at a respectful distance behind. He was dressed in white, an iron badge hanging from his neck though he was only seventeen, and he carried a spear wrapped in shimmering green shadesilk. His hair was long and thick, tied back until it flowed behind him like a black river, and some of the less flattering rumors said he spent as much time caring for his hair as he did practicing his sacred arts. His gaze did land on Lindon, cold and calculating, but passed by in a breath.

The hammering of Lindon's heart redoubled. The Foundation fights weren't important, but now the Patriarch and his grandson—a future disciple of the vaunted Heaven's Glory School—were *both* here to witness. What was happening? Surely they had something more important to be doing besides watching Lindon try to beat up ten-year-olds.

Seconds later, he had his answer, but it was no comfort. Rather than joining the Wei section and sitting among their family, Sairus and Amon greeted some of the elders and moved on. They walked over to the stairway leading up to the box reserved for visitors from the four Schools.

And Lindon realized there were people up there. Actual School disciples, the elites of Sacred Valley, there to see him fail.

Now that he was watching, he could pick them out. A young woman with purple robes and a crown of ivy represented the Fallen Leaf. The boy wrapped in white and gold, seemingly even younger than Lindon, would be there for the Heaven's Glory School. The man for the Golden Sword wore plates of iron sewn onto his clothes, and his goldsteel sheath gleamed. That left the old woman in gray to represent the Holy Wind, and as far as Lindon could tell, she was absolutely ordinary.

He turned around and heaved, spewing his breakfast all over the ground behind the bench.

The three clans didn't account for the entire population of Sacred Valley—far from it—but they ruled by virtue of superiority in the sacred arts. Those who followed the Path of the White Fox were stronger and better-trained than those wild practitioners without the support of a large family, and the Wei could afford to produce elixirs that the most powerful sacred artists needed to advance.

The four Schools were on another level entirely.

They focused *completely* on the sacred arts, to the exclusion of all else, and their disciples were selected from among the best of the clans. Wei, Li, or Kazan...it didn't matter, so long as the disciple was promising enough, and wasn't so old that they couldn't still switch Paths. It was said that any Jade expert from the Schools was on par with the Patriarch of a clan, and each School had enough Jades to tear every Wei to pieces.

A School disciple would be well within his rights to strike an ordinary clansman down with no explanation. If Lindon's fight offended the senses of the honored guests overhead, they could kill him from where they sat. The Patriarch would more than likely apologize for wasting their time.

A hand rested on his shoulder, and Lindon turned to see his father, face twisted in disgust. "Wipe your mouth," he said. "We can't have the Kazan seeing you like this."

Lindon hurriedly swiped at his lips with the back of his sleeve. "Apologies, Father. I did not realize the esteemed guests from the Schools would be in attendance today."

"Ah, well, best not to shame us then. Though there are worse things than a clean death."

Seisha pushed him aside, drudge still floating over her shoulder. "Keep your eyes open. Learn what you can. However it turns out today, it's not the end of your path."

Behind her mother, Kelsa nodded. "Don't push yourself too hard. If they shame you too badly, I'll pay them back in the Iron trials."

Lindon looked at his family. Each of them had shown up for a word before the matches, which was more than he expected or deserved. He was warmed by the mere fact that they had tried, and he dipped his head to show his gratitude.

But the warmth was balanced by cold knowledge: none of them expected him to succeed. Even his mother, who knew he planned to cheat. Even his sister, who had helped him train. Even his father, who led him to speak with the

First Elder and leverage an additional reward. None of them actually believed he could do it.

In the end, he could only rely on himself.

There was an elaborate welcome ceremony involving the booming voice of the Patriarch, the blessing of each of the four Schools, and a parade of illusory snowfoxes from the Wei clan elders on the sidelines. Lindon watched none of it. His attention was inside, following the blue-white energy of his madra as it traveled through the complex network of lines inside his body. He guided it, matching it to his breathing, purifying the energy. Cycling it.

When the other children on his bench stood, he was ready.

There were hundreds of Foundation children participating, and he was fortunate—or unfortunate—enough to be in the first batch. He and fifteen others walked onto the stone stage, as directed by an elder of the Wei clan. He walked into a square, an eighth of the stage, against a boy with the jewelry of the Li clan. The boy looked no more than ten, and his eyes were wide as he took in the size of his opponent.

A few laughs drifted Lindon's way from the Li and Kazan sections, and he imagined them noticing the fifteen-year-old with the wooden badge. It didn't hurt as much as he'd expected.

He and the boy bowed to one another even as the other seven pairs did the same. A purple star flared in the air above them, created by a White Fox technique, and the elder's voice filled the arena. "Begin!"

Lindon stepped forward, bending to get low enough, and drove an Empty Palm into the boy's stomach.

The boy fell to his knees, his spirit failing him, and cupped both hands to his gut with a look of astonishment. Lindon shoved him over the lines marking the boundary of his square.

"Winner!" the elder announced, powerful Iron lungs carrying his voice into the distance. A second after the match had started, Lindon walked away. Bands loosened on his lungs, and he felt as though he could breathe again for the first time that morning.

He wasn't doomed after all. His trump card had worked. It had *worked.*

When the jeers sprouted up among the audience, even among the Wei, he only smiled.

"Cheater!" someone shouted.

"Coward!"

"Trash!"

His smile became a laugh, and he walked back to the bench chuckling. Their insults couldn't touch his sheer delight. Words were nothing, less than nothing, compared to the facts: he had used the sacred arts to overthrow another sacred artist in battle. He was winning like a Copper.

Not like an Unsouled.

He tripped a girl after an Empty Palm, and she stumbled to her hands and knees. When she started to cry, the crowd's shouting redoubled. He grinned all the way back to his seat.

In the weeks leading up to the Seven-Year Festival, he'd trained every day to deal with possible threats. What if an opponent could resist the Empty Palm? What if they had a technique they could land on him first? What if his madra was exhausted before the later rounds?

But as the sun crept past noon and Lindon defeated his fifth opponent, he realized there was one scenario he'd never prepared for: easy victory. None of these children had a countermeasure for the Empty Palm, and once their sacred arts were disabled, superior size and strength made their loss trivial.

His hidden weapon, sealed in a jar and buried beneath the stage, would stay hidden.

He hoisted a Kazan boy by the red sash, tossing him out of bounds. The Kazan section rose up in a furious sea of red and gray, but he just waved at them as he walked away from the stage.

Joy burned in his chest like a torch.

●

Wei Shi Seisha stopped watching the exhibition matches as soon as it was clear her son would win. She had expected he would; he was older than all of his opponents, and had finally found a technique he could use in spite of his deficiency. She had every confidence that he would grow into a productive member of the clan now, though once she had doubted.

She began to pace the arena, checking scripts on the conductive pillars that held the illusory images of Elder Whisper. Sometimes visitors would deface scripts like this, but the mere presence of an inspector would reduce such occurrences significantly. She had almost an hour before Lindon would have to fight an opponent at the Copper level, which was plenty of time to make at least one lap around the arena.

The first anomaly appeared when she was passing the Li clan entrance. She happened to glance between the seating sections and noticed a Li clan elder—his jewelry all gold and jade, befitting his status as a Jade-stage practitioner—slipping out the door. She paused, curious, and another Li elder followed a moment later.

Seisha reached up and tapped the side of her drudge, carrying a drop from her spirit. The construct whistled an affirmative.

Drudges were all the tools a Soulsmith required rolled into one. They could measure madra output, determine its aspects, analyze the parts of a Remnant, and even help separate that Remnant into its components with minimal loss. Soulsmithing primarily revolved around deconstructing and reconstructing Remnants to take advantage of their unique properties, and without a drudge, it was almost impossible to do so accurately. Like a surgeon operating with her hands taped together and one eye shut.

In this case, Seisha had anticipated trouble from the Li clan, and so had gone to great lengths to acquire samples from Remnants similar to the ones they'd recently captured: the teleporting rabbit, vanishing bat, and space-warping mole. Her drudge could track a Remnant based on a sample like a hound taking a scent, and while trying to track three 'scents' at once would be complex, it was worth attempting.

With a specific pattern of madra pulses, she activated the drudge's tracking feature. It complied with a burble, unfolding tiny antennae as it executed the search. Those antennae were always the first thing to decay on any drudge, so she tried to use them sparingly, as they were expensive to replace. But this was a worthy cause. If the Li clan was attempting some kind of coup on the first day of the Seven-Year Festival, she had to clip this bud before it flowered.

Her drudge honked only seconds after the search had begun, startling her. The range on such detection was incredibly limited, and even more so when she'd packed three samples at once. There was always the chance of a false positive, but with such a quick response...

The Remnants, or something that reminded her construct of their power, was here. Possibly inside the arena.

She signaled the two closest of her assistants, young men with iron hammers on their badges. She had trained them for years, even if neither of them made promising Soulsmiths, and they had volunteered to help her secure the arena. Both came running.

"Li clan elders are slipping away," she said. "One of you report to the First Elder, and the other can follow me." She turned toward the Li entrance, leaving it to them to decide which would take on which task.

The arena had been constructed on the edge of Wei land, so it was enveloped on three sides by a forest: a sea of green dotted with the occasional purple island as an orus tree was mixed in with its more mundane counterparts. Aside from the gravel path leading away from the exit and back toward the main property, she saw nothing.

But her quarry was more advanced in the sacred arts, and she had to respect that. With a whisper of White Fox madra and an effort of focused will, she Forged a disguise.

The Wei clan Forgers trained in the Fox Mirror technique for years, learning to create illusionary copies with a dizzying degree of detail. Her peers specialized in creating copied faces, full-body duplicates, or even camouflaged walls that would render the user invisible. There were imperfections in each of these techniques, specifics that violated reality in ways that could be noticed.

She specialized in clothing. Layered robes of white and purple turned to green in an instant, jewelry glinting on each finger and both ears. Illusory necklaces hung down to her chest, and even her iron badge dangled from a gold chain. Her face would remain the same, but it wasn't as though the Li clan knew her on sight. Her hair could be a slight problem—brown hair was more common in the Kazan clan, but not the Li. She would have to risk it. In the shadow of the trees, her hair looked more black than brown anyway.

As her escort Forged his own disguise, a clumsy green cloak that he threw over himself, she followed the direction of her drudge into the forest. It clicked or whistled to her occasionally, changing her direction, but the chase took much less time than she'd expected.

Less than five minutes after leaving the arena, she spotted a flash of pink light through the trees, along with a man's raised voice. She silenced her drudge, cradling it in her arms like an infant, and signaled her guard to quiet. Carefully, she crept forward.

The Li clan disguise would stop them from attacking her outright, but it wouldn't save her from a thorough questioning...which she would prefer to avoid. Ideally, she wouldn't be caught at all.

Her skin tingled as she slid quietly closer, heart pounding, her well-practiced breathing technique strained by excitement. She hadn't worked against other clans since she reached Iron in her twenty-second year, but she'd missed it. She felt a rare pang of empathy for Jaran; he'd fought far more than she had, in his youth, and the lack of that thrill must add to his bitterness.

Seisha stopped when she was close enough to see the Li. They weren't all Jade, but a mix of Jades and Irons. The youngest was older than she was. Nine in total, though she was staring through a flowering cloudbell bush, so she could have missed one or two in the back. They were gathered around a circle in the forest floor, a circle made of tiles. A script.

They'd brought tiles the size of an open hand, each etched with a rune or sigil. When connected properly, they would function as well as a full-size script circle. It was a technique she'd seen before, mostly in cases where the circle might have to be redesigned quickly.

The three Remnants had been caged and placed at three distinct points around the circle. The blue rabbit chewed frantically at its prison, clutching at the bars with hands that looked almost human A pink series of swirls that might generously be called a bat flapped in place, fading in and out of existence but still unable to shift through the scripted cage. Finally, a brown-and-black mass with huge silver shovels for claws sat motionless, watching its captors with beady eyes.

All of the Remnants here, and all whole. No wonder her drudge had located their signatures so quickly; she hadn't expected them intact and so close.

The Jade man at the head of their party continued speaking, dictating to them as though repeating a lesson taught many times before. "...first the anchor, and *then* the call. If he doesn't answer, we have to be fresh enough to try again as soon as the next window opens. Shao, have you confirmed our location?"

Seisha didn't know the speaker, but she knew Shao, one of the Li clan's most accomplished Forgers. He was bald and tiny, with an appearance closer to a fresh disciple than an expert at tracking and locating Remnants.

His own drudge, like a gleaming steel sword too fat and dull to be of any use to anyone, sprouted antennae like a pincushion. He listened to its whistles, checked something on a scroll, made a note with chalk and slate, and then consulted a map. Finally, he nodded. "We are, honored elder. He should emerge at exactly this spot, if we time the doorway correctly."

"If we fail again, he will punish all of us," the highest-ranking elder said, voice grim. A palpable shudder moved through Shao, as well as a few of the others. "Let us see that doesn't happen. Are we ready to begin?"

Shao checked a few more notes, his bald head bobbing up and down, before he shot up abruptly. "It's *now!*" he screamed. "Ignite the script now, now, now!"

The Li elders scrambled for their tiles on the ground, injecting madra into them with a novice's haste. The script glowed white, irregularly at first, but within seconds it had settled into a smooth pulse.

The three Remnants, inside the circle, obviously sensed something was wrong. One and all, they began to screech in the peculiar way of their kind—the mole sounded like an avalanche, the bat like wind whistling through high peaks, the rabbit like the swift beat of a heart.

This is it, Seisha thought, but she hadn't been prepared. From her discovery to the activation of the script had only taken a minute, maybe two. Should she disrupt the script and face the consequences, or run back and tell the First Elder? The Li elders technically hadn't done anything yet. But if she watched, it would soon be too late.

Ultimately, the decision was taken out of her hands.

Only a breath after the script's first light, the Remnants popped and bubbled, as though the ink that painted them on the world had begun to *boil.* Their complaints grew louder and louder until their bodies fizzed away into motes of light.

That in itself was not so unusual. As they expended power, Remnants dissolved back into the madra that formed them. But she'd never seen it happen so *fast*, and never to such an effect.

The spots of color, pink and blue and dark brown, swirled around inside the script like snakes in water. They spun closer and closer, getting tighter and tighter, before gathering into a single form that looked like nothing so much as a muddy inkblot.

Only a blink after the process had begun, it was finished. A tiny blue spark flared to life in the center of the ink-stain, glowing brighter every second.

"It worked," Shao breathed, before the light shot into a single line the height of a man. It looked like the edge of light down one side of a doorway, and as she watched, that doorway slid open.

She never saw anything but a rectangle of deep, textured blue light before the whole construction collapsed, the energy of the Remnants dispersing, the power that had animated the script fizzling out. For a breath she believed they had failed, that whatever summoning they were attempting had fizzled and died. Then the light cleared.

A man stood in the center of the circle.

His clothes were an oddity for Sacred Valley: he dressed in fine black furs, with a broad belt holding various tools. A sword hung from that belt, straight-bladed and unsheathed. Diamonds glistened in each ear, silver chains held diamonds on his chest, and yet more silver and diamonds on his fingers, as though he'd chosen to bedeck himself in imitations of ice. He wore his black hair short, but streaks of white ran through it like a tiger's stripes.

Those were his ordinary features, though, the facts about him that her panicked mind couldn't help but catalogue. They were not what she noticed first.

When he appeared in the circle, he stretched his wings.

They unfolded at least thirty feet from tip to tip, and the structure of bones and tendons were coal-black. But the skin that stretched between them was pale and colorless, as though he'd stripped the wings from some giant arctic bat.

He grinned, flashing fangs. "There is nothing so grand as a second chance."

The Li clansmen all but collapsed to their knees, grinding foreheads against the dirt. Seisha was tempted to do the same.

"This one is humbled by your mercy, Grand Patriarch." The elder who had spoken earlier still spoke for the group, even when he was too terrified to raise his face. "Thank you for allowing this modest group the chance to atone for our failure to serve you the first time."

Grand Patriarch. Sickness rolled through her gut. He was a previous-generation Patriarch of the Li clan, but she'd never heard of one surviving. Which left only one terrifying possibility: an ancient immortal had come home.

The Grand Patriarch grunted, rolling his shoulder in its socket. "I have not returned to this realm in some time. Tell me, have the Four Beasts come home?"

The elder hesitated, but the Grand Patriarch laughed in response to his own question. "No need to answer. You still live, so they remain abroad. I should like to test myself against them, once the Valley is united."

"Yes, Grand Patriarch. Ah, forgive this one your lowly servant, but this one has prepared something for you." Without raising his head, the elder lifted an object in both his hands.

It was something as mythical as the wings on a human being; something Seisha had never expected to see.

A gold badge, etched with a scepter.

The Grand Patriarch took it, chuckling. "I had forgotten this custom. Are there any other sacred artists of the Gold stage currently in Sacred Valley?"

"Not to this one's poor knowledge, Grand Patriarch."

"Then it will do." The Grand Patriarch slipped the

shadesilk ribbon over his own neck, then lifted the badge so he could examine it. "If there were, I would have had you craft something more valuable. Gold is entirely deficient to describe the current state of my advancement."

Judging by the gasps and whispers that traveled through the gathered Li experts, they found that statement as shocking as she did.

The Gold folded his wings, ran a hand through his black-and-white hair, and started off through the woods without another word. The Li hurried after him, clearly startled.

Fortunately for Seisha and her guard, the Li party passed far enough by her that they remained undetected. Unfortunately, the Gold was headed straight for the arena.

As they marched through the woods, the elder hesitantly spoke up. "Forgiveness, Grand Patriarch, but the Festival has only recently begun. The children of the Foundation stage are fighting. Were you to appear now, it would only be an insult to your grand status. This one had planned an event to display your glory, wherein those from other clans could approach—"

The Gold waved him to silence. "In the face of absolute power, of what use is respect? This task is not worthy of more than one day of my time. I am here today, and so they will bow today."

The Li clan finally left, taking their Grand Patriarch with them, but leaving Seisha in a cold sweat.

"What do we do?" her guard finally asked, whispering even though minutes had passed since their enemies disappeared into the woods.

"We can't risk running into them here," she said, matching his volume. "We should go around. We might not make it in time to warn the Patriarch, but at least there's a chance."

The sun darkened overhead, a gust of wind blasted down on her, and when the Grand Patriarch of the Li clan settled down to the forest floor next to her, she knew there was no chance.

She closed her eyes and accepted death.

CHAPTER TEN

The final round of the Foundation stage tournament should have been a nervous affair for Lindon, with his family's reputation and his own future at stake. The stage seemed broad as the entire valley with no one but his opponent to share it, and the crowd's dull noise wavered between supportive cheers and mockery.

But this round ended as all the others had. Lindon drove his Empty Palm into the core of the girl across from him, folding her in half. She was almost as old as he was, and therefore only inches away from advancing to Copper, but no one in all the clans trained to fight without their madra. Despite having witnessed his previous matches, she still froze in horror after feeling her power abandon her. After tasting, for the length of one breath, the life of an Unsouled.

Lindon pushed her off the stage and walked away before the elder could announce the results of the match. He was prepared for the jeers of those watching, the dark humor rising up in him again, but this time there was no scorn. There wasn't much applause either—a handful from the Wei clan, clapping slowly or voicing a few halfhearted words of praise—but the artists of Sacred Valley acknowledged victory above all else. Even when it tasted sour, even when they suspected him of cheating in some way, they still respected success.

He glanced at the side of the stage, to the square beneath which his jar was buried. He hadn't been forced to *really* cheat. The reality slowly set in, like water seeping into soil. He'd won a tournament, even a small one, using *actual* sacred arts. He was a sacred artist, and all of Sacred Valley knew it.

Lindon almost walked straight into a barrel-chested man wearing robes of purple-and-gold shadesilk. The Patriarch of the Wei clan smiled at Lindon through his silver mane. "You have the congratulations of our clan, Wei Shi Lindon. There is honor in overcoming a deficiency to achieve victory."

Resisting the urge to drop to his knees, Lindon bowed at the waist, his fists pressed together in respect. "This one does not deserve such kind words, Patriarch." It was the first time the head of the Wei clan had ever addressed him directly.

Sairus rested a broad hand on Lindon's shoulder. "A sacred artist should never be so humble as to refuse what he has earned. You have earned victory today. Let that be enough, and return to your family with honor."

Lindon hadn't spoken with the Patriarch before, and had only rumors to judge the man's character. But he could hear the unspoken message in Sairus' words, and his joy dampened. Even the lingering cheers of the crowd faded in his ears.

"Your pardon, but this one is meant to exchange pointers with a senior disciple at the Copper level."

Though Lindon did not move his eyes from Wei Jin Sairus' feet, he could feel the man's frown. "Some of our guests from the Schools were uncomfortable with your performance. It would ease them greatly if we could conclude our events today and begin anew with the Copper fights tomorrow."

He meant that the elders from the Schools had been offended by the sight of a fifteen-year-old Unsouled claiming victory. His bet with the First Elder would go unfulfilled, his test incomplete. Lindon glanced up at the stands, to try and catch a glimpse of the First Elder's face, but the old man's seat was empty. No help there. The chance of real training was slipping from Lindon's grasp, but he clawed desperately to keep it.

"Our honored guests from the four Schools have yet to witness a true demonstration of our clan's sacred arts, Patriarch. When this one can compete with the Copper from another clan, they will see the strength of the Wei clan. If they are then dissatisfied with this one's performance, this one will of course fully atone."

An unsettling pressure settled on the back of Lindon's neck, like a snake sliding between his shoulder blades. The effect of Sairus' irritation, nothing more, but it still pushed him toward the ground.

"I would not wager the honor of my clan on an Unsouled." Painful words, but Lindon reminded himself they were fair. "Give me some face, disciple, and renounce this exhibition. I do not forget my debts."

Thoughts of the parasite ring, still in the keeping of the Patriarch, flashed through Lindon's head. He could take his cycling to the next level with such an artifact, perhaps enough to catch up with his peers. If he could leverage the Patriarch's debt to even borrow the ring, he could leave his current weakness behind. But he had no promise from the Patriarch. From the First Elder, he did.

Lindon weighed his own future against the honor of the Wei clan. He found the clan wanting.

In one motion, Lindon dropped to his knees and pressed his forehead against the ground. "Your pardon, Patriarch, but this one must prepare for his exhibition match."

He squeezed his eyes shut, anticipating a wave of pain. As a Ruler on the Path of the White Fox, Sairus could make him suffer hours of agony in seconds. He could force Lindon to bow to his will, or even kill him outright.

Instead, he walked away.

At the sound of footsteps, Lindon raised his head hopefully, squeezing a glimpse out of the corner of his eye. The Patriarch was already signaling to the elder in charge of the tournament, waving him to continue.

Lindon shivered with the released pressure and let out a long, heavy breath. He wasn't sure where he had found the courage to defy his own clan's Patriarch directly.

But the First Elder had promised him more. To travel his own Path, Lindon had to reach higher and farther than anyone else. Only then would he be able to hold himself with pride in Sacred Valley. Only when he was strong.

"Due to a request from our honored ally of the Heaven's Glory School, there has been a slight change in the Foundation stage exhibition," the Wei elder announced, his voice carrying to every corner of the arena. The four illusory snowfoxes turned toward him at once, as though he'd caught their attention.

He'd certainly caught Lindon's.

"The champion of the Foundation tournament, Wei Shi Lindon, will immediately exchange pointers with a senior disciple. This will be an invaluable learning opportunity for both children, and will allow the Foundation champion to test the limits of his potential."

Lindon's spirit was strained and weak, after almost a full day of exertion, and he doubted his ability to use the Empty Palm too many times in a row before he would have to rest. But all things considered, he was in good enough shape to fight. The Patriarch wouldn't get him to surrender this easily.

"And the champion's Patriarch, Wei Jin Sairus, has volunteered none other than his own grandson for this duty. Honorable sacred artists of all Schools and clans, the Wei clan presents to you Wei Jin Amon!"

Suddenly, surrender sounded like a much more appealing option.

Black hair tied back and spear propped over his shoulder, Amon leaped from the box at the top of the arena all the way down to the stage. He landed with barely a flex of his knees, iron badge swinging against his chest. "Wei Shi Lindon," he announced, his voice full and rich. "I invite you onto the stage that we might learn from one another."

The hornets. They were his only chance of making it off that stage. Having to fight against an Unsouled was an insult to Amon, and he would take it out on Lindon personally. If Lindon could make it back to his seat with only a pair of limbs broken, he would count himself lucky.

He scarcely dared to hope that the Remnants he'd hidden might be enough to save him. But if they were... If, by cheating and trickery, he managed to fight Amon to a draw...

The Wei clan would practically *have* to support him. He would have proven himself the match of their star disciple in front of the entire Sacred Valley, and if they denied him training then, they would look like fools.

He straightened his back, focusing on the hope of victory rather than the bleak chasm of probable defeat, and started to walk toward the stage.

His sister grabbed him by the elbow, hauling him back. "Let me take your place," she whispered urgently. "Say you aren't worthy of the honor, and you need a family member to replace you. They will allow it. Amon will push for it. And if I can beat him, no one will disrespect you like this again."

Lindon gently extracted himself from Kelsa's grip. "This is for me."

The doubt was so plain on her face it might as well have been painted across her forehead. "What are you saying? Fighting children does *not* prepare you to face Wei Jin Amon." Then something occurred to her, and she jerked away from him. "Wait. No. This is one of your...Lindon, what have you done? What are you doing?"

He jogged away from her, onto the stage, in order to avoid having to answer. When he hopped up onto the blocks of white stone, the audience cheered. Looking forward to seeing him torn apart, he judged.

He could only hope they would be disappointed.

Lindon pressed his fists together and bowed. "Wei Shi Lindon is honored to accept your instruction, cousin Amon."

Without returning the greeting, Wei Jin Amon spun his spear down, flipping it in a circle so that the shadesilk wrapping slid off and drifted to the ground. He ended in a ready stance, half-turned and crouched with his spear angled forward and down. "You have one last chance, Unsouled," Amon said, his voice too low to carry.

His grandfather walked onstage between the two of them, his arms raised to quiet the crowd. "Courage can be cultivated by the weak and strong alike, and Wei Shi Lindon has already demonstrated his courage today. Our clan honors courage, and when it is warranted, we also value humility. Young Lindon, there is no dishonor if you remove yourself from the stage. Rather, we would respect your wisdom in deferring to your betters."

In Lindon's place, no sacred artist would be able to refuse. He would lose too much face by contradicting his Patriarch's words in public. This was a perfect strategy on Sairus' part, cornering him between a physical threat and the looming reality of humiliation. He had left Lindon only one honorable way out.

He'd forgotten that Unsouled had no honor to lose.

"The Patriarch's words are a privilege to hear," Lindon said with another bow, "but the opportunity to learn from a disciple as skilled as Wei Jin Amon does not come often. This one would be a fool to pass it up."

Sairus scowled even as the sky behind him darkened. "Very well," he said, nodding to Amon. A shadow passed over the sun even as purple foxfire flickered around the head of Amon's spear.

Clouds gathered over the arena, slowly blackening as the Patriarch spoke. "Assembled experts of Sacred Valley, I hope this exhibition proves pleasing to...your..." His words trailed off as he looked into the sky.

Lindon had assumed that the Patriarch had used his mastery of illusion to make the sky seem dark, perhaps in an attempt to intimidate Lindon. He'd barely given it a thought. But Sairus stared at the black clouds as though a gate to the Netherworld had opened overhead.

"Amon," Sairus began, but he was cut off by a voice that boomed through the arena, tearing the air apart with its sheer volume.

"Are you the Patriarch of the Wei clan?"

The crowd shook under the voice, a few people screaming. Lindon glimpsed one woman sprinting for the exit. That, more than anything else, convinced him that something was profoundly wrong.

A man descended from the dark clouds like an angry messenger of the heavens. His whole being was defined by shades of black and white, from his black-veined white wings to his black-and-white striped hair. He wore black furs, and diamonds glistened everywhere he could fasten jewelry.

His right hand rested on the hilt of a silver-chased sword, and his left hand clutched a rough sack. Dark stains spread slowly over the bottom of the sack, giving Lindon a gruesome guess at its contents.

But his most startling feature, even considering the enormous wings that spread from his back, was the badge that rested against his furs. It was made of solid gold.

Lindon found himself unable to take a breath, and only part of it could be attributed to the man's oppressive atmosphere. Here, descending from the sky, was a Gold. A real Gold, in the flesh, someone who had mastered the secrets of madra beyond mortal dreams.

The arena filled with a sound like muffled drums as everyone, from every School and clan, fell to their knees. Even Sairus dropped to one knee, as was appropriate in the presence of a Gold, but the sight of him kneeling struck Lindon as *wrong*. Like an eternal mountain suddenly swaying with the wind.

"This one's humble name is Wei Jin Sairus, and he indeed has the honor to lead the Wei clan," Sairus said. "May this one know the honored elder's name?"

The man of black-and-white landed before Sairus, his wings extending to fifteen feet on either side of the Patriarch. The shadow of his wings fell across Lindon's face, and though Lindon shivered, he didn't avert his eyes. Sudden though it was, this event was going to redefine the history of the Sacred Valley, and he couldn't miss it. No matter how the sight of a Gold turned his guts to water.

For a few seconds, the stranger stood over Sairus, his golden badge the only color on his person. He finally spoke in a casual tone, though wind aura carried his voice to every ear in the arena. "I am Li Markuth, Grand Patriarch of the Li Clan."

Sairus' silver-maned head snapped up in shock. One breath later, Markuth's hand blurred, and a spray of blood slapped Lindon in the face.

He fell backwards, heart hammering, scraping warm and sticky blood away from his eyes. While he was blind, he couldn't fight the panic—he had to see, to know if the white-winged horror from the Li Clan was coming for him next.

The first sight to greet his eyes was the Patriarch's headless corpse collapsing to the stone, staining it red. Markuth had struck his head entirely off.

"The sins of the father pass to his sons, as the sins of the mother pass to her daughters," Li Markuth intoned, wiping blood from his fingers on his dark furs. "To pay for the evil of your clan's founder, every beating heart from every living Wei descendant would not be enough. So I will settle for two."

The Grand Patriarch spun around, thrusting his clawed hand into empty space.

Slowly, Wei Jin Sairus' body dissolved into foxfire. Even the blood on Lindon's face flared with heat before dissipating, revealing itself as a Forged dream.

Light lurched, and the Patriarch appeared out of nowhere. His head was attached, but now his chest was impaled on the Grand Patriarch's fist.

Sairus tried to speak, but Li Markuth tore his hand back, clutching what must have been the other man's heart. Blood dripped from the Grand Patriarch's gore-soaked fist.

Out of tricks, the Wei Patriarch fell to the stage and died.

Markuth opened his fist, and a heart dropped on top of the corpse with a splat. "One heart. I will collect the other in time."

Black-and-white wings folded up behind the Grand Patriarch, trailing him like a leather cloak. A white-and-purple Remnant began to peel itself from the Patriarch's corpse, but Markuth crushed it beneath his heel and the madra dispersed.

He looked straight at the box containing the elders from the clans and the guests from the four Schools. "I believe in solving my problems directly. Let it be known that I intend to claim the whole of Sacred Valley as my personal territory. If there are any challengers, step forward now. All at once, if you please. I will not waste my entire night fighting every Jade in the valley one at a time."

Markuth lifted the bag that had been in his left hand since he'd descended, upending it over the stage. A pair of heads fell out, leaving a trail of blood as they rolled on the pale stone. He tossed the empty sack aside, but Lindon's gaze was fixed.

One of the heads belonged to a man he'd never seen before. He didn't care about that. He was focused on the other head, the second head, the one whose features were veiled in long hair. Long brown hair.

His body shivered uncontrollably, madra racing through his veins in a pattern unrestrained by any cycling technique.

He knew who that head belonged to. He didn't need to see the face. He knew.

The world took on a feeling of unreality, as though he'd been struck by Kelsa's Empty Palm. It was too absurd. Just this morning he'd been preparing to fight a bunch of children and now...now Golds were descending from the sky? His mother was dead?

It was stupid, that was what it was. Idiotic and ridiculous. The world didn't work like this; the world made *sense*. Only dreams operated without rules or reason, and even his insane dreams of singing flowers and dancing clouds held more logic than this.

Jades began to gather at one end of the stage, old men and women from Kazan and Wei gathering together, mingling under both banners. They argued fiercely, none daring to walk up onstage, but they did gather. In ones and twos they hurried together, banding together to fight and die with pride.

Not all the Jades joined them. Some stayed in the stands, on their knees.

Markuth laughed, shaking droplets of blood from his fingers. "Is this it, then? Don't hold back, come up. I won't begin until you are ready."

Hatred boiled up in Lindon, and he found himself wishing he could join the Jade elders. Even a Gold wasn't immortal. In fact...

The idea illuminated his soul like a sunrise. Li Markuth might be even more dependent on his madra than an ordinary person. If the legends were true, Gold bodies were partially *made* of madra, like a Remnant's.

What would an Empty Palm do against such a being?

Lindon would die landing that blow, but that wasn't worth consideration. He'd grown up with stories of mythical heroes who were killed trading strikes with a blood rival. If he succeeded here, he would live on forever in the myths of the Wei clan. It would be a good death. An honorable death. The death of a sacred artist.

If even the Empty Palm wasn't enough, Lindon had one more card to play. The hornet Remnants were still sealed in their jar beneath the stage, waiting for him to release them. If they could distract the Gold for even a breath, even the fragment of an instant, Lindon's life would be well spent.

The sense of unreality crashed in on Lindon once again, shattering his beautiful delusion. What was he thinking? Here *he* was, Wei Shi Lindon the Unsouled, considering throwing his life away in a battle against a Gold. It was a bad joke, or the fanciful poem of someone with too much ego. He couldn't do anything. He would only die, with no plan or purpose whatsoever.

He stared at the Li Clan monster, and his hopeful idea died. The truth settled on him like the fall of night: there was nothing he could do. No reason to try. He was too weak.

Li Markuth spread his arms and his wings, and the sky darkened even further, until night fell over Sacred Valley. The whole arena shook as he called on the vital aura of the world, the four White Fox pillars crumbling to rubble. Only Markuth shone in the darkness, his body outlined by white power. "The world is wide outside your narrow Paths," he said, even as the crowd of Jades prepared their techniques. "Let me guide you."

The Jade elders of the Wei and Kazan clans walked onstage in a solemn procession, summoning foxfire or Forging bright red blades. They spread out in front of Markuth, some forty or fifty of them, and from their faces Lindon knew they were each prepared to die.

And in that moment, Lindon decided to die with them.

Maybe he *was* too weak, and his death would accomplish nothing. But it was better to bet on the tiny chance that he was wrong than to wait for death without even trying.

When Lindon stood up, Markuth didn't so much as move his eyes. It was as though anyone less than Jade didn't even exist to him. When the first ranks of Wei elders moved toward him with madra readied, the Grand Patriarch condensed wind and shadow around each of his fists.

Lindon crept in front of him, still unnoticed. He didn't even glance down, paying Lindon no more attention than he did the stones beneath his feet. The sky overhead flashed white.

And Lindon, ignored by the Grand Patriarch, landed an Empty Palm on Markuth's core.

It was as though he'd splashed water on a boulder.

Even legends never suggested that a Foundation-stage child could harm a Gold. It was like a fly attacking a tiger...no, attacking a mountain. If everyone at the Foundation stage in all of Sacred Valley joined hands and pooled their madra, they couldn't do so much as ruffle the clothes of the Grand Patriarch of the Li Clan. Lindon should have known better.

He should have remembered his place.

His force vanished uselessly, and Markuth backhanded him in the midsection. Even in the end, he didn't give Lindon a single glance.

The casual slap of a Gold struck hard enough to knock him backwards off the stage, but somehow it didn't hurt. He landed in the dirt, but the air had already vanished from his lungs. His mouth flapped open, trying to grab a breath, but it was as though the air had disappeared.

He tried to sit up, but nothing happened. He remained on his back, his head shaking from side to side. Lindon strained his eyes, looking down, to see how bad his injuries were.

I'm still dreaming, he realized, when he didn't see his legs. That was the only explanation. He'd been a fool to consider any of it real. Golds didn't descend from the sky, the Patriarch couldn't bow, his mother didn't die for no reason, and his legs were supposed to be at the end of his body.

It was comforting to know that he was dreaming. Soon he would wake up, and then everything would make sense again. In fact, he could feel exhaustion pressing down on him like a blanket. Maybe that was what waking up felt like, in a dream.

His head flopped to the left, and he caught a glimpse of his father and sister. Kneeling, like the rest. Kelsa's eyes were fixed on his, glistening with tears, her face pale. Why was she so sad? This was just a dream, she shouldn't worry so much.

Jaran wasn't looking at him at all, but was fixed on the battle between Markuth and the Jades. He had to admit that hurt, even if it wasn't real.

He let his eyes slide shut to hide the sight of his kneeling father. When he woke up, everything would be all right again.

That was Lindon's last thought before he died.

CHAPTER ELEVEN

With the assistance of her Presence, Suriel watched her
target location from a thousand kilometers away. The fated
arrival point was an empty stretch of forest in the territory
of a local clan, one marked by images of a white five-tailed
fox. [The Wei clan,] her Presence informed her, spooling
out lines of explanatory text in her vision. She willed the
explanations away, scanning the area.

There was some sort of festival nearby, where children
from various clans engaged in combat games. She watched
the matches idly for a while, waiting for the spatial violation destined to occur nearby.

One boy in particular caught her attention—tall,
broad-shouldered, with a wooden badge and a rough face.
He was the oldest of the group, and he won as easily as
someone of his size should defeat younger children. The
crowd treated him with disdain, but he seemed to carry
himself with pride, as though pushing nine-year-olds out of
bounds was an achievement.

She looked a little deeper, examining his soul.

She spotted his flaw immediately. He'd been born with
a madra deficiency; that could be corrected, given time,
but primitive clans like these often ostracized or margin-

alized the weak. Only the strong could contribute to the greater good.

She ordered her Presence to pull up the boy's story, digesting it in an instant. It was as she'd expected. He was born with nothing, less than nothing, and others increased his burden because of it. Yet today, he still fought. She could admire that.

His fate unspooled in front of her, a series of images stringing from one to another. She would have seen clearer images, even branching paths, had she left her eyes functional, but in her current disguised state this was the best she could do.

The boy fights against a relative of his, a young man with long black hair and an iron badge. The boy cheats, releases emerald hornets, ekes out a technical victory.

With a bulky brown pack on his back, he bends his head over a scroll, studying a Path by candlelight in someone else's home.

The same boy, years later, weeping as he earns his copper badge.

As a man with gray in his hair, he and his wife and their children gather around before a ceremony that sees him promoted to Iron.

He dies in a Dreadgod attack that claims a quarter of the valley, decades hence.

Suriel willed the fate away, wiping aside the pathetic collection of images. These would be his dominant fate, the most likely path for the boy's life, and a thousand little things could change it. But left to his own devices, he would overcome his handicap to live a happy and satisfying life, dying a little early.

That was all.

Her interest waned, shifting as the Presence chirped in her mind. [Spatial violation imminent]. The spot in the empty forest flared red, glowing brighter and brighter.

Suriel launched herself from the ledge on which she'd been standing, shattering the air in an explosion as she moved faster than sound. She was late.

Predicting events based on fate was an art more than a science, and not her specialty. She had chosen to stay a few thousand kilometers away for safety, to avoid undue interference. She'd known it was a risk, but now the event was upon her, and she couldn't arrive in time without tearing the atmosphere apart. She could bend space to transport directly in, but her target might sense the distortion and flee to another world. Even so, she wasn't unduly concerned.

Anything this trespasser could do, she could undo.

He descended from a class six spatial rift, little more than a slit in the Way that was repaired immediately. She watched as he gathered some followers around him—he must have been communicating with this world for some time, which would add to his sentence—and decapitate a couple of observers. The spines were severed cleanly, but she would reverse causality rather than attempt a manual reattachment. No sense taking a risk.

As she reduced speed for her arrival, the trespasser fully unveiled his spirit, darkening the sky with storm aura and smashing nearby pillars to frighten the locals. He was going for full dramatic effect.

"Is this it, then?" the black-and-white striped trespasser taunted his enemies. The audio quality had improved now that she was within two dozen kilometers. "Don't hold back, come up. I won't begin until you are ready."

Suriel prepared to descend when she noticed a detail that the winged man had overlooked. That boy, fifteen and clad in white, was sneaking around to the front of the trespasser. He gathered his meager madra together, terror and resolve and muted self-loathing radiating in a psychic wave.

With the same move he'd used on the children earlier, the boy drove his palm into the Gold practitioner's core.

Suriel winced even before the trespasser tore the boy in half, sending his torso flipping up and out of the arena. The boy had to have known it was useless.

[He knew,] her Presence confirmed.

And he tried anyway, Suriel thought. This was the sort of person the Abidan were created to save: the weak who stood against the strong. The sort of person the Phoenix was meant to save. The sort of person who might, with a little outside help, even reach beyond their fate.

His life guttered out, visible to her eyes, but that meant nothing before Suriel. He was only dead.

She changed her plan. She had meant to freeze time, retrieve the trespasser, revert the damage he'd done, and leave. With a delicate adjustment of memory, the locals would never notice their day had been interrupted.

Now, she had a new goal. Makiel wouldn't be pleased, but this event now fell officially under her purview. She could handle it as she saw fit.

And she saw fit to make the trespasser sweat.

●

Death looked surprisingly like the last moments of his life, Lindon found.

His vision had fuzzed away for a second in a haze of gray, but now it returned, and he found that everything looked exactly the same. Markuth had his hands raised above his white-striped hair, madra gathered in balls of force and wings spread. The Jade experts of two clans ran at him with weapons and foxfire ready, resignation in their wrinkled faces. Blood splattered the arena, and his legs lay next to his mother's head.

When Lindon was a child, he had once nudged a table carrying a ceramic vase, an heirloom from previous generations of the Shi family. The table shook, and he looked up to see the vase teetering on the edge. That moment had seemed to stretch, a single image imprinted on time so that it seemed to last forever before the vase at last began to fall.

At first, he thought that was happening now. The world

seemed frozen around him, as though time had stretched once again. He noticed it, and waited for the battle to resume.

But it didn't.

A few breaths of time later—though Lindon wasn't breathing, and felt no urge to—the tableau before him remained exactly the same. He wondered if this was what death was, a single instant lasting for eternity. He hoped not. Boredom seemed like a worse fate than otherworldly torment.

Then something changed. The sky, masked by the dark clouds summoned by the Li Clan's Grand Patriarch, began to glow blue. Azure light lit the underside of the clouds as though a blue sun rose, spilling its light over the entire arena.

And in that light, pieces of the world began to move.

Though Li Markuth remained locked in his pose of triumph, the Jade combatants still frozen before him, blood slithered along the floor around his feet. The severed heads tumbled across the arena, gathering blood as they rolled, bouncing off the stone and rolling away toward the forest.

His own legs slid across the stone, as though his blood had become a rope pulling his body together. Panic tightened his chest, and he tried to struggle, but he couldn't even widen his eyes. No part of him responded to his control, and he had to wait and watch as his flesh pulled itself together. It wasn't painful, but he *could* feel it, an uncomfortable squirming below his ribs as muscle and bone reassembled themselves.

All the while, the sky grew brighter and brighter.

Markuth slowly moved his head on his neck, thawing gradually, first looking around him at the frozen world and then at the brightening sky.

He stumbled backward in shock, flapping his wings like a panicked bird to keep from falling over.

"No!" he screamed, hurling the balls of his madra into the sky. "Wait, *please!* I belong here! This is my homeland!"

The clouds parted, revealing the source of the blue light. It blazed like a sapphire sun for an instant, sending a painful lance through Lindon's eyes and making him wish he could close them.

The light dimmed somewhat, revealing its source: two sweeps of blue fire, like a pair of wings formed from iridescent flames and big enough to cover a third of the sky. It gave the impression of a blue phoenix, or perhaps a phoenix Remnant, descending from the heavens in glory.

Markuth roared at the phoenix, drawing the sword from his belt. It was shaped like a straight, simple sword, but it fuzzed and flickered, buzzing oddly as though it weren't quite real.

The phoenix faded further as it descended, until its flames no longer hurt Lindon's eyes. When he could see again, he made out a person at the phoenix's heart: a woman, drifting down toward them and bearing flaming blue wings.

Beautiful she was, but it wasn't the word that occurred to Lindon first. The first thing he thought was, *Perfect.* It was as though someone had taken a real person and perfected her, smoothing every blemish in her pale skin, arranging her cloud of dark hair so that nothing was out of place. Neither too short nor too tall, too thick nor too thin, she looked like the template from which every other human being was wrought. She was so flawless that she couldn't be real, reminding Lindon forcibly that he was dead now. Maybe she was a messenger from the heavens, here to usher him into the netherworld. That would explain the burning wings.

Though, aside from her inhuman perfection, she didn't look like he would have imagined. Her body was sheathed in white, liquid armor that moved effortlessly with her. Gray ribbons of hazy smoke started at the fingertips of her right hand, winding up her arm and terminating in her neck. Her hair looked brown at first glance, but upon further reflection, he would call it a deep green. And her eyes, large and human, were undoubtedly purple.

The heavens must be a strange place to produce people like her. But with her here, he found that he could relax. Maybe when she brought him to the next life, he would be more than Unsouled.

Markuth stood with his chest heaving and a sword in his right hand, but he didn't attack. "I have not violated the Pact, nor upset the balance of this world, nor defied the Abidan. I demand a trial before—"

An invisible rope grabbed Li Markuth around one ankle, pulling him off-balance and dragging him to a point just behind the woman. He flapped his wings, kicking up a powerful wind, straining against his unseen bonds, but to no avail.

[Li Markuth,] said an impassive voice in Lindon's mind. [You have been sentenced to trial for spatial violation and attempted domination of local inhabitants. You will be imprisoned until the Court of Seven determine a date and location of your trial.]

A black spot appeared behind the green-haired woman, a point of absolute darkness. It widened so that Lindon could see a few spots of color within, like a distant cloud of rainbow-colored fireflies. Markuth continued being dragged backwards, as though that spot called him inexorably toward it.

As the Gold came closer to the woman, he roared and spread his wings wide, raising his strangely twisting sword. With both hands, he slammed the blade down on her unprotected head, and the force of his madra was such that it pressed against Lindon even across the arena. The stones beneath her cracked, and wind blew away from the impact. The air rang with a sound like steel on stone.

And the woman continued drifting over the ground, undisturbed. Not a single strand of her hair moved out of place, and she never looked in Markuth's direction.

He screamed like a child as the darkness swallowed him, slurping up the tip of his sword last. The black hole in the world closed.

The woman continued toward him, having never acknowledged the Grand Patriarch of the Li Clan for an instant. From the beginning of her descent, her eyes had remained locked on Lindon.

She reached the ground just before she reached him, her smooth white boots tapping down on the stone. The blue-fire wings vanished at the same moment. She regarded him first, then motioned for him to stand.

"Stand," she said. "Do not be afraid." The words sounded strange, as though she were trying a different accent with every syllable, but they were completely understandable. He was surprised enough that she'd spoken directly to him, instead of using the dispassionate impersonal voice that had sentenced Li Markuth. Her real voice sounded so different that he wondered if they had even come from the same person. Maybe the words earlier were straight from heaven.

When he realized he hadn't immediately obeyed this celestial messenger, he scrambled to his feet, only an instant later remembering that he should be in agony.

He wasn't. In fact, he felt better than he had before the tournament, his spirit restored to full capacity and his body clean and well-rested.

Lindon considered dropping to his knees, but she had just ordered him to stand, so he bent in half at the waist. "This one thanks you for the attention, honored immortal. Please, how may this one serve you?"

An afterlife in the service of a celestial immortal was infinitely better than his mortal existence. If there was any truth in the myths, he could still practice the sacred arts now that he'd left his physical body behind, so this might be an unimaginable opportunity.

Death could well be the best thing that had ever happened to him.

He couldn't see her face, but she considered for a few seconds before speaking again, her expression as pleasant and unyielding as a mask. "This one would not require so much of you."

This one? He wondered if she was mocking him, or if he had somehow offended her. "Please, honored immortal, do not speak to this one so humbly."

"Humbly? Ah."

She considered a moment longer before clearing her throat. This time, she sounded as though she'd spent her entire life in Sacred Valley. "Raise your head and speak freely. I have no patience for the manners of this world."

He straightened, taking the chance to look her in the eyes. It was technically rude of him, but she said she didn't mind, and he was willing to take her at her word. Besides, this might be the only time he ever met her, and he was determined to commit her faultless face to memory.

But there was one answer he needed. "May I ask, if you don't mind...am I dead?"

A smile tugged at one corner of her mouth, a crack in the mask. "Do you not feel alive?"

He thought he did, but then, who could say what death felt like?

"If you've brought me to life, then..." he hesitated, looking around at the frozen world. The Jade elders were stuck rushing forward to oppose an enemy that no longer existed.

Purple eyes surveyed the scene, her face pleasant and impassive once again. She might as well have been looking over a field of flowers. "Li Markuth was not permitted to return to this world. His attack was a deviation from fate, which I have reversed. When I depart, it will be as though your festival continued uninterrupted."

"What about me?" Lindon asked immediately. "You restored me to life. Will I forget this kindness as well?"

"Yes." This didn't appear to disturb her in the least.

"You don't think you could...leave my memory? So that I could be properly grateful?" He was the only one to receive special treatment from the heavens; he couldn't allow himself to walk away as though nothing had happened.

She reached over with her left hand, stroking the lines

of gray smoke on her right as though tenderly playing an instrument. "Temporal reversion is not memory modification. When I'm done here, nothing Li Markuth did will have happened. Your festival *will* have continued without cease. To spare you, I would have to temporarily withdraw you from the flow of fate."

"Thank you for your consideration, honored messenger," he said, as though her words were a promise. "I am ready."

Her lips twitched, and he suspected she was using her neutral expression to suppress a smile. "It's not a complex process for me. I can draw you out of fate with a thought."

"Fate. So then, if you're not offended by this one's humble questions...can you see the future?"

"Fate is not the future. What is destined to occur does not always occur."

He bowed before her three times. "That is enough for me, thank you. Would you tell me my destiny?"

This time she did laugh, and he was almost surprised that it sounded so human. "I'm pleased to have descended personally, Wei Shi Lindon." A thrill rolled through him. The celestial messenger *knew his name.* "I can show you some limited details of your fate, if you are willing to see them."

"This one would be honored." He tried to hide the eagerness in his voice. Even the most trivial knowledge of the future could be used to great advantage.

The tips of two white-plated fingers met his forehead, like cool eggshells. "Then *see.*"

The frozen world was wiped out, replaced with another. He was still standing on the stone of the arena stage, but the clouds Li Markuth summoned had never appeared, and the sun beat down out of a clear sky. Wei Jin Amon faced him, and though he resisted longer than anyone expected, he still lost.

That night, he nursed his wounds alone when the First Elder barged in without knocking. The old man slapped a book down on his table: *Path of the White Fox.*

Lindon's eyes shone at this vision. He *had* succeeded after all. He expected the immortal to return him to reality, but the future flowed on, coming in faster and faster images.

He watched a version of himself, years older, receive a copper badge with tears in his eyes. The First Elder smiled in pride.

His sister led Wei clansmen to fight around a carriage, while armored members of the Kazan fought. She wreathed one man's face with foxfire, then drove her sword through a second man's gut and left it there. Kelsa wrenched the door to the carriage open, revealing a finely wrought box. Her expression lifted.

More years passed, and Kelsa was personally awarded a jade badge by Patriarch Sairus himself. She didn't even look thirty. Lindon and his family cheered for her from the crowd, though his father looked as though he'd bitten something sour.

An unknown time later, Jaran slipped out of his house in the middle of the night while his wife slept. He hobbled on a cane, but he took an overcoat and a sword with him.

Lindon's stomach dropped.

The three remaining members of the Shi family, wearing white funeral robes, clustered around an iron tablet with Wei Shi Jaran's name on it. Seisha lit the candle herself.

More years silently slid by, and Lindon saw himself sitting on the edge of a roof under the stars, side-by-side with a girl he'd never met. She had a wide, open smile. He passed her a bottle, and she drank.

Now they stood together in the Hall of Elders, both wearing red, with a white ribbon tying their clasped hands together. The First Elder said something and everyone laughed, but the vision-Lindon gazed only at his new wife.

The Lindon of the present felt his eyes burn and hurriedly wiped them away. He shouldn't show tears to a heavenly immortal, but...Unsouled weren't allowed to marry.

Time moved on in the blink of an eye, and he saw himself cycling in a meditative position next to his son. Applauding his daughter as she conjured foxfire for the first time. Pouring tea for his wife.

Fate, it seemed, was good to him. Was this why a messenger had descended from heaven? To show him the rewards for a young life spent suffering? If so, he welcomed it.

He saw himself grow older, his children grow tall.

Then Sacred Valley collapsed.

The image passed so quickly he almost didn't catch it. A monstrous creature that towered into the clouds waded through the mountains like a man through waves, washing over the valley and burying it in earth. Everything was wiped out in an instant.

And Lindon returned to reality, standing before the white-armored woman. Her green hair drifted behind her, and the ghostly lines leading from her fingertips to her skull flickered with light like swallowed stars. She watched him with that same mask of an expression, though now he saw a tinge of pity in her eyes.

His cheeks were wet with tears, and he felt as though his chest had been hollowed out. "I...my future, I..."

"Not your future," she said. "Fate is only a direction. That is the direction your life would have gone, like a river flowing downhill, had Li Markuth not intervened. That is how your story is fated to continue, and how it is destined to end."

"And now, you've...undone what he did. Is that still what will happen to me?"

Her smile was sympathetic, and the pity in her eyes deepened. Her compassion scared him almost as much as the visions, because that meant she knew. "It is a good fate. You only die after a full, rich life."

"When my home is destroyed!" He'd never considered Sacred Valley his home before. Sacred Valley was the entire world.

"Not every thread is cut. A few survive, and they will go on to join greater powers in the world." She reached over for her lines of gray smoke. "This is why I take the memories, Wei Shi Lindon. Fate is not considerate."

"How do I fix it?" Lindon asked.

Her fingers froze on the lines.

Taking that as encouragement, Lindon continued. "There has to be some way to fix it. If it's a direction, then direction can be changed. There has to be some... sacred arts, or some weapon, or..." Lindon still felt the countless tons of cold earth, pressing down on his family. "If I were strong like you are, I could change things. This one begs you. Please."

Purple eyes watched him, weighed him. Her hand withdrew from the smoky strings, and she paced a half-circle around him as though to consider him from a new angle.

The immortal glanced to her left shoulder. He could glean nothing from her face, which remained somehow pleasant and impassive both. "Suriel requesting clearance for unbound transportation within Iteration One-one-zero. Verbal response, please."

A woman spun itself into existence on her shoulder, like a doll made of gray smoke. That didn't surprise him much; Forgers of the White Fox created illusions more solid than this one every day. The ghost spoke with the all-surrounding neutral voice he'd heard earlier. [Acknowledged. Consulting Sector Control.]

Silence reigned as the ghost waited for a response, but Lindon was caught by another detail: the celestial messenger had called herself Suriel. He'd never heard the name before, but he filed it away like a scroll in the clan archives.

[Clearance granted.]

"I would like a tour," Suriel said, with a glance at Lindon.

[For what purpose?]

"I'm looking for combatants."

[Acknowledged.]

Suriel reached up to rest an armored hand on top of Lindon's head. "Steel yourself," she said. "Do not be afraid."

She'd told him that already, but before he could ask what he was supposed to be afraid *of*, they vanished. An intense pattern of blue light washed over him, devouring every other sight. It was like being covered in a blanket woven with millions of threads, and each thread was a distinct shade of blue light. His ears rushed with overwhelming noise...but only for an instant.

Then the blanket fell away, and they stood in the middle of a royal court such as he had never imagined. Lanterns held glowing, golden jewels a hundred yards overhead, and the room stretched so far that it vanished in any direction. Lindon was next to Suriel, the both of them standing in the middle of a vast crowd of old men and women in intricate formal robes. Each of the elders wore a fortune's worth of jade, gold, and exotic metals that Lindon couldn't identify. Some had sacred beasts with them—a red serpent coiling around an arm here, a two-headed tiger curled up there. He could feel their wealth and authority hanging in the air; these were people that could have Lindon executed with a gesture.

He dropped to his knees even as the smoky ghost said, [The Ninecloud Court.]

Suriel flicked her fingers, and he found himself gently pulled to his feet though nothing touched him. "They cannot see us unless I allow them to." She herself stood with hands clasped at her waist, gazing straight ahead as though none of the opulence could attract her interest for a second.

Lindon glanced around, prepared to fall back to his knees at any second. Indeed, none of the crowd so much as glanced at them.

This is the power of an immortal. With even a small piece of that power, he could do anything.

A hatch in the ceiling opened up, and a rainbow-glistening cloud descended. As it drifted down toward the floor, he saw that someone was *riding* on the cloud: a girl perhaps ten or eleven years old, wrapped entirely in glistening peacock feathers. Her hair was an impossible, fiery red, and she surveyed her elders as though looking down on her subjects.

[Luminous Queen Sha Miara,] the ghost said. [Path of Celestial Radiance.]

The girl reached out a hand and Forged a sword of blinding rainbow light. "Kneel," she said, and the sea of people knelt. Lindon had to focus to keep standing. The blade radiated power and authority, such that it seemed to affect his soul directly.

Suriel nodded to the girl. "Sha Miara inherited her madra from a noble lineage stretching back to the birth of this world. In three days, she will use that sword to sink a fleet of cloudships, saving her capital city from attack by air. If you had her power, you could save Sacred Valley."

Lindon stared at the redheaded girl and her rainbow sword. He'd never heard of this "Ninecloud Court," and of course no one had left Sacred Valley for a hundred generations. It was a desolate landscape beyond the mountains, a nightmare from the lowest hells. All the books said so.

"Where is she?" Lindon asked. He might be able to recruit her, or beg her for help, if he couldn't learn the secrets of her training.

Suriel gave him a sidelong glance around the curtain of her dark green hair. "If you walked the length of Sacred Valley end-to-end, you'd have to do it more than a hundred times—"

[One hundred and fourteen times,] the ghost said.

"—one hundred and fourteen times to reach the outer border of her country. The Ninecloud Court is in the Nine-cloud Country, for which it was named, and that country is four hundred times—"

[Three hundred and ninety-four times,] the ghost said.

"Verbal response not required for calculation corrections. Three hundred and ninety-four times bigger than Sacred Valley. You would never get there. Here, your fate is an absolute certainty. If you tried one million times to go to the Ninecloud Court from where you are at this moment, you would die before you reached her one million times."

He started to ask for advice when the blue flash came

again, and then they were standing in midair over an end-less ocean. When Lindon saw the slate-gray waves tossing under his feet, his breath left him. He hurled himself onto Suriel's armored shoulders before he fell.

She stood with perfect equanimity, every hair in place, as an invisible force peeled him off her shoulders and placed him next to her. His feet were firmly planted on air. On *air.* He couldn't trust it. His gut was certain that he would be dropped at any second.

"Do not be afraid," she reminded him for a third time.

[The Trackless Sea,] the ghost announced.

And then they dropped.

Stomach lurched, and he plummeted into the ocean. He panicked as water closed over him, flailing his arms even as he squeezed his eyes shut, holding his breath. He'd learned to swim in the Dragon River, as any Wei child did, but it rarely ran deeper than his shoulders.

"Breathe," Suriel commanded, and he realized he was still dry. He cracked his eyes open, but almost shut them again. Aside from a bubble of air surrounding him, the immortal, and her pet ghost, water stretched infinitely in every direc-tion. Light glimmered above them, increasingly distant, but they plunged lower and lower. Into the darkness.

He finally caught his balance, forcing himself to breathe normally and not to cling to the white-armored woman as though to a raft. She seemed to be treating this as nothing out of the ordinary, so he took his queue from her. But he did stand very, very close. Not only was he trusting her to save him, she was the only other person in this world of black water.

As they fell, Lindon saw that they weren't alone after all. Someone else dropped alongside them, a man sinking through the water like his bones were weighted with lead. The stranger was a mass of muscle, his eyes glowed golden, and he had his arms folded as though impatiently waiting to reach the ocean floor. As they fell into darkness together, the ghost spoke again. [Northstrider. Path of the Hungry Deep.]

The absolute black beneath them shifted, and Lindon slid closer to Suriel. A dragon's head emerged from the dark, followed by a serpent's body that coiled endlessly. It must have been *miles* long, and its jaws gaped open into a pink tunnel lined with teeth.

Northstrider unfolded his arms, revealing hands gloved in pitch-black scales. With one hand he seized a fang longer than he was tall, but the monster's momentum carried him past Lindon. A wall of scales rushed past him, blocking out everything else.

"Northstrider consumes sacred beasts in the deepest places of the world," Suriel said. "He takes their power with him to the surface. He could level Sacred Valley on his own...and you could save it, if you had skills and powers like his."

She'd said that already, but she had withheld the most important part. "Honored immortal, *how?* I am Unsouled. Where could I possibly learn his skills?" He hoped she would answer him, but feared she would call it impossible.

She smiled at him as though she knew his thoughts, and another blue flash took them away.

Inside an ordinary inn hewn from rough logs, eight people in intricate golden armor laughed and clinked glasses together. A woman tossed a gold shield down, saying something with raised eyebrows. A man pulled his helmet off, revealing a red eye in the center of his forehead.

[Western Chi Ning City. The Eight-Man Empire. Path of the Eightfold Spear.]

"These eight call themselves an empire because they conquer wherever they roam," Suriel said, striding through the room. She let her hand drift behind her, as though she meant to run white-plated fingers over the local men and women, but she never touched a thing. "So far, they have not been defeated. They could easily save Sacred Valley, as could you, if you earned a place with them. Their armor is a cross between a Remnant and a construct, and when one of them dies, they pass it on to a successor."

"Are they all Gold?" Lindon asked. He hadn't seen anyone outside the valley wearing badges, but he supposed the armor might serve a similar purpose.

Suriel stopped with her palm hovering over one member of the Eight-Man Empire, a woman with yellow hair who lay facedown on a table, snoring. "Larian was raised in a noble household. Her father wouldn't let her play with the other children until she reached the level you know as Gold. When she was six years old, she did. Today, an army of ten thousand Gold-ranked sacred artists couldn't scratch her armor."

Larian grunted in her sleep.

The blue blanket fell again, but this time it lingered. He and Suriel drifted in a blinding sapphire void. She stood in the same position as in the inn—arm outstretched as though to deliver a blessing, her visage all the more inhuman for her green hair and seamless white armor. Without turning around, she spoke. "You have twenty, maybe thirty years before disaster strikes."

[An average of twenty-eight years, seven months, four days,] the ghost put in.

"Verbal response *not* required." She turned to face him, arm still raised. "I have showed you some of the most powerful sacred artists in the world, on three very different Paths. What do they have in common?"

"They're incredibly strong," he said. He hadn't seen much from the girl in the court or the eight in the tavern, but the man fighting a sea dragon bare-handed had definitely caught his attention.

Suriel's expression told him nothing, but she flipped her hand palm-up. "They have nothing in common, save their commitment. They each have different motivations, different goals, different levels of talent, but all of them pursue the sacred arts with absolute dedication."

Lindon met her gaze with resolve, drawing himself up to his full height. He was taller than she was, he realized, though it made him feel somehow wrong. "I am dedicated."

"Are you?" Her purple eyes were cold and unflinching, her lips still as a carving. "Each of those sacred artists risked their lives, gave up their pride, endured beatings and public humiliation. They sacrificed comfort for lives of brutality and pain. And *none* of them built their power from nothing in a mere thirty years."

"I will do it."

"Not even I had reached their level in thirty years."

Now he wasn't so confident.

"Your first step, if you wish to take it, begins today. You have to abandon your family and leave Sacred Valley as quickly as possible. There is nothing here for you."

"I can do that," he said without hesitation. He'd been prepared for that requirement ever since she'd shown him the girl in the Ninecloud Court. It would hurt, but his family would actually encourage him if they knew he was journeying to practice the sacred arts.

"No, you can't. Not without help." The blue light vanished, leaving them floating thousands of feet in the air. Four mountains surrounded them: one crowned in light, one robed in purple trees, one made of red stone, and one wreathed in a rushing river.

This was his home, but he had never seen Sacred Valley from this perspective before. It looked so...small.

Suriel surveyed the land like a judge. "By the standards of the outside world, anyone below Gold is considered powerless. Unworthy of being called a sacred artist at all. Your only chance, and it's a distant chance, is to leave this place where Jade is the greatest height."

"If I *do* leave, then can I..." He was afraid to ask the question, afraid the answer would be *no*. "...can I become a Gold?"

"You'll have to," she said, eyes still on the landscape. "That is where you must start."

Abandoning his home was a sad thought, and he couldn't deny a rush of fear at the idea. But more than that, his soul *lifted*. She might as well have told him he could become a celestial immortal and live in the heavens. He was capable of reaching not just Jade, but a level *beyond* Gold. It was such a bright, tender dream that he almost didn't dare to touch it.

He wouldn't even have dared to dream such a bold dream...but Suriel's words were those of fate itself.

Lindon couldn't drop to his knees in the air, but he bowed at the waist. "Honored immortal, this one begs one more answer from you. How should I leave the valley?"

Suriel waved a hand, and four green lights shone like beacons in Lindon's vision. One on each of the holy peaks, burning like emerald bonfires. "There is an exit on each of the peaks, guarded by one of the Schools." She hesitated a moment as though searching for a specific memory. "But leaving will be very difficult. If there is a way..."

She glanced at the ghost on her shoulder, which responded almost instantly. [Nine-point-eight kilometers northwest.] A smaller point of green light appeared on the slopes of Mount Samara.

The invisible bubble containing them rushed forward, and Lindon's body shuddered with the instinct to protect itself, but Suriel spoke as though reciting a poem. "There are a million Paths in this world, Lindon, but any sage will tell you they can all be reduced to one. *Improve yourself.*"

Lindon was still somewhat worried about offending this visitor from another world, but he dared to say, "That doesn't sound like enough."

The mountain rushed closer as they descended into its shadow. "It's been my path for longer than you would believe. Do you think anyone dares to attack *my* homeland?"

Near the peak of the mountain, where patches of snow still lingered despite the summer heat, and where the enormous halo of light seemed close enough to touch, there was a deep chasm. Without hesitation, Suriel directed them down into the darkness.

At the bottom of the chasm, there stood a girl with the lean, ragged look of a wandering warrior. She was perhaps his age, with the look of Sacred Valley about her: the pale skin, black hair, and dark eyes that characterized virtually every clan.

But the sacred artist's robes she wore were black, which fit no clan or school he knew, and she carried a sword on her hip...but no badge. Her hair was cut absolutely straight, as though sliced with a razor, and she wore a coil of thick, bright red rope wrapped around her waist like a belt. She had obviously been treated roughly: her robes were torn and stained, her hair frayed and matted, every inch of her skin covered in layer after layer of razor-thin scars. Most of those scars had to be years old, but some were obviously pink and fresh. She stared death down the chasm, sword gripped tightly in both hands.

At first, Lindon thought she was glaring at *him*. But a glance behind him told him the truth.

She was cornered by her enemies.

The Heaven's Glory School of Mount Samara wore white and gold, and each of these young men and women had badges of iron around their necks. There were eight of them—two with spears, two with swords, two who carried weighted nets, and two whose hands glowed with light.

[Mount Samara,] the ghost announced. [Yerin, Disciple of the Sword Sage. Path of the Endless Sword.]

Suriel's boots crunched in the snow as she walked forward, though she left no footprints. "She might not have the skill to save Sacred Valley, but she can help you leave it. With her guidance, you may both leave this valley alive. She, too, has a fate that needs changing."

The girl stepped forward to fight.

Blue flashed, and an instant later they were standing amid the arena of the Seven-Year Festival, but Lindon fixed the image of the black-clad girl in his mind. *Yerin, Disciple of the Sword Sage.* She was his path forward. The Heaven's Glory School would never allow him access to the mountain, which only meant that he had to find another way in.

Suriel lifted into the air again, surveying the frozen sacred artists beneath her with that same pleasant mask of an expression. She spoke to Lindon without looking at him. "If I let you keep these memories, it will change your fate. Your life will be harder, and most likely shorter. You have one last chance. Would you forget, or remember?"

He should spend longer considering such an important decision, but he'd already made up his mind. "I would never choose to forget you, honored immortal," Lindon said with a bow. "You restored my life."

She smiled at his words, though she still examined the still tableau beneath her. White-armored fingers strummed the smoky cords on her right hand. "Then watch closely. This is a rare sight."

Blue flashed, covering everything, and time ran backwards.

The Jade elders who rushed up on the stage now reversed themselves, returning to their seats. The sky overhead cleared up. The pillars crumbled upward, rebuilding themselves from rubble until the illusions of Elder Whisper danced on them once again. Only those she had already repaired were excepted: the Patriarch, his body rebuilt, stood on the side until she pointed to him. As though carried by invisible strings, he drifted up and onto the stage, assuming a pose with his hands in the air. She'd already cleaned up the severed heads, for which Lindon was grateful. If she had returned him to life, surely she had resurrected his mother as well.

Soon, the world was as he'd left it. Before reality had gone mad, and ancient Golds descended from the sky followed by celestial messengers. She had undone everything. Given them a fresh start.

He bowed again, with no other way to express his gratitude. If he lived for a thousand years, he would never be able to repay such a debt. "This one thanks you a hundred times for the guidance, honored immortal. Will this one ever have the chance to return some small measure of your kindness?"

Around him, the day still crawled in reverse as Suriel's hands danced in accordance with some sacred art. She still spoke to him while regarding her handiwork. "I will give you a token so that I may find you easily, wherever and whoever you are. When the time comes, I will return for you. If you're lucky, you might be able to ascend to a higher world."

"Do you mean the heavens?" Lindon asked. "With you?"

Suriel turned to face him, green hair falling to frame her pale face, and finally the world was still again. This time, everything was as it had been only a handful of hours before: the Patriarch of the Wei clan stood in the arena, disapproval on his face. The crowd shouted in the stands. Wei Jin Amon crouched with his spear, ready to do battle. Even the sun had reversed its course, shining golden in the late afternoon. Among it all, the celestial messenger stood out, her purple eyes growing brighter.

"My organization has a name for this world, Wei Shi Lindon. We call it 'Cradle.' It's where we keep the infants."

She reached out and dropped something into his hand: a glass bead, slightly bigger than his thumbnail, with one blue candle-flame trapped inside. The flame burned evenly as he turned it in his hands.

"This is my token. You cannot use it to contact me, but I can sense it across worlds and beyond time."

"Apologies, honored immortal, but...what if it breaks?" It was glass, after all.

She favored him with a little laugh. "It can't break, and it cannot be lost, as it is tied to you with strings of fate. Move forward, stay alive, and I will come retrieve you when you've grown." Behind her, a gateway opened on a layered field of solid blue, as though it opened underneath the surface of a shining sea. "Go with the Way, Lindon."

In a flash, she vanished.

Sound returned in a rush, and even the crowd's hushed whispers—they had softened themselves out of respect for the Patriarch—sounded like thunder in his ears.

Wei Jin Sairus lowered his arms, which had been raised to settle the audience. "Young Lindon, there is no dishonor if you remove yourself from the stage. Rather, we would respect your wisdom in deferring to your betters."

Only recently, Lindon had wondered if he was trapped in a dream.

Now the same sensation returned in full force, as everything his senses told him suggested he had never left. His mother paced the arena, her eyes locked on him. His father glowered from the stands, angered that the Patriarch had put his son in such a position. Kelsa sat next to him, anger plain in the way she perched on the edge of her seat.

Between his fingers, he rolled a warm marble. He looked down to see a ball of glass surrounding a single blue candle-flame.

If this was a dream, it was one sent by the heavens.

He turned from the Patriarch and bowed to the representatives of the four Schools.

CHAPTER TWELVE

Sacred Valley is a paradise nestled within a mountain range. It is protected by weather and terrain, by the inhospitable nature of the surrounding regions, by ancient legend, and by a few significant individuals with vested interest in keeping the valley unexplored. Most of the world has forgotten Sacred Valley, overlooking it as nowhere of interest.

But it has a long history, and that history has left its mark.

The four mountains bracketing Sacred Valley are known to the locals as the "holy peaks," locations of myth and mystery. The four largest schools in the region have each claimed a peak as their home, and the secrets found within have given these organizations strong roots.

To the north, Yoma Mountain is carpeted in purple orus trees for most of the year. The Fallen Leaf School processes the fruits of these trees into products to be sold, as well as secret elixirs to strengthen their own students. They also possess the largest and most obvious entrance into the labyrinth that forms the foundation of the entire Sacred

Valley, an entrance they call the Nethergate. The door stands thirty meters high, and is carved with the image of a Dreadgod. Every ten years, it opens, and the Fallen Leaf elders are able to retrieve some treasures from the shallowest levels of the labyrinth within.

To the west, Mount Venture shows off its distinct mineral composition with rust-red cliffs. It is the shortest of the four peaks, and most of the mining in Sacred Valley takes place here. This is the home of the Kazan clan and the territory of the Golden Sword School, and the profits of the mine are split between them. Goldsteel and halfsilver are the primary output of these mines, though a further report can be requested on especially rare or trivially mundane materials.

To the south, the mountain called Greatfather is broken, its peak shattered into a shape resembling the mouth of a bottle. Water pools up there, cascading down the cliffs in a stream known as the Dragon River. Fueled by the water aura at the top of the mountain, storms wrack these slopes year-round, and the Holy Wind School maintains shelters for unlucky travelers caught outside. Favored Holy Wind elders can bathe in the pool known as Greatfather's Tears, regenerating their vitality of body and spirit.

To the east, Mount Samara rises as the tallest of the four holy peaks. It is blanketed in snow, and crowned in a ring of pale white light that circles the summit. The halo appears at sundown and disappears at sunrise, so that no one in Sacred Valley has ever experienced a dark night. Samara's halo is a construction of light aura bound into form by an expert centuries past, and it is the reason why so many sacred artists in the valley practice light-aspect arts. The Heaven's Glory School has claimed this peak, using the power of Samara's ring to gather light aura even on a moonless night.

SUGGESTED TOPIC: ORIGIN OF THE HOLY PEAKS.
CONTINUE?
DENIED, REPORT COMPLETE.

Without the lungs of an Iron, Lindon couldn't make his voice heard in every corner of the arena, but he shouted as loud as he could. "Honored representative of the Heaven's Glory School! This one regrets that his display has caused you shame, and he begs one more chance to prove himself."

In the box above, the boy in white-and-gold stepped forward. His expression was cold and forbidding, as though he wished to have Lindon executed before he said another word. "Why should I give you such a chance?"

"Wei Jin Amon is to become a disciple of your school, is that not so?" Amon, startled, looked from Lindon to the Heaven's Glory agent. "If this one manages to force him out of the ring, or cause him to admit defeat, then this one has surely demonstrated his own value. This one requests a place in your school, under those conditions."

The boy let out a single, high laugh. "My school only receives those with potential. You have none."

"This one does not dare to contradict you, honored guest, but if this one can by chance overthrow Amon...then surely, this one has proven his skill. And with the tutelage of the Heaven's Glory School, surely such skill has future potential."

Wei Jin Sairus had too high of a status to seize Lindon and hurl him bodily from the stage, but it looked as though he wanted to. "You go too far!" he thundered, but the Heaven's Glory elder raised a hand to stop him.

"We've wasted too much time already on this nonsense," the boy said. "Let him fight. Wei Jin Amon, ensure he has no time to admit defeat."

The cold words sent a chill up Lindon's spine, but he bowed again. "Does that mean the Heaven's Glory School accepts my words?"

"We do. So long as the Wei clan accepts the consequences of your loss."

"Certainly," Sairus declared. "One Unsouled is no loss to my clan. An honorable death in a duel is more than he has earned."

Lindon glanced up in the stands. Kelsa looked horrified, Jaran was half-standing in fury, and the First Elder shook his head sadly. None of them could intervene.

Only his mother frowned, as though considering something.

"Sacred artists, prepare yourselves!" the Patriarch shouted. His grandson ran a hand along the spear, face as cold as his iron badge. Lindon leaned forward as far as he could, as though he meant to dash into Amon immediately.

"Begin!"

Lindon ran the other way.

A surge of laughter burst from the stands as they watched the Foundation-stage child run from the Iron practitioner. Amon didn't deign to pursue, but straightened up, his spear locked in his fist. "Do you want to shame me into chasing you?" he asked, in a tone too low to carry. "Is that your plan?"

Lindon didn't answer. When he reached the edge of the stage, he turned to face his cousin. "This one patiently awaits your guidance," he said politely.

When Amon moved, Lindon could barely see it. He seemed to cross a dozen yards in a single step, the foxfire gathered around his spearhead tracing lines in the air like shining serpents.

But he wasn't faster than Lindon's spirit. He sent a pulse of madra down through his heel, into the stage, undoing the seal he'd placed on a jar three days earlier.

Be free, he urged mentally, and the Remnants shattered their prison. They followed the weak thread of his power up and through the stone, passing through like ghosts.

A swarm of green-light hornets spun around Lindon like emeralds, buzzing with fury. His command still bound them: *Attack*.

As one, the Remnants turned to face Wei Jin Amon.

The Iron fighter pulled himself up short, skidding to
a halt on the stone, but he'd been moving too fast. He
couldn't stop in time. Not that the Remnants would have
allowed him to escape anyway.

They were on him like a school of ravenous fish, stingers flashing as they stung. No one could display the dignity
of a sacred artist under such a condition; he screamed like
a child, flailing his spear as though he'd never had an hour
of weapons training, swatting wildly at the air around him.

For a few seconds, Lindon only watched. When he saw
pulses of hazy purple-and-white force emanating from
Amon's body, causing hornets to pause or turn spirals in
midair, he knew that his cousin had focused his spirit on
defense. Now was the chance.

Lindon walked forward, and the Remnants parted
before him. Amon was still dangerously strong, his spear
sweeping through the air, and Lindon took an instant to
judge its path before he reached out and caught it.

The wood smacked painfully into his palm, but not with
nearly the force a true attack would have carried. Amon's
spirit was in chaos, his madra bent to swiping away hornets, and he had not focused his strength.

With both hands, Lindon wrenched the weapon away.
Amon didn't seem to understand what had happened, as he
stumbled blindly forward.

While everyone in the clan who reached at least Copper received instruction in a basic weapon, Lindon had
never had such an opportunity. He had no idea how to use
a spear beyond imitating what he'd seen in others. Fortunately, he didn't need much skill.

He gripped the spear in both hands like a club, and
began smacking Wei Jin Amon everywhere he could. The
sharp edge of the spear caught him a few times, drawing
blood, but Amon was an Iron. He was in far more danger
from the Remnants than from Lindon's pathetic attacks.

Lindon couldn't deny a *little* excitement. He'd dreamed of this moment for years.

Under assault from the hornets and his own weapon, Amon's screams turned to sobs. "I...don't..." he tried to force out, but Lindon didn't lessen his assault. "I...give..." he began, and that was too much.

Lindon walked around to the other side of his cousin, reversing his spear until the butt rested against Amon's chest. Then he gave a shove.

The Iron-ranked fighter tumbled to the ground outside the stage.

The arena was silent except for Amon's sobs and the buzz of the Remnants, who continued their attack until they received another wave of Lindon's madra. When they did, they responded as a swarm: "TASK COMPLETED." Then they flew off into the sky.

No one stopped them. Someone like the Patriarch could surely have destroyed them had he wanted to, but even he seemed paralyzed. His face grew red as he stared at Lindon, his mouth gaping open as though he couldn't give voice to his fury.

Before he could say anything, Lindon bowed to the foreign guests once more. "Wei Jin Amon has admitted defeat and left the bounds of the competition."

Another instant of silence, except for the pathetic sounds made by Amon, and then the boy from Heaven's Glory began to laugh.

"Is this the honor and dignity of the Wei clan, then? One child attacks another for a lowly position in my school, fighting over our scraps?"

The air warped around Patriarch Sairus, and Lindon was sheathed in absolute darkness. The Patriarch had blinded him.

Only that morning, Lindon would have panicked and begged forgiveness. But after seeing Suriel's display of power, this one was somewhat lacking.

"Forgive us, Elder Whitehall," Sairus said. "We will

punish the Unsouled." *Elder?* That child was a Jade? Lindon hadn't gotten a look at the boy's badge, but that seemed incredible.

"No!" Elder Whitehall barked. "The Heaven's Glory School has given its word, and a child cannot cause us to break it. We will harbor Wei Shi Lindon for as long as he can perform up to the standard of a Heaven's Glory disciple."

Which wouldn't be long, Lindon was sure, but it didn't have to be. He only had to find Yerin, the Sword Sage's Disciple, and leave the valley.

"But we only came down from Samara for one disciple," the elder continued. "We have no room for two. Have your grandson meditate on his failures, and perhaps when we again have space for a new disciple, we will consider him once more."

The darkness over Lindon lifted, and he dropped to his knees to press his forehead against the cold stone. "Disciple Lindon greets Elder Whitehall."

"Don't buy your own lies," said the boy in gold and white. "If you last a week on the mountain, I'll tutor you myself."

The rest of the Seven-Year Festival passed without incident, as far as Lindon was concerned. His veiled questions to his family about a Gold from the Li Clan, or the phoenix that descended from the sky, were met with confused looks and careful inquiries. His mother, at least, was worried that someone on the Path of the White Fox had tampered with his perception.

Kelsa ended up as the highest-ranking young Iron in the Wei clan, as Wei Jin Amon was too busy recuperating from his injuries to participate. She ultimately lost to a Kazan girl, but that wasn't enough to tarnish her achievements.

The Patriarch himself presented her with a pair of valuable elixirs, announcing that she would "Redeem the shame of the Shi family."

After receiving her prizes, Kelsa returned to the Shi family compound with Lindon by her side. She spoke about the Festival with great enthusiasm and without interference. He walked in silence.

"...I'll need one of these elixirs to stabilize my core after reaching Iron, but the second won't help much. They say it takes *twenty* of these to get close to Jade, can you imagine? They're five thousand chips apiece. And that's *with* years of cycling in between each one." She glanced to the side, giving him a wry smile. The box of elixirs was tied in a cloth bag, and that bag dangled carelessly from her hand as she walked.

"I'd share one with you, but I doubt you'll need it. Heaven's Glory. You'll be eating spirit-fruits for every meal and drinking elixirs like water. Instead of sharing with you, I should be asking you to share with me."

Lindon knew Kelsa. She wasn't angling for a handout, just making an idle comment. If he actually offered to share any elixirs from Heaven's Glory with her, she'd refuse unless he tricked her into it.

But the thought gave him a pang of loss and regret. If all went according to plan, he wouldn't see Kelsa or the rest of his family for more than twenty years. It was an impossible amount of time to him, incomprehensibly vast.

She read his silence and stopped, stretching out an arm in front of his chest. He ran into it as though into a tree branch, her forearm striking his ribs with the strength of a club. He coughed out a breath, and the weight of his pack pushed him forward, straining his neck.

He staggered back, wondering if his chest would bruise. "What was *that?*"

"You're too quiet," she said, folding her arms. The box of elixirs hung down in its blue shadesilk bag. "Something happened."

He pressed fingers into his sternum, feeling for tenderness. "I'm *listening,* I'm not meditating on boyhood trauma. Maybe I should do all the talking from now on, and you should take the punches."

She stared him down. "You can punch me as long as your knuckles hold out, but when you're done, I need an answer. You've won everything you've ever wanted. More than I did; there are people who would kill you for a spot as a School disciple. And you're not proud of it, you haven't gloated, you haven't tried to get something extra out of the clan before you leave. You haven't even redeemed that *deal* of yours with the First Elder, and he told me he'd expected to see you before sunset on the day of the Foundation tournament. When you didn't show up, he thought you were dead."

The deal he'd made with the First Elder, a copy of the White Fox Path in exchange for displaying his abilities in the Seven-Year Festival, felt like it had come from a different life. He'd been dreaming before he met Suriel, and now he was awake.

Not that he could say that to his sister.

"My end of the scales doesn't balance," Lindon said. "I was supposed to defeat a Copper from another clan and show them the power of the Wei, but I ended up humiliating our own clan's best disciple."

Kelsa placed the elixirs carefully on the ground, then grabbed him by the shoulders. She leaned forward, her face inches away from his, dark eyes heavy with concern. "*Are* you dead? Because that is nothing my brother would say. *My* brother would have tried to convince the First Elder that beating Amon was *better* than beating some Copper from another clan."

Lindon shrugged, averting his eyes. "I'm going to a School. I won't need it anymore."

He wasn't concerned about keeping Suriel a secret. Spreading rumors about her couldn't harm her, and receiving a visit from the heavens was a source of pride, not shame. If that had been all, he would have been trying to convince his sister to believe him, not keeping it a secret.

But he'd seen more than just a celestial messenger. He'd seen the end of the world.

There was nothing Kelsa could do to change that, nothing she could do to help him. Even if she completely believed him and was willing to leave Sacred Valley at his side, how could she help? She wasn't a disciple of Heaven's Glory, so she couldn't follow him up the slopes of Samara, and she wasn't strong enough to survive the terrors outside the valley any more than he was.

If he failed, if he died on the way as he was more than likely to do, he didn't want her to live helpless under a cloud of doom. She'd be happier if he said nothing.

All that was true, but he still wanted to tell her.

She was still watching him from an inch away, still looking into his eyes with selfless concern. He found himself saying, "Was there....anything you can remember from that day at the Foundation tournament? Anything strange?"

Her eyebrows raised. "I'd say so. You set a swarm of hornets on Wei Jin Amon and beat him with his own spear."

"Anything else?" Now it was his turn to search *her* eyes, looking for any sign of recognition, any uneasy recollections. "You didn't feel like you were somewhere and then somewhere else? You didn't lose any memories, or forget some time?"

"How would I know if I did?" she asked. Whatever he was looking for in her eyes, he didn't see it.

He took a step back, and she allowed him to break her grip. "I'm nervous, that's all it is," he said. "Heaven's Glory won't accept a disciple like me, and they'll try and force me out as soon as they can."

Kelsa watched him a moment longer, then plucked her bag of elixirs from the ground. "Likely they will. What does that matter? You'll take what you can from them, then if it gets too dangerous, you just come back down. Maybe you'll get an elixir or some treasures from the top of the mountain. This could be exactly what you need to make the clan proud."

They reached the Shi family complex, a square of tightly packed houses, as night fell. The ring of light around Samara glowed white, illuminating the snowy peak and casting a blanket of light all over the valley.

He took in the sight of his home under Samara's ring as though for the last time.

In the morning, his mother and father said their good-byes casually, and they'd all assured him that he would be welcomed back exactly as he was. They didn't understand why he fought back tears as he wished them farewell, because they expected him to return in no more than a week or two.

But in the end, he still had to leave. He'd seen too much to stay home.

The party from Heaven's Glory was led by Elder Whitehall, who was indeed a head shorter than Lindon. He looked no more than eleven or twelve, despite his intricate white-and-gold robes and the Jade arrow badge on his chest.

He waited with two disciples from his school before a carriage pulled by a pair of Remnants. The carriage itself looked finer than anything the Patriarch would ride, inlaid with golden clouds and dancing sacred beasts, and the Remnants were a pair of transparent oxen. They seemed to be made from heat haze, or perhaps incredibly fine glass, and—like most Remnants—they made sounds totally unlike a living creature. When they stomped their hooves, thunder rolled, and their fractious snorts were like the crack of a whip.

"You've made us wait," Elder Whitehall said, though it was still an hour until dawn. Samara's halo still shone brighter than the moon, crowning and illuminating their destination. "Stow your belongings before you set us further behind."

The two disciples glanced at Lindon more out of curiosity than pity, he was sure. Then they climbed into the carriage behind their master.

Lindon had tied his bulky pack to the roof before he noticed what they were missing: a driver.

"Hurry yourself, Unsouled," the elder called from inside the carriage. "I have business to attend to at the school."

Without a word of dissent, Lindon clambered up onto the driver's seat behind the oxen. Even this was cushioned, though the only carriages he'd ever ridden in the Wei clan had undressed boards for the driver. He was grateful for the comfort, and for the lack of company.

With an instant of concentration, he sent a drop of madra into the reins. A line of script ran down the inside of the leather straps, carrying his power down and into the ox-Remnants. They bellowed like a couple of thunderstorms, transparent forms rippling with light, and they began to pull.

After that, the trip was easy. At first, Lindon was concerned that he might have to ask Elder Whitehall for directions, but he discovered that the path toward Samara was clear and wide. They rode for hours as the sun rose, the terrain sprouted hills, and the purple-leafed orus trees gave way to foliage of mundane green.

Mount Samara's halo faded and dimmed as they approached, eventually vanishing for the day. The mountain's slopes were sparse, sprinkled with the occasional copse of twisted trees or the spot of color from a flying Remnant. The mountain loomed over them as noon broke, like a wall taking up half the horizon.

The road terminated at the base of the mountain, transforming into a dirt path that twisted upward in a series of hatchbacks. Lindon hesitated as he saw the trail, but the oxen didn't, hauling their way up the mountain with dogged determination.

Within seconds, Elder Whitehall must have sensed the change. "Halt!" he called, and Lindon had no choice but to urge the Remnants to stop their advance on a steep slope. They supported the carriage as though their hooves had been nailed to the side of the mountain.

The childlike elder hopped out of the carriage, his disciples following like chaperones. But when they reached the ground, they bowed to Elder Whitehall, saluting with their fists pressed together.

Lindon left the driver's seat and did likewise. There was no sense in disrespecting an elder before even arriving at the school.

Whitehall paid them no attention, walking to their right, skirting the edge of the mountain. "The three of you will walk a different path up the mountain. This is the first test of any disciple in the Heaven's Glory School."

Lindon was somewhat surprised to learn that the other two were in the same category as he was. They were both older, but only by a year or two, and very little set them apart. One was as tall as Lindon, with brown hair a shade darker than his mother's, the other shorter with black hair. Otherwise, they were wholly unremarkable.

Unremarkable except for the iron badges on their chests. Every glance they shot at Lindon's wooden badge poked a needle in his pride.

He only had to bear with it. They would never make it past Jade; they were almost to the end of their Path. His was just beginning.

A number of boulders dotted the landscape where part of the mountain must have slid down years before, and each step of Elder Whitehall's took him from one boulder to another. The Iron disciples followed him without difficulty, but Lindon strained his body to the limit just to keep up. More than once, he came teetering within an inch of falling off the rock and smashing his head, and he was sure he wouldn't receive the best of medical care from the Heaven's Glory School.

They arrived in less than an hour, with the elder and the other two disciples as fresh as if they'd simply stepped outside. Lindon's clothes were caked with sweat, each breath heaving, his spirit fuzzy and weak from the madra he'd drawn to support his failing limbs.

Whitehall and the other two were looking up the mountain, and though it pained him to even turn his neck, he followed their gazes.

Into the slopes of Mount Samara there was a staircase. Rather than the rough gray-brown stone that surrounded him, these stairs were polished and white. It was so wide that a hundred men could march up side by side, and it appeared to progress up the mountain in a straight line. Beyond a few hundred steps, Lindon could see no further.

After that, the path was obscured by clouds of light. Shapes moved within the light, shadows with twisted antlers and gaping jaws. Even the two Iron disciples eyed the cloud with apprehension.

"Behold the Trial of Glorious Ascension," Whitehall said proudly. Lindon had to admire whichever ancient leader of the Heaven's Glory School came up with the name. It was only a staircase with some Remnant formations on it, but they had left such a proud and lofty title.

"Within that cloud are a few of the spirit-aspect and mind-aspect Remnants our school has tamed over the generations," Whitehall continued. "They will test your resolve, your determination, and the solid foundations of your spirit. With each step you climb, the Trial will become heavier. Past a certain point, retreat is impossible. If you have no confidence, you may give up your title as a Heaven's Glory disciple and return to your home. I will tell you that one in three disciples who challenges this Trial either dies or has their spirit broken, unable to practice the sacred arts again."

The boy stared directly at Lindon. "I expect that statistic is especially appropriate today. Would any of you like to withdraw?"

All three of them looked at Lindon, but he maintained an open and honest expression, as though he didn't realize what they expected of him.

After a minute of silence, the elder dismissed Lindon, turning to the other two. "If you reach the top, you will have passed, and will be considered a disciple of the Heaven's Glory School. If you reach the top before sundown, however, then we will consider you to have a bright future. In that case, you will be allowed to select one item from the school's Lesser Treasure Hall for your personal use. There are weapons, training supplements, elixirs, constructs... even some elders cannot choose freely from the hall. Use whatever means you have at your disposal, and do not take this Trial lightly."

The other two disciples straightened up, and the short one's eyes lit up. But Lindon's heart blazed. Even the Wei clan's treasure hall was enough to stir his imagination and longing, but the Heaven's Glory hall had to be an unknown number of times greater.

Now he had to reach the top before sunset. Only...

He glanced up at the cloud, where a pair of silhouettes clashed with each other in a silent, distant battle. Shadow-liquid sprayed in the air. That was a test designed for promising young Irons and genius Coppers. There was no way he could survive.

So he had to find a different way.

Elder Whitehall jumped at the staircase, skipping six steps at a time. "When I reach the cloud, you may begin. I'll see those of you who survive at the peak."

In seconds, he vanished into the light. The two Iron disciples exchanged a few brief words with each other and then ran after, not sparing Lindon a glance. That suited him, as he had immediately left.

CHAPTER THIRTEEN

Lindon wasn't insane. No matter how resolved or determined he was, there was no way someone at the Foundation stage of advancement would survive a trip through the Trial of Glorious Ascension. He'd barely been able to withstand the illusions created by his sister's madra, much less an all-out attack from a mind Remnant. But he still had to make it to the top of the mountain before the sun set, and it was already early afternoon.

It wasn't pleasant, but he did have one lone idea. Heaving a sigh, he started running back over the boulders.

The trip here had taken an hour. He was able to slow down a little on the way back, at least enough to ensure his safety, but his soul was already exhausted. By the time he arrived back at the carriage, his vision was swimming and his breath came in gulps.

Fortunately, the carriage was still here. If it hadn't been, Lindon would have cursed himself for rushing.

He untied his pack from the roof, slipping his badge inside it. Then he rolled around in the dirt for a few minutes—painfully, as many of the rocks around here were sharp—until he looked pathetic enough.

When he did, he collapsed facedown.

As soon as Elder Whitehall had abandoned the carriage, Lindon had noticed. The Remnants might be intelligent enough to drag it back up to the Heaven's Glory School, but they couldn't necessarily be trusted to do so. Remnants always acted according to their nature, after all, and it was not in the nature of most Remnants to be perfectly obedient.

The carriage required a driver, and Whitehall had climbed up the Trial with his two students. Which could only mean that someone was coming down the mountain to pick up the school's property. And since Remnants were valuable and prone to madra decay without proper care, that someone would be coming soon.

His only worry had been that he might arrive and find the carriage already gone. Now, he only had to wait for the servant of Heaven's Glory. He could have driven the carriage up the mountain himself, but then he might face some awkward questions. Better to wait.

As the first hour of waiting stretched to two, Lindon's confidence in his own theory began to thin. Someone should have been here by now, but he couldn't lift his head to check too often, or they might see through him.

He finally gave in to the temptation and lifted his head only to see a stick-thin boy, barely Lindon's age, staring at him from inches away.

They both gave a shout at the same time, scrambling away from one another.

The boy was wearing the uniform of a Heaven's Glory disciple, white and gold with a red sash. His badge was copper, which explained why he was junior enough to be sent on such a menial assignment, and his eyes were wide.

"Honored stranger, do you need help?" the boy asked hesitantly.

Before he answered, Lindon lifted a hand to his head and winced. He made a show of checking his entire body for wounds, moving tenderly as though his every muscle ached. With his face and white robes matted in sweat and marred with dirt, he should look like someone who had just survived a calamity.

"Are you a disciple of the Heaven's Glory School?" he asked, injecting his voice with heavy exhaustion.

"Yes, honored stranger."

Suddenly Lindon propped himself up on his hands and knees, and bowed until his forehead pressed into the dirt. "This one has failed you. This one has failed your esteemed school, and he deserves a thousand lashes for his weakness."

The disciple clearly didn't know how to respond, but Lindon raised his head and swept into his story. "This humble one is only a gatherer of herbs, and was on his way to deliver his monthly supply to the magnificent Heaven's Glory School. But he was set upon by a group of honorless *dogs...*"

Lindon choked as though unable to go on.

Fortunately, the disciple was intelligent enough to piece it together. "Truly unfortunate. Did they not even leave your badge?"

The boy's voice was sympathetic, but Lindon had to quell any suspicions immediately. "A copper badge will not fetch them much, but they took even the bread I kept for my meals. I am blessed by the heavens that they overlooked this meager pack, so at least I will have clothes for the return journey." He held up his pack voluntarily, so he wouldn't notice it and become suspicious. "I spotted your carriage from afar, and I waited for you to return, but I am afraid weakness overcame me and I fell into sleep. Tell me, what must I do to redeem myself in the eyes of the Heaven's Glory School?"

The boy hesitated. "I'm just a lesser initiate. You would need to speak to an elder..."

With obvious difficulty, Lindon levered himself to his feet, strapping the pack to his back. "Then I must go acquit myself before an elder. Thank you, honored disciple." He bowed deeply and hobbled off, as though he meant to climb the trail on foot.

The disciple rushed over and caught him by the arm before he'd even passed the transparent ox-Remnants. "Hold a moment. With your injuries, you'd never survive the mountain."

Lindon looked him dead in the eyes and tried to imitate his father. He knew he looked stronger than he actually was, so he was hoping to approach the prideful stare of an expert. "My failure is my own, and I must walk my own path."

He took two steps and sagged, barely catching his balance. This time, the Copper boy sighed and pushed him back toward the carriage.

"I know you have your own pride, but I have mine as well. If I were to let a fellow sacred artist die on the side of the road when I could have helped, how would I show my face among the disciples? What would people think of my Heaven's Glory School? I must take the carriage up the trail either way, and these Remnants will not mind a little extra weight."

With a show of reluctance, Lindon allowed himself to be ushered inside.

●

Elder Whitehall only *looked* like a child. As a young man, old age had frightened him more than anything, so he had tested his fledgling refiner's skills on all the spirit-fruits and sacred herbs he could gather. He'd finally refined an elixir that he was convinced would allow him to extend his youth.

It had almost worked.

An eight-year-old boy's body was not developed enough to use the full extent of its spirit, no matter how powerful that spirit was. Nor was it strong enough to handle the most powerful sacred arts. He could accept that if it meant an increase in longevity, but for reasons he couldn't fathom, this state put an increased burden on his internal organs. In only another decade or so, he would die of old age while trapped inside a child's body.

That he had achieved Jade in spite of his handicaps was a testament to his own genius. Unfettered, he was certain that he could have become the first sacred artist in hundreds of years to reach Gold. The other elders thought his condition added a mystique to the Heaven's Glory School, as though they'd trained a child to Jade, so they sent him to other factions. He especially resented it now, as a young woman in disciple's robes told him what he'd missed while he visited the Wei clan.

Having to crane his neck to look this seventeen-year-old girl in the eye didn't improve his mood.

"Elder Harbek, Elder Nasiri, and Elder Serenity were all confirmed slain in battle," the girl reported, her voice heavy. "Four Irons are still missing, and thirteen dead."

"But the Sword Sage was destroyed?" Whitehall was very intent on this point.

"There can be no doubt. His Remnant was the one to kill Elder Serenity, forcing the rest to retreat. The Remnant was sealed in the Grand Patriarch's tomb."

"And the corpse?"

She bowed, averting her eyes from his. "Pardon this one's insufficient knowledge, elder. This one presumes the corpse is still inside with the Remnant."

Of course it was. If the elders had been able to bypass the Remnant and loot the corpse, they wouldn't have locked the tomb.

"His disciple is still in hiding," she added as an afterthought. "The elders say she will be caught soon, and she may provide insight into the Remnant's powers."

Whitehall rubbed his chin, wishing for a beard. He hadn't missed anything too important after all; he was only too late for the danger. The reward may still await him. "That will be all, disciple."

The disciple bowed again—her hair dangled close to his

face—and then ran off. She would be only too happy to leave; no one liked standing here, on the edge of the cliff at the top of the Trial of Glorious Ascension. The stairs were steep here, and covered in a pink-tinged cloud, and occasionally a slashing claw or flickering tail would emerge as the Remnants fought within.

Whitehall had just climbed the stairs himself, so he couldn't be bothered, but many of the disciples harbored nightmarish memories of their time in the Trial. They didn't want to spend a second longer near that cloud than they had to.

Nor, at the moment, did Whitehall. His heart itched with impatience, as he longed to go explore the tomb. There was every possibility that he could find a method to disperse the sword-Remnant, and if he did...

The Sword Sage had come from beyond Sacred Valley. Only the most favored of the Heaven's Glory elders knew that truth, as many believed there were no settlements outside the valley. It was almost true; he'd seen the land beyond from a distance, and it was a barbaric world of slaughter and violence. Better if people stayed here, to meditate on the sacred arts in peace.

But this visitor from outside could be the key to Whitehall's greatest problem. During his stay in the Heaven's Glory School, the Sword Sage had demonstrated not only his proficiency with weapons, but his skill as a refiner. He'd brought out herbs and ingredients that Elder Whitehall had never seen before, from an Infant Songroot to the bones of a thousand-year-old sacred beast. With materials of that quality, Whitehall was sure that he could restore his body. He was close already, even with the pathetic sacred herbs he'd been able to scavenge from the clans.

Whitehall had attempted to buy what he wanted from the Sage, as had many of the other Heaven's Glory elders. The visitor had laughed and insulted them to their faces, saying they did not deserve such treasures.

That was why the elders had collectively decided to kill

him and take his wealth for their own. He was a lone expert, after all, not backed by any significant power. Whitehall had only hoped that they would wait for him to return from the Wei clan, but obviously the others had rushed ahead without him and bungled everything. This presented him with a unique opportunity. If he could dispel the Remnant and loot the man's treasures on his own, then he wouldn't have to settle for a small cut. Even if he couldn't undo this curse on his body, his powers as a refiner and as a sacred artist would leap forward. It would be a heaven-sent opportunity either way.

He only lacked time, and now here he was waiting for disciples. What a waste. He'd already stood here for three hours, and if the two children were especially slow, he could be here for three more before the sun set.

As for the third disciple candidate, Whitehall wouldn't even bother waiting. If the Unsouled hadn't turned back for his clan, then the boy didn't know what was good for him. He could die on the steps, and it would be no less than he deserved for embarrassing Whitehall in public.

A more substantial shadow loomed in the clouds, and Whitehall raised an eyebrow. Perhaps he had underestimated the boys. The tall one, Kazan Ma Deret, actually had a bit of talent. If he'd managed to climb the stairs this quickly, Whitehall might even consider taking him on as a personal disciple.

The figure that lurched from the stairs and collapsed, panting, on the cliffs was certainly tall. His hair was too dark for the Kazan boy, and though his robes were white, they were not the Heaven's Glory robes that Deret had started with. And he was carrying a bulky brown pack that Whitehall didn't recognize.

He lifted his face, and Whitehall saw that his jaw was clenched with apparent anger, his eyes sharp as spears. From his face, you'd think him rebellious and defiant.

The Unsouled.

Wei Shi Lindon crawled to his knees, kowtowing before

him. "This one...greets...honored Elder Whitehall," Lindon said between breaths. "This one tried his hardest, and hopes he has not shamed the Heaven's Glory School too much with his tardiness."

Judging by the sun, they still had at least two hours until sunset. The goal of reaching the top by sundown was not an easy one; only one in five disciples who survived the Trial of Glorious Ascension were allowed to select from the Lesser Treasure Hall. As a boy, Whitehall himself had not made it, and he had used that failure to push himself in the following years.

Had he been outdone by an *Unsouled?*

The boy's clothes were shredded and caked with dirt, as though he'd crawled on his belly the whole way up. Scratches covered his knees and hands, and it looked as though part of his face would swell up. He was crusted in layers of sweat, as though he'd wrung every drop of effort from his body for hours. He certainly *looked* like someone who had passed the Trial.

But he remembered the final demonstration of the Seven-Year Festival, how Lindon had "beaten" his Iron opponent by conjuring Remnants out of nowhere. This wasn't a proud potential disciple of Heaven's Glory, but a scheming child whose spirit was trapped in a body that had grown without him. A twisted mirror of Whitehall himself.

Whitehall walked over and kicked Lindon in the shoulder, tossing the boy up and making him shout with pain. "Did you have a winged Remnant carry you up? Hm? Do you have a construct that protected you? Are you a genius scriptor? Because the heavens will *crumble* and the earth will sink into the *sea* before I believe you climbed up here on your own strength."

Wei Shi Lindon looked up at him with hurt in his eyes, but rather than looking pitiable, he looked like he was angry enough to pick a fight. But there was no hint of anger in his words. "Forgiveness, honored elder, but the honored elder himself was very specific that we should climb the steps by any means at our disposal. If the honored elder did not mean it, I would be willing to return to the bottom and climb back up, only I don't believe there is still time..."

Whitehall slowly glanced over his shoulder. Several disciples, in their red sashes, had gathered to watch this scene. They had paused their end-of-day training to see who'd made it up the Trial of Glorious Ascension.

With no witnesses, he would have tossed Wei Shi Lindon off the side of Mount Samara himself. No one would believe the Unsouled had a chance to make it in the first place, and they would all assume he'd died on the way up.

Besides, the stairs were scripted to prevent anyone who started climbing them from leaving. People could enter the Trial late, but even Whitehall himself couldn't move off the trail once he'd begun.

Whitehall hurled a small wooden piece at Lindon's head hard enough that it would probably leave a bruise. The Unsouled flinched and raised a hand to his scalp. The token was polished orus wood, bearing the mark of the Heaven's Glory School: three crossed swords on top of a blazing sun, with clouds surrounding it all.

"Take that to the Lesser Treasure Hall and give it to the elder there," Whitehall said, restraining his anger. He had more important things to be about; this Foundation-stage cripple wasn't worth his time. "Tell him you're not worth anything too valuable."

Lindon returned to his knees and kowtowed one more time, pressing his forehead to the ground. "Gratitude, honored elder. This one is grateful for your generosity."

"*Go!*" Whitehall shouted, and the Jade madra powering his voice sent pebbles scattering and a flock of birds fleeing from the top of a distant tree.

The boy scrambled away, token in hand, leaving Elder Whitehall to seethe alone.

CHAPTER FOURTEEN

Lindon's plan had worked better than he expected. He'd ridden the carriage almost all the way up the mountain before dismounting, telling the Copper disciple that he had to walk the final distance for the sake of his pride. As soon as the carriage wound out of sight, he had walked around the slopes to the Trial of Glorious Ascension, which he had only experienced for about a hundred yards.

Certainly, it was a grueling hundred yards. Spirits scoured his mind, tormenting him with doubts and dreams and phantom rage. He stumbled up each step with voices screaming in his head, and when he finally reached the top, he felt as though he'd escaped the cold grasp of death.

If he'd tried to climb the whole thing, he really might not have made it.

He flipped Elder Whitehall's token in his hand as he asked a nearby disciple where he might find the Lesser Treasure Hall. She was delighted to direct him once she realized he'd passed the Trial before sunset, although his wooden badge gave her a look of clear confusion.

As expected, the Heaven's Glory School was much more impressive in appearance than the Wei clan. Each building was sculpted from riverstone, a delicate and expensive material that glistened in the light as though drenched. Under the light of the setting sun, every wall sparkled.

The buildings were each large enough to be a family dwelling of the Wei clan, and next to each was a carefully cultivated garden that was dense with life. Disciples, in their white-and-gold robes with red sashes, were often tending the flowers or trimming trees in these little garden patches.

With the mountains in the background, the shimmering buildings and luxuriant plants gave this school the look of a celestial village, torn from the heavens and set down on the side of a peak. As a son of the Wei clan, Lindon could appreciate the dedication that had gone into designing such an image. Impressions were important.

The Lesser Treasure Hall of the Heaven's Glory School was no larger than any other hall, but a towering sign boasted its name in letters of gold. A script around the edges gathered vital aura into light, so that it could be clearly read even in the night.

Sitting on the porch of the hall, next to a pair of Iron Enforcers, sat an old man that looked as though he would shrivel away to nothing at any second. His hair was white and wispy, his skin so thin and dry that it looked like it might crumble, and his eyes were little more than beady black dots. His heavy jade badge—carved with a hammer— trembled as he climbed to his feet, hobbling over to see Lindon.

"Welcome to the Heaven's Glory School, new disciple," the elder said. "Your token, if you please."

"This humble student greets the elder," Lindon said, pressing his fists together in a salute. Only then did he hand over the wooden piece.

The elder slipped the token in his pocket and studied Lindon. "You have a wooden badge."

There was no point in hiding it, even if he could. Lindon didn't plan on staying at the Heaven's Glory School very long, and his weakness would cause him trouble even if he tried to deny it. "I am Unsouled, elder."

"Elder Rahm. For an Unsouled to pass the Trial of Glorious Ascension before sundown is a fine achievement indeed. No matter how you did it." A bit of wry humor crept into Elder Rahm's voice before he turned and waved Lindon after him.

Lindon followed, deliberately looking away from the Irons on the side. He already had a good impression of the elder, and he didn't want to ruin his mood by seeing looks of ridicule or doubt on the faces of the guards.

"I have supervised the Elder Treasure Hall for forty years, and if you need a more detailed explanation of any of the items, you have only to ask. This is the least of the three treasure halls in our school, but do not let that dim your eyes. These are still priceless artifacts that any of the clans would ransom their sons and daughters to afford, and only outstanding disciples are given a chance like this."

Lindon was hardly listening. The Heaven's Glory treasure hall looked much like the Wei clan's archive, but on a grander scale. The building was one huge room, broad and open like a dancing hall, with display cases stretching out in vast rows. Each case only came up to his chest, so he was afforded an almost uninterrupted look at the whole spread.

And the treasures he saw—at least, the ones he recognized—were enough to make any Wei elder sick with envy.

"How do you leave them all in the open like this?" Lindon asked. It was the first thought on his mind, because he imagined any disciple coming up from the clans would be tempted to rob this place clean.

The elder's wrinkled face stretched into a smile. "The Path of Heaven's Glory does not require you to set aside evil and selfish desires, but it is to your own benefit that you do so. If you had any ideas of slipping out with something extra in your pack, put them aside now." The elder pointed one gnarled finger at the frame around the door, through which they had just entered, and Lindon could just make out the delicate etchings of a script.

"That script is a defensive formation that calls battle-constructs out of the ground. Some of them use Heaven's Glory madra, but not all of them. Only the Grand Elder and I know the full configuration. Their power is enough to destroy even a group of Jades. Besides," he gestured to the cases, "each case is sealed. If you try opening one without me, the alarms will wake the whole school. And set off the constructs."

He cackled and slapped Lindon on the shoulder. "So if you want to try and steal something from me, Unsouled, go ahead and try. If you survive, you'll learn a good lesson."

Lindon pressed his fists together to salute the elder, glad the man hadn't taken offense. But in the back of his mind, he still noted that those security measures didn't seem unbeatable. He'd learned a bit about scripting and a bit more about constructs from his mother, and he was sure he could slither his way through a loophole.

Not that a disciple should ever steal from his school, but Elder Whitehall had made it abundantly clear that he wasn't a real disciple. So why should he treat the Heaven's Glory School with extra respect?

But those were matters for another time. He stepped up to the first case, eagerly snatching the attached tablet. This was a fine, slightly-curved sword of polished steel, short enough to wield in one hand, with a delicate spiderweb of script over the flat of its blade.

Flying Sword, the tablet read. *When powered by Iron-quality madra, this weapon is capable of levitating through vital aura and striking with the force of a real sword. Used for personal defense, distant attacks, or even transportation for advanced practitioners.*

Aspect requirement: none.

Already, Lindon's heart burned with desire. He'd heard stories of sacred artists standing on flying swords, or controlling clouds of the floating blades to shred armies. Even he could face a stronger opponent by using the sword from behind, fighting as though he had an invisible partner. It didn't even require a particular aspect, so his pure madra could power the script.

It was only suitable for sacred artists of Iron and above, but Suriel and Elder Whisper had both suggested that he would reach that level eventually. Why not take the treasure now and prepare for when that day came?

Eventually he pried himself away from the first case and moved to the next one. This case contained only a polished wooden box, but the tablet included a picture: the sketch of a hovering, plated ball with what appeared to be a single eye in the center.

Glasswater Sentinel. A transparent construct that is almost invisible, intended for personal protection. Strikes down attacks aimed at its owner. Crafted by Soulsmith Serenity of the Heaven's Glory School.

Involuntarily, Lindon reached out a hand to hover over the glass case, as though he could sense the construct's power. This would be even better than the flying sword! He could use it now, as constructs were fueled by vital aura, and it would keep him alive at least until he reached Copper and could somewhat protect himself. He almost picked this one immediately...but there were dozens, perhaps hundreds, of other cases.

Nightflame Spirit-lamp, said the tablet for a shuttered black lantern that gleamed with a cruel edge. *Gathers fire-aspect vital aura during the day, sprouting a flame when the sun sets. Allows easy access to fire aura, and provides any practitioner with a source of light.*

Spirit-seals sat in their own case, but he brushed by these. They were rectangular sheets of paper about the size of a palm, covered in scripts of daunting complexity, which could be attached to a Remnant in order to weaken them for capture or dissection. Spirit-seals were valuable, but they were almost useless for anyone aside from a Soulsmith. He left that one aside.

One case had a small garden inside, complete with tiny trees, grassy hills the size of a mouse, and a river running around the border that was still flowing. The glass of this case seemed twice as thick as the others, and it took him a minute or two of examination to realize that there was actually a glass box *inside* the glass case. Inside this garden, a finger-sized Remnant of ocean-blue flame darted around like a playful wraith. It slid inside the river, made a lap of the terrarium, and then frolicked on a hill for a few seconds. When Lindon leaned over the case, it paused, tilting its featureless head up as though to look at him.

After a few seconds, apparently bored, it returned to skimming around on the grass.

Sylvan Riverseed. The seed of a nascent Sylvan with water and other, unidentified aspects. Can be nurtured by a supply of pure madra, but its future growth is not guaranteed.

Aspect requirement: pure.

This case fascinated Lindon, and he stared at it for more than ten minutes. It seemed tailor-made for him, as it required purity, though he had little idea what a Sylvan was. It looked like a Remnant, and Remnants were indeed capable of becoming more powerful, but they didn't grow from a seed. If this was something like a cross between a Remnant and a sacred beast, it could serve him long after he left Sacred Valley.

But in the end, he moved on to other cases. It had the same drawback as many of the other riches here: it would take too long before he could use it. He needed something useful *now.* Then again, he didn't want something that would be useless to him as soon as he hit Copper...

Elder Rahm appeared in front of the Sylvan Riverseed's display case, smiling gently. "It's good that you make this decision with patience. The treasure you select here can guide your entire Path, and my soul shudders every time a young disciple comes in here and grabs the first weapon they see. If you tell me what has caught your eye, I might be able to enlighten you."

If Lindon didn't walk out of here with at least half a dozen treasures, he would be leaving pieces of his spirit behind. He gave the elder a helpless look. "I could take it all, and it still wouldn't be enough."

Rahm gave a hearty laugh, smacking his palm on the flat of a glass case. "Good! Very good! That's how a young sacred artist should be. If you're not greedy for more, always more, how could you ever advance?"

Lindon suspected he may have just heard something profound, but the elder was already ushering him forward. "You're weaker than you should be, yes? Let this old man give you a few suggestions."

Elder Rahm toured him through the aisles, past a few eye-catching items that made Lindon want to twist around and take a look. Finally, he stopped in front of a velvet cushion displaying a twisted halfsilver ring.

Lindon's eyes widened even before he read the tablet. The parasite ring would burden his cycling so that it took twice the effort, but it would result in twice the reward as well. Since cycling was one of the only ways to strengthen his spirit without drawing on the vital aura in the atmosphere, the parasite ring would help him build up pure madra.

Elder Rahm gave a brief explanation, but before Lindon could say that this was exactly what he was looking for, the old man moved on. He passed a rack of weapons that weren't under glass; goldsteel breastplates, mail, and shields, as well as halfsilver knives, daggers, awls, sabers, and spearheads. Halfsilver looked like ordinary silver that had caught sparks from stars, so it glittered; it was more brittle even than its mundane counterpart, but it had disruptive effects on madra. Those properties made it desirable for Soulsmith tools and certain weapons.

Goldsteel looked like polished gold, except whenever it caught the light it reflected pure white. That was an odd sensation for the eye, so that the mind was never sure exactly what color it was. Some in the Wei clan used goldsteel to gather light-aspect vital aura for training the Path of the White Fox, as it reflected light in a deceptive manner.

Goldsteel did not disrupt as halfsilver did, but it provided protection against Remnants. It was best suited for trinkets that warded off small spirits or armor to protect against larger Remnants in combat.

Lindon's fingers itched to examine the weapons and armor more closely, because such pieces had been far too valuable for him back in the Wei clan. But Elder Rahm had him firmly by the elbow, and soon had him in front of another case. This one contained a pinkish-white lotus flower, clenched halfway into a bud, perched delicately in a ceramic cup. It seemed to be made of pure color, like a Remnant, as though it had been painted onto the world with a brush of light.

"The bud of a Starlotus," Rahm said reverently. "Despite its appearance, it's classified primarily as a spirit-fruit. Its herbal and medicinal aspects are considered low-grade, but if you eat it directly...well, I normally recommend it to talented Copper disciples who are having trouble advancing to Iron. For you, it might very well allow you to step into the Copper realm immediately."

Immediately. After Suriel's visit, Lindon had begun thinking of advancing as something inevitable, but he hadn't even imagined breaking through *instantly.* He could catch up to his peers *today.*

Of course, Copper was only average by the standards of the Wei clan. The Heaven's Glory School rarely accepted anyone under Iron, and outside Sacred Valley the standards were apparently even higher.

"This is the one I need," Lindon said, trying to make his voice sound firm. There were still at least five other items he wanted, but he had to be practical. The first step wasn't as exciting, but it had to come first.

Instead of listening to him, the elder had already gathered him by the elbow again, pulling him away. "Don't be hasty, now. The school already gives one elixir and one spirit-fruit to each disciple when they join, as well as every half a year. You'll claim your first batch today, and the mid-year celebration for Sun Day is in only a few weeks. It's very possible you'll advance then, using materials much less valuable than the Starlotus."

"Pardon, honored elder," Lindon said, even as he tried to extract himself as gently as possible from the man's grip. "But if I break through, the Starlotus will still be beneficial. It's intended for Coppers, isn't it?"

"Certainly it is," Rahm said, stopping before a cage that softly shone. "But if you can advance with the resources provided you by the school, why would you waste your one chance in the Lesser Treasure Hall? Pick a treasure that will truly serve you even if you one day reach Jade."

Lindon thought the elder might have overestimated him a bit too much. An Unsouled reach Jade? How?

He firmly stopped that line of thinking. *Jade isn't where I'll stop. Neither is Gold. When I return to the valley, they won't be able to measure my power.*

Suriel had practically promised him.

Elder Rahm gestured to the case, where a dense, rust-colored cloud filled the box. "This is known as the Thousand-Mile Cloud, but it will let you move even farther than that." Only with the elder's explanation did Lindon realize that the cloud itself was a treasure. He'd been trying to peer through it, to see what the red fog was concealing.

"It's a construct. When you power it, it can carry you through the air for as long as your madra lasts."

Flight. Who hadn't dreamed of that? Suddenly advancing to Copper seemed trivial. Any child could reach Copper— any child except him—but what Jade could fly?

As he was picturing the glorious scene of himself returning to the Wei clan on a flying red cloud, the case next to him caught his eye. It was a vertical column of glass, rather than an enclosed podium like the rest, and it contained a stack of purple banners that stood only as high as his knee. One side of the banners were stitched with three intricate script-circles, but on the other side was the image of a five-tailed snowfox.

Without a word to Elder Rahm, he moved over to the tablet next to the case.

White Fox boundary formation. These seven banners, when placed in conjunction with one another, gather light- and dream-aspect vital aura. This can be used for training Paths such as the Path of the White Fox, or for baffling enemies. By holding one of the ward keys (provided), the owner can enter and exit at their discretion.

Aspect requirement: light or dreams.

"This is the one," Lindon said.

The rest of his ambitions notwithstanding, Lindon had spent every day since he was a child dreaming of being a sacred artist...and more specifically, a sacred artist on the Path of the White Fox. A master of illusion who could strike with the force of a thunderbolt while his foes were still trying to catch a glimpse of his shadow. This boundary formation would allow even him to use power that should be limited to a Ruler of the White Fox.

And the *one* thing he could do as an Unsouled was power a script.

Elder Rahm drifted over, making a noncommittal sound. "You're from the Wei clan, I take it. It's not a bad choice, as formations are restricted only by your flexibility. You can use White Fox madra even without cultivating it yourself, which has its uses. But formation flags have to be placed in a circle, which takes time. It takes planning, it takes foresight. If you're attacked, these banners won't save you, and they won't help you advance either."

But the more he thought about it, the more convinced Lindon became that this formation was the right choice for him. The banners were only useful with planning and insight, but those had nothing to do with his spirit's advancement. Only his mind. They would serve him now, last him even when he left the valley, and they would serve as a reminder of his family.

He picked up the tablet, handing it to Elder Rahm with both hands. "Thank you for your guidance, Elder Rahm.

This is my choice. Perhaps if I can render some merit to the school, I'll see you in here again."

Rahm laughed and took the tablet, which—if the treasure hall worked anything like the Wei clan's archive—he was supposed to file away. Instead, he tucked it under his arm and waved his free hand over the glass.

The "glass" shimmered and dissolved into motes of white-gold light, and only then did Lindon realize that it wasn't glass at all, but Forged madra. Of the Heaven's Glory Path, he assumed.

"Take them, I'll update my records when you leave. I'll tell you now, this is likely to be your last visit. Most people don't serve the school well enough to earn a second trip until they hit Jade, and by that time you'll be qualified to enter the Greater Treasure Hall. These are toys compared to what you'll find in there."

Lindon's imagination soared, and he'd already started coming up with ways to impress the Heaven's Glory elders in hopes of receiving another treasure, but he knew he was being foolish. *I'm not staying here,* he reminded himself. *I have a much longer path to follow.*

The surge of importance he felt helped, but even with the banners tucked under his arm, he couldn't resist a last longing look at the Thousand-Mile Cloud.

Elder Rahm pushed him out by the small of his back. "You're a disciple here now, boy. You can visit me every once in a while and drool over my treasures, though I won't let you take one. Maybe I'll let you help out here, from time to time."

Lindon bowed and thanked him, but before he'd even finished saying his goodbyes, a shout from outside distracted him.

"Bring him out here!" a man's voice said, with barely restrained fury.

Elder Rahm pushed open the door, revealing a tall young man—about Lindon's height—with brown hair and a dark gaze. Blood ran down his scalp, he'd lost his red sash, and his white-and-gold training uniform looked like it had been torn apart by a beast's claws. His iron badge was the size of two spread palms together, which was the detail that made him fit Lindon's memory.

He was one of the other potential disciples from the Seven-Year Festival, the one from the Kazan clan. And he stared at Lindon with undisguised anger.

CHAPTER FIFTEEN

Night had fallen while Lindon browsed the Lesser Treasure Hall. He could tell why the Kazan disciple was furious; obviously he hadn't made it to the top in time. He couldn't swallow the idea that an Unsouled could succeed somewhere he'd failed.

"You're making a ruckus in my hall," Elder Rahm said, and the cold in his voice made even Lindon shiver. The Kazan curbed his anger, bowing.

"Apologies, elder. I forgot myself. I am Kazan Ma Deret, and I have had my honor *trampled* by the trash behind you."

Deret glared at Lindon, but Lindon was already sliding away down the side of the porch, clutching his bundle of seven white banners. The Kazan disciple turned as though to stop him, but Rahm placed a hand on the boy's shoulder.

"By ignoring me in favor of your rage, you have dishonored *me*," Elder Rahm said. "Explain. How has an Unsouled insulted an Iron?"

Deret looked briefly surprised, as well he might; even in the Wei clan, anyone with an iron badge would have been able to dispose of Lindon as they pleased without question. Lindon's own grandfather wouldn't have stood up for him as Elder Rahm had just done.

But he couldn't rely on others to defend him, especially not from the Heaven's Glory School. However Rahm felt, the other elders certainly wouldn't be excited about an Unsouled joining their ranks. That suited him. Once he found the Sword Sage's disciple, he was gone.

Until then, he needed to defend himself.

Lindon slipped in between the Lesser Treasure Hall and another building, its stone walls slick with the appearance of rainwater. He stood over a flower-bush, in the center of one of those densely packed gardens he'd noticed before. As soon as he was out of sight from the street, he scrambled to untie his bundle.

Seven three-foot poles attached to purple banners spilled over the grass, but they weren't the only contents of the treasure he'd taken from the hall. A pair of polished wooden placards followed the banners, each the size of Lindon's hand and banded with script-circles that wrapped around each edge. Ward keys.

He slipped both keys into the sash at his waist and scurried around the edges of the garden, stabbing poles into soft earth. Boundary formations worked on the same principle as smaller script-circles: if they were evenly placed in a ring, they would activate the vital aura in an area to fuel some result. If their placement was too sloppy the boundary wouldn't trigger at all, and it would only work at peak efficiency if the banners were a precisely equal distance apart.

Lindon didn't need peak efficiency. He needed whatever he could get.

When the seventh banner was placed, Lindon initiated the script on the back. It flared blue-white...and, a second later, the other two banners visible to him through the undergrowth flashed as well.

The madra rushed out of him all at once, almost exhausting his spirit. He stumbled as he walked away, only holding himself upright with a hand on the wall. In his mind's eye, the light traveling through his madra channels was dangerously dim.

Before he'd eaten the orus spirit-fruit, he wouldn't have been able to activate this boundary at all. Even now, though a Copper could likely use it with ease, he had to be careful.

He suppressed the instant longing he felt for all the other treasures inside—the ones that would advance him to Copper, or that he could use without feeling like he might lose control of his body at any moment. He had chosen, and now he would prove his choice useful.

As he left, he glanced back at the boundary. He didn't feel anything from the boundary, as he carried the ward keys with him, but a faint suggestion of white haze had gathered between the boundaries. He even thought he heard a distant eagle's cry.

He'd lived among a White Fox aura his entire life, and he could tell when it was gathering.

When he rounded the building again, Kazan Ma Deret was stating the facts of his case. "I saw Shet die. He lost himself, crying and moving in circles, until he finally threw himself at the feet of a Remnant and begged it to kill him. That is what the Trial did to a strong, honorable sacred artist. I ask you now, how could that trash have possibly survived where Shet did not?"

More than ever, Lindon was glad he hadn't tried to walk up those steps. They sounded brutal.

"It seems he has come to answer for himself," Elder Rahm said, turning to squint in Lindon's direction.

Lindon squared his shoulders, drawing himself up to his full height. Deret was a year or two older than he was, but he looked the Kazan straight in the eyes. "Do the Irons of the Kazan Clan have nothing better to do than oppress their juniors?"

Elder Rahm turned toward him slowly, like a tree bending in the wind. Kazan Ma Deret looked like he was about to erupt.

"Very well," Lindon said. "I'll give you some pointers. Elder Rahm, will your humble disciple be punished if I injure a peer in the course of a supervised duel?"

Deret's face turned slowly red, and madra clenched over his shoulders, forming squarish boxes of rippling haze. The hammer on his badge said he was a Forger, and the Kazan walked the Path of the Mountain's Heart. He would be able to conjure weapons of crushing force. Even half-formed, the constructs floating over his shoulder could smash Lindon's limbs to pieces.

"Are you sure about this, boy?" Elder Rahm asked.

"I can't render any merits to the Heaven's Glory School if I can't even put down a dog from the Kazan Clan," Lindon said, bowing over his fists.

Deret choked out his own agreement to the duel, all but incoherent with rage.

For once, Lindon's appearance worked in his favor. He looked like he was eager to fight, even as his hands shook and cold sweat ran down the back of his neck. He hated provoking people like this, especially people capable of crippling him, but he needed Deret angry enough to follow. And he was confident in his plan. Well, reasonably confident.

His mind spat out a dozen ways this could go wrong, eroding his certainty by the second, but he was committed now. Elder Rahm raised one ancient hand in the air, even as Kazan Deret's Forged madra began to take on shape and definition. They were definitely bricks, appearing line by line as though sketched in midair, and they would gain heft and weight as soon as he finished Forging them. For now, they remained floating.

"To incapacitation or surrender," Elder Rahm reminded them. Lindon leaned onto the balls of his feet, shifting his weight as though he meant to dash with all his speed straight toward Deret.

A blinding golden light flashed from the elder's hand even as he called, "Begin!"

Lindon turned and ran.

Most Forged madra did not float. Soulsmiths had to craft their constructs with special techniques in order to get them to levitate, and Mountain's Heart bricks were very dense. The Kazan used their Forgers to build walls, constructing intricate scripted arrays to keep the madra from dissipating.

So Deret couldn't simply will his bricks to blast Lindon from a distance, which was the only reason why Lindon had a chance. But he was an Iron. He could simply throw them.

Without looking behind him, Lindon ducked to one side just as a solid brick smashed into the stones at his feet, blasting into rolling pebbles of Mountain's Heart. He felt the impact through his feet, and it seemed to rattle the air like thunder. Even the stone it landed on showed a faint crack.

Lindon's frantic, heavy breaths had very little to do with physical exertion. He had started only a few dozen yards from the edge of the Lesser Treasure Hall, and in the seconds it had taken him to cover that distance, Deret had almost destroyed his legs.

As soon as he crossed the corner, stepping into the dense garden, he snatched the ward key from his belt. Otherwise, he didn't slow down; the Iron would be only a breath behind him, and he would have another brick ready to hurl.

Lindon dove into the bushes and waited.

Sure enough, Deret followed a second later, one brick raised in his hand, another forming over his shoulder. He stopped when he saw the garden.

Lindon couldn't allow him to inspect the area for too long, so he rolled away from the bush, intentionally shaking its leaves. A brick blasted the bush to pieces, shredding the branches and tightening the bands of fear around Lindon's throat. If Deret didn't approach, if he just stood there at the mouth of the alley and threw bricks...

"I knew a Wei coward wouldn't fight," Deret called, a freshly formed brick dropping into his hand. "All you have are your tricks...but do you even know any? Did they teach the Path of the White Fox to an Unsouled?"

Lindon trembled as he stared at the spot where he'd hidden the formation banner. Deret was *one step* from crossing the boundary. But if Lindon moved again, he'd need the luck of a Gold to avoid getting smashed to pieces by a brick.

The leafy branches of the undergrowth had prevented Deret from finding him so far, along with the barely-perceptible distortion the White Fox aura left in the air, but if he moved, Deret would see him for sure. There was one thing he could try, the same old trick every child tried when playing with their friends in the woods. He could throw a rock.

Lindon reached into one of the smaller pockets in his pack, where he usually kept a few halfsilver chips, and grabbed something small. He lobbed it out from behind his hiding-space.

It was the glass bead that Suriel had given him. Its blue flame shone like a tiny star.

Deret whipped his arm forward like a striking viper, reacting with a speed that made Lindon instantly glad he hadn't tried to make a break for it, but he stopped before the brick left his hand. He stared at the rolling marble for a second as though trying to figure out what it was. He took a single step forward, his foot landing on grass.

When the boundary activated, the White Fox aura that had gathered in the atmosphere ignited. Lindon saw it as though he looked into someone else's dream: the blue flame of the bead split again, and again, until seven illusory blue stars spun around Deret's head. He swung the brick at them, staggering away, but his feet actually took him deeper into the boundary.

He spun around at the cry of a bird, only to see—instead of an alley wall—an endless forest that stretched out for miles.

Lindon observed all this as though it were painted in front of him. He witnessed it all clearly, even as Deret launched his brick at the descending talons of a swooping

Remnant. The Forged madra sailed over the rooftops of the Heaven's Glory School, vanishing in the distance.

Though Lindon could see it, it deceived him no more than a painting would have. The ward key shielded him from the effects of the dream aura, protecting him as long as he carried it.

So as Kazan Ma Deret screamed and battled with creatures in a dream, Lindon slipped away. He had to lean on the rainstone wall to even leave the alley; the last minute had taken more energy from him than the entire trip up the mountain. He slipped around the corner of the Lesser Treasure Hall to avoid any stray bricks, then slumped down against the wall, every muscle in his body trembling out of control. He let his eyes drift shut.

"The Heaven's Glory School is very strict about preventing its disciples from killing one another," Elder Rahm said. Lindon pried his eyes open and tried to stand, to show some modicum of respect. The old man didn't seem to care.

"Otherwise, we mostly leave our students to their own devices. You should be careful now. There is plenty young Deret can do to you short of killing you."

A tiny object, flashing blue, rolled out of the garden and along the stones of the road. The elder stared at Suriel's bead even as it came to a stop, its bright blue flame shining steadily.

Lindon leaned over and picked it up. "I apologize, elder. This is merely a toy left to me by my mother."

"A strange toy," Rahm said softly. "I would not lower myself to steal from a child, but I would like to examine this bead someday. When you have settled in to the school."

Lindon attempted a shaky bow. "I owe you at least that much, Elder Rahm. For your advice and for the treasure, which has already saved my life once."

The elder chuckled as he walked around the alley. "Yours was a very clever choice." He paused before he was out of sight, catching Lindon's eye. "But cleverness is an unstable foundation. Wisdom, loyalty, strength...in the sacred arts, only these things are firm."

Then he ducked into the garden, and a second later, the illusory bird-calls and shrieks from the White Fox boundary faded away. He must have removed one of the banners. Kazan Ma Deret's labored breathing echoed between the buildings.

"The victor of your contest is Wei Shi Lindon, by virtue of incapacitation. As it was a duel for honor, to seek revenge or recompense would shame you greatly, and by extension my Heaven's Glory School. I will not allow you to bring shame to my school, do you understand?"

Elder Rahm was clearly speaking for Lindon's benefit, and he was grateful. With Rahm's protection, he might actually last long enough among this school to find the Sword Sage's disciple.

"He did not fight me honorably!" Deret insisted, his voice filled with anger.

"Was it honorable for an Iron to challenge a boy at the Foundation stage?" A snap resounded through the alley, and Deret yelped. "This was foolishness, and I want no more of it."

Lindon hid himself inside the Lesser Treasure Hall as Deret left the alley. If the Kazan knew that Lindon had overheard that lecture, he would be further shamed, and would have one more reason to pursue his feud. Lindon wouldn't be able to endure attacks from an Iron forever.

After Deret left, the elder emerged with a bundle of purple banners in his arms. "Take care of these, and don't leave them lying about. I will confiscate them if I feel you have not valued them properly."

With further thanks, Lindon took his banners.

Another disciple was helpful enough to guide him to the quarters for initiates, which were nothing in comparison to his home back in the Wei clan. It was only one room, with a thin mattress and hardly enough space to lie flat.

His pack was stuffed with everything he could think to bring, from lights to ink to travel food, but he hadn't brought a change of clothes. Heaven's Glory School required its disciples to wear clothes indicating their station, and these were provided. Two identical outfits—white and gold, with a red sash—sat folded on top of his thin bed.

"You receive one spirit-fruit and two Clearblood elixirs when you arrive, and again every half a year," the disciple reminded him while handing over his room key. "You'll get yours from the Outer Disciple Hall in the morning, it's up the mountain at the very center. The road heads straight for it. Eventually you'll have duties assigned to you, but for now, you're expected to cycle twice a day and keep practicing your Path."

Those had the feel of an official declaration, but what he said next sounded much more formal. "Watch out for the more advanced disciples. They'll take what they can from you, and if you don't know anyone at the school, they won't hold back."

Lindon took the advice to heart.

After the massive ring of light around Mount Samara had begun to dim, but before dawn rose over the peak, Lindon was already waiting in front of the Outer Disciple Hall. He huddled around one corner, letting the building break the icy wind. Even so, he had to cycle his madra to keep from shivering.

An hour or so later, after the sun peeked over the horizon, a man with a short gray beard and some mixed black in his hair came strolling up to the hall, carrying a heavy key. He stopped when he saw Lindon, an amused smile on his lips.

"Wei Shi Lindon?" he asked.

Lindon pressed his fists together and bowed. "This disciple greets you, elder."

"Only new disciples are so eager. I am Elder Anses, and I will assign you your chores during your stay with us." As though the cold didn't touch him, Anses took his time unlocking the door and lighting an oil lamp before ushering Lindon inside. He accepted gladly.

The first room of the Outer Disciple Hall was scarcely bigger than Lindon's room, and packed with rows of shelves, stacked drawers, and desks covered in paper, tablets, and scrolls. There were other doors in the back, but Anses didn't head for them; he squeezed by Lindon, sliding open a drawer and removing a shallow wooden box from inside.

He walked over to his desk and made a note before handing the box to Lindon. "Fate was kind to you. The middle of the year is coming soon, so these won't have to last you long." He slid open the lid, revealing a pair of round pills colored in swirls of blue and white, next to a fruit like a miniature golden pear.

"These Clearblood pills are refined from a unique blend of herbs grown only here on the mountain," Anses said, in a tone that suggested he'd given this speech many times. "They will remove impurities from your core and from your blood, increasing the speed of your cycling and preparing you to advance to the next stage. Take one and cycle it for at least three days before taking the second, although you may wish to save the second until you are attempting to advance."

He pointed to the pear. "The spirit-fruits we give to disciples are different depending on the year's harvest, but you're exceptionally lucky this year. One of our elders happened to find a thousand-year dawnfruit tree just on the other side of the mountain. The dawnfruit has absorbed the vital aura of heaven and earth for centuries, and it will nourish your soul directly. I recommend you wait until completely digesting at least one Clearblood pill before eating the fruit."

After hearing those descriptions, Lindon slid the box out of the elder's grip before Anses had quite released it. He slid the lid closed, cradling the box like an infant. The only thing he wanted to do was run back to his room and cycle, especially before Deret came hunting for him, but he had one question first. "An elder found this outside the valley? He actually left Sacred Valley?"

Elder Anses grimaced. "I forgot myself. We try not to speak of the outside world to disciples until they're ready. You've heard that the land around Sacred Valley is all wild and untamed?"

Lindon nodded.

"But have you also heard that there are people living outside?"

"I have." His clan had sold crates of orus fruits to the Fallen Leaf School for generations, and always they were told that the fruit was a delicacy to the people outside the valley. As a child, Lindon had never thought particularly hard about how people living in a forsaken wilderness could afford to buy sweet delicacies.

"Then you're better informed than most," Anses said. "Many families don't tell their children that there's anything beyond the mountains. And for good reason." He rolled up his sleeve, revealing an arm that had been absolutely mangled. Huge chunks of flesh were missing from the forearm, so that Lindon could see tendons and bone pressing directly underneath the skin. The upper arm, just under the shoulder, had been shredded by what looked like three claws.

It had clearly happened years ago, as the skin had grown back and the man's hand was in perfect working condition, but the shock of the sight was a slap in Lindon's face.

Unperturbed, the elder slowly rolled his sleeve back down. "I've been outside Sacred Valley for a total of six hours. I was lucky not to lose an arm. The man who discovered the goldfruit tree disappeared after returning four baskets of fruit to the school. He said he was checking the tree one more time, and he never came back."

"People *live* out there?" Lindon asked in a hushed whisper. If it wasn't safe for a Jade, how could anyone raise children?

"Only nomads," he said dismissively. "Barbarians. They have tamed some sacred beasts, and they roam around in caravans avoiding the greatest dangers. They're hardly better than Remnants themselves, acting according to their base instincts with no civilization to speak of. Only savages can live in such a savage land, while culture flourishes *here*." He gave Lindon a fatherly smile. "Be grateful for what you have. I expect you to work hard, use those resources well, and advance to Copper before Sun Day."

As Lindon left the Outer Disciple Hall, his imagination swam with thoughts of barbarian nomads and their tame sacred beasts, living in a land so harsh that the Jade elder of a powerful sacred arts school could only survive for hours. He imagined wilderness stretching on to the end of the world...

That may have been what the Heaven's Glory School believed, but *he* knew better. Suriel had shown him palaces the size of the whole valley, vast courts, paved roads and rugged taverns. Civilization had taken root somewhere else, not just here. And he'd be the first person from Sacred Valley to see it.

Yerin and the Sword Sage had come in to the valley from the outside, after all. With her guiding him, why couldn't he make it?

He pictured a savage beast, all teeth and gleaming claws, leaping out of dark trees and shredding his arm until it looked like Elder Anses'. If he thought about that too long he'd lose his courage, so he focused on the elixirs in his arms instead.

Under the dawn light, he made his way back to his room with dreams of Copper filling his head. These pills were the sort of medicine that the Wei clan had never been able to afford, and the spirit-fruit was beyond anything he'd ever heard of. A *thousand* years' worth of vital aura? And they had so many they could afford to give some to disciples? The ancestral orus fruit would be nothing next to this.

He had the box tucked under one arm and one hand on his door when something smashed into the side of his chin.

Pain flowered in his head as though his jaw had cracked, swallowing his vision. The box tumbled open, sending the blue-and-white pills spilling onto the ground. Weakly he reached out a hand for them. They were far too valuable to let them get dirty.

A hand reached down past him, plucking both pills from the ground. It gathered up the box as well, which still contained the goldfruit, and lifted them all out of Lindon's vision.

Those are mine, Lindon tried to say, but his jaw felt as though someone had stuffed it with live coals. Through watery eyes, he squinted into the dawn-lit sky.

Kazan Ma Deret loomed over him, brown hair hanging down into his eyes, iron badge heavy and black against his chest. Before he spoke a word, Deret lashed out with a foot.

Lindon curled up in instinctive reaction, but the kick still landed, slamming into his ribs and arm like the Iron had driven a spike through his elbow and into his chest. He gasped for breath, but his lungs wouldn't cooperate.

"If this was Kazan territory, you'd be dead."

Deret spat, and something warm and wet splattered against Lindon's cheek. He was in far too much pain to even wipe it away. "On Sun Day, you'll bring another box to me. If you make me come down here to pick it up myself, I might lose my temper. Do you understand me?"

Lindon nodded with his cheek pressed against dirty stone, even though every tiny motion of his head was agony.

Deret snorted in disgust, tossing the empty box down so that it clattered next to Lindon's face. He stepped heavily on Lindon's arm as he walked away, his footsteps retreated into the distance as Lindon was swallowed by pain and shame. It was one thing having everyone know that you were weak, but it was many times worse to be beaten like a stray dog and left in the street. He wished desperately to lose consciousness.

Instead, he heard the murmurs of disciples around him. They whispered to one another, but he still caught snatches of their conversation. It was exactly as he'd expected.

"...both new disciples?"

"...too weak..."

"...Unsouled?"

Finally, hands lifted him up by the shoulders, causing him to groan in pain. It was all he could do to avoid screaming.

"Hold on," the boy carrying him said, and Lindon recognized his voice. It was the disciple that had delivered him to his room the day before. "I'm taking you to the Medicine Hall."

Lindon wondered how many halls there were in the Heaven's Glory School, but idle thoughts didn't survive long amid the sea of pain. The disciple had lifted him off the ground and was carrying him over one shoulder, which was no doubt easy for someone with Iron strength, but every step sent agony shooting through Lindon's body.

"I thought something like this might happen," the disciple went on. "I was going to take you to see Elder Anses myself so no one singled you out, but I didn't think I'd be too late."

Lindon tried to say *I was stupid,* but it came out as "Shtupid."

The disciple grunted. "They let the disciples compete against each other for everything. The strongest rise to the top, and they only want the strongest. As long as nobody dies, the elders don't care, but I don't know why they let an Unsouled in here. Even the Coppers will be eyeing you."

He ascended some steps, which Lindon's ribs did not appreciate, and then a pair of doors swung open. The smell that wafted out was equal parts metallic blood, putrid sickness, and a sharp herbal scent that Lindon associated with medicine. The moans and muffled screams within were less than comforting.

"Another casualty?" a man asked.

"No, this one wasn't *her.*" Lindon's benefactor laid him down on a bed gently, but the impact still made him choke back a shout.

"New disciple," he added.

"Ah. Leave him here, we've got limbs to sew back on first."

The disciple tossed a blanket over Lindon and hesitated before leaving.

Gratitude, Lindon said, but it passed his injured jaw in a garbled mess of syllables. The disciple looked at him as though debating whether to say something or not. Finally he let out a heavy breath and leaned closer. "Listen. They don't let disciples leave once they're here, not unless something goes really wrong. But you...I don't think the elders would chase you down if you just left. You're from a clan, so go *home.* You won't die here...but you might find that you want to."

He left, leaving Lindon thinking fond thoughts of home. His bed was soft, the air didn't have this permanent chill, and while no one treated him with any respect, they didn't beat him in the streets either. And this was only the *beginning* of his journey. The outside world was a thousand times more dangerous.

Lindon's bed was not private, crammed as it was between dozens of other beds filled with men and women with injuries at least as bad as his own. As his heart grew heavy and he blinked away tears of self-pity, he couldn't help overhearing a conversation from the bed only inches away.

"We had her cornered," the girl said through gritted teeth. "She was—go *slower,* that burns—backed up against a cave. Fifteen of us, one of her. Then she drew her sword, and we were all cut."

"Was she that fast?" a woman asked. "Bite down on this, it will sting."

A minute or so passed with the girl groaning in pain before she finally responded. "Not...fast. She's not an Enforcer, I think. Probably a Ruler. When she drew her sword, we were all cut. Out of nowhere. She didn't move."

"The Sage was an Enforcer. Would he take a disciple with a different spirit?"

"How could I guess the thoughts of the Sword Sage? But she cut fifteen of us to the bone in one move, then she ran away. A few Enforcers followed her, since they held up better than the rest of us."

Lindon gingerly craned his neck to the side, speaking as clearly as he could. "Forgive my curiosity. Where was this?"

CHAPTER SIXTEEN

A woman of about forty carried a fistful of wild grass in one hand and a knife in the other. She leaned over the girl in the bed, smearing a paste on the girl's wounds with the flat of her blade. The disciple's face was red and covered in sweat, but both of them looked over after Lindon's words.

He shifted position to make sure his badge was hidden beneath the sheet, so the girl would assume he was a fellow Iron. It must have worked, because her tone became defensive immediately. "We almost had her. Our Rulers put down a barrier formation to stop her from escaping, but she's...if she's not Jade already, then her sword must be some kind of treasure."

"She couldn't have escaped you without some dirty trick," Lindon said. He'd learned years ago how to flatter a sacred artist's ego, but the pressure of speaking clearly was burning his jaw. He tried to shorten his sentences as much as possible. "I'm tracking her down. Where did you see her?"

Something of a lisp had crept into his voice by the end, and he had to cut off the last word before pain brought tears back into his eyes. Hearing this, the girl looked at him in sympathy. "Did you run into her after us? Heavens grant you favor, but I'm not going after her again. My pride isn't worth my life."

She hissed as the healer applied another dose of the paste. The woman spoke with the tone of one who had great experience, "Pride is more important than you think. The elders haven't acted against the girl because it lowers their status to treat a disciple as a threat. But now she's killed six Irons and incapacitated nigh-on forty. At this rate, we won't have anyone left with a whole body by Sun Day, but which elder would lower their station to fight a disciple? At a certain age, pride is all you have left."

Lindon tried to speak, but his mouth might as well have been wired shut. The healer noticed and put her herbs down, rinsing her hands in a nearby basin. She moved over to Lindon's side, cold fingers probing the side of his face.

The injured girl winced as she shifted position. "If you want to go after her, you'll be going by yourself. I don't know anyone else who's willing to risk their lives for it by this point, no matter how much the elders are offering. We saw her in a cave on the north side of the mountain, a few miles up from the Ancestor's Tomb. Don't know how she survives the Remnants out there every night. Samara's ring gathers them like flies to honey."

The healer poked at his ribs, making him grunt in pain, and then tested his elbow. "Nothing broken," she announced. "You're lucky. You'd heal in a few weeks on your own, but we just got a delivery of herbs from down in the valley. Had extra thorngrass, so we made a batch of these. Elder's orders: anyone who has to fight against the Sword Disciple gets one of these to bring them back to fighting shape."

She pinched a tiny pill between her thumb and forefinger. It was red and green, and it smelled so sharp he thought his nose would bleed. "This won't do anything for your spirit, and you won't like the way it feels, but cycle it for a few days. If you don't feel fresh as a Copper in three dawns, come back and see me. The problem might be deeper than I thought."

Lindon gave her the hint of a bow, which was the best

he could manage from a seated position with his ribs as tender as they were. She accepted it, bowing back, and handed him the pill.

Taking it was almost worse than the beating. He swallowed it and began cycling, and only seconds later, it felt as though needles were pricking the *inside* of his skin. He broke into a sweat, cycling faster, focusing his madra on the areas that needed healing. In only two or three breaths' time, he wanted to quit.

The girl next to him looked on with sympathy. "I had one of those already. All the more reason not to go after *her* again, because I'm not taking a second one." She watched longer before adding, "It helps if you cycle it a little at a time. Takes a day or two longer, but it's not as much of a torture."

Lindon appreciated the advice, but he couldn't answer. He forced the pill's energy through his veins, pushing his spirit to the limit and holding it there through sheer force of will. His earlier melancholy had evaporated.

Before, finding the Sword Sage's disciple had been a distant thing. Now, it was right in front of his eyes. She could take him away from Sacred Valley, and that was his only hope. As long as he stayed here, there would always be another Kazan Ma Deret. He would never be anything more than Unsouled.

All day and into the night, Lindon cycled. It never stopped prickling him from the inside out, but he let the pain wash through him. If this was all he had to endure to escape his life, he would consider it a small price to pay.

Whitehall stood before the other elders of the Heaven's Glory School. It was rare enough that they would all gather at once, even the elders from the various halls, but the

Sage's Disciple was a disaster big enough to warrant their full attention.

The room was humble enough, with reed mats on the floor and unadorned walls of orus wood, and each elder knelt on a flat cushion and sipped tea from a mug. This was meant to be a civilized meeting, held in an atmosphere of peace and equality.

Elder Whitehall stood in the center, having accepted neither cushion nor tea. Peace did not fit his agenda here. "Every Jade left in the Heaven's Glory School is in this room. We can march on the tomb right now, together! Even if the Sword Sage had been a Gold, his Remnant would be no match for all of us combined."

Several of the elders exchanged glances, and many others simply sipped their tea in silence. They didn't take him seriously, he knew. How could they, when he spoke with the squeaky lilt of an eight-year-old throwing a tantrum?

"We would not lightly disturb the Ancestor's rest," the Grand Elder said. The Grand Elder served a role in the school not unlike that of a Patriarch or Matriarch of a clan, and the Grand Elder of the Heaven's Glory School was perhaps the most powerful Jade he'd ever personally seen in action. Even the Sword Sage, that strange wanderer from outside, had expressed admiration for their Grand Elder's accomplishments.

"Is the Ancestor's rest not disturbed by the presence of another corpse? Or the wild Remnant accompanying it?" Whitehall countered. "I do not understand why you haven't cleared the tomb already!"

"You were not here," Elder Rahm said, sounding as though his voice might crumble to dust. "We acted against the Sage for the good of the school, but he was far more powerful than we expected. I still have not recovered from the injury he left to my spirit, and I was luckier than some of our brothers and sisters."

Whitehall had not missed that. There were three or four gaps around the room, places where Jades had not survived their ambush of the Sword Sage. And as Whitehall understood it, they had attacked full-force while the man slept. Even so, the Sage had left a number of casualties.

Their tragedy could be Whitehall's great fortune, if he placed his pieces just right. "I wasn't there, and that's why I am all the more eager to do my part. If only a few of you accompany me, or even allow me to bring a group of Irons, I will survey the tomb and return. Together, we can devise a way to retrieve the stranger's treasures. And his sword."

Whitehall was far more interested in the rare sacred herbs the Sword Sage always carried on his person, but he knew that many of the other elders coveted the man's sword. The Sage had performed miracles with that blade, and they believed that an artifact of such power could form the cornerstone of their entire school.

So it baffled Whitehall that they had simply left the weapon where it lay.

Elder Anses rubbed a hand along his short beard, as though to emphasize that Whitehall could no longer grow one. "That's more complicated than you perhaps think. The Remnant has the sword."

Whitehall stared at him, searching for any signs of a joke. Remnants did not use weapons. Even the Remnant of such a powerful warrior, made up entirely of sword-aspect madra, would grow its own blade rather than picking one up. Remnants could advance over time, just like humans and sacred beasts, but it was a joke to think that one could advance so far, so fast.

"It's that stable?" he asked, looking to the Grand Elder for confirmation.

The Grand Elder was at least as old as Elder Rahm, but age had not diminished him. He was a mountain of a man, a huge slab of muscle that took up twice the space of anyone else. "We tried to lay a boundary formation to force it out," the Grand Elder said. "It used the sword to destroy the first banner. Every time we tried to lay a script, it either broke the script...or broke the one laying it."

Remnants could speak and reason and make deals, but they were very narrow in scope. They had only fragments of their memories from life, and could understand nothing outside of those memories. They were shadows, nothing more, even if they did gain more detail over time.

But this one had proven itself capable of understanding script, planning action against it, and striking its enemy's weak points. It was thinking strategically.

"Is it even a Remnant?" Whitehall asked.

"It is," one of the other elders responded. "Its appearance is very clear, but we had a Soulsmith scan it anyway, in case the Sword Sage had simply used a technique to somehow imitate a Remnant. We're confident this isn't the case. It has simply left a Remnant that is far, far beyond anything we've ever seen."

Whitehall's mind staggered at the thought. To leave such a Remnant...the Sword Sage might *actually* have reached the Gold stage. His desire for those sacred herbs redoubled. Anything a Gold carried on his person would be a priceless treasure.

"I now understand," Whitehall said, and he did. A Gold's Remnant was the stuff of legends and nightmares. The elders would have to tread cautiously, in case the spirit had the ability to destroy their entire school. "You were wise to treat the situation with such care, and I spoke from ignorance." He bowed to the Grand Elder in apology. "But what about that girl, his disciple? If the Remnant remembers her, we might lure it away from the corpse."

He had very little impression of the Sword Sage's disciple. She had always followed him around, but at the time, Whitehall had thought of the Sage as nothing more than a wandering Jade. As such, his disciple wouldn't be anything special. But if he was a Gold expert, the picture changed.

Another elder, an old woman with a completely shaven head, sighed. "We have sent practically every combat-capable Iron in the school against her for weeks now. She sends them back dead or wounded. We planned on exhausting her spirit, pressuring her until she broke, but our disciples might be the ones to break first. Now that we know how powerful the Sword Sage was, it makes some sense; a Gold's disciple must be extraordinary."

Whitehall had just apologized, so it would be unbecoming of his dignity to make a scene, but it was hard to hold himself back when he heard *this* stupidity. "The Irons failed to capture her, so you...sent more Irons?"

The Grand Elder rumbled deep in his chest. "The enemy is only a disciple, and a young girl. Which elder from the Heaven's Glory School would throw away their face to deal personally with a child?"

Elder Whitehall very carefully stopped himself from exploding. This was a good thing for him, he reminded himself, and their foolishness was to his advantage. He still felt like strangling every one of them. "*This* elder does. The Sword Sage's treasures could make us the strongest power in the valley, or his Remnant could ruin us. This concerns the survival of our school. How could I value my pride over that?"

"It is not our pride that concerns us," Elder Rahm said, "but the honor of Heaven's Glory. Without its reputation, a school is nothing. The clans will send their young geniuses to the Fallen Leaf or the Holy Wind, and we will be forced to harvest all our sacred herbs in our own gardens. Even the outsider nomads might not deal with us if they did not trust in our honor."

Whitehall waved a hand at himself. "Then let a child deal with a child. The pride of the school is untarnished, yes?"

The other elders shifted, uncomfortable, but none of them spoke out. He knew how their minds worked. Elder Whitehall's condition was not common knowledge outside this room; they allowed all outside parties to assume that he was really a precocious genius that had managed to achieve Jade at a preposterously young age. His plan wasn't honorable, because it meant propping their reputation up on a misconception. Therefore, none of them wanted to be the first to agree.

But it would work, so none of them tore it down either. They each waited for someone else to give in first.

"You may do as you see fit," the Grand Elder said, which was the least enthusiastic approval Whitehall had ever received. But it didn't matter, so long as he was allowed to do as he liked.

"I'll need Irons that have fought the girl in the past," he said. "As well as some fresh ones."

"A group of five will be released from the Hall of Healing tomorrow morning. I'll have them report to you. As for your fresh fighters, didn't you bring in a pair yourself only yesterday?"

Whitehall almost hated to admit that Lindon had been one of his, but since the elders already knew, there was no sense in denying it. "Yes, Grand Elder."

"Take them as well. It will be a good education for them, however it turns out."

None of them were worried about the safety of the new disciples; there was a Jade along, after all. The matter was practically settled.

Whitehall would work with what he had. Kazan Ma Deret was appreciably strong, and a Forger. He had learned the Path of the Mountain's Heart, so he would never walk the Path of Heaven's Glory, but he could still benefit the school. He could build walls, which ought to help back the girl into a corner.

The Sword Sage's disciple wouldn't be short of weapons or secret techniques, but now she was out of options.

It was the middle of the night when Lindon shocked himself out of his cycling trance, and the light from Samara's ring cast an eerie light over the interior of the Hall of Healing. He'd grown up with the ring overhead every night, but down in the valley, it didn't actually provide much light. It was only an interesting feature of the sky-line. Here, it acted like a full moon...but its light was thin, somehow stretched, giving the surroundings a pale and dreamy quality.

All the other patients had collapsed into an exhausted sleep, and even the healer on duty was slumped against the wall at the far end of the room. She had exhausted her spirit dealing with the wave of wounded.

Lindon wasn't sure how he had managed to stay awake. His clothes and sheets were drenched in sweat, and while the thorns under his skin had lessened in intensity, his veins still itched. His madra was ebbing low, so that if he did too much more tonight, he'd overdraw his spirit and be trapped in bed for days. Even his head pounded after hours concentrating, stuck cycling.

But he hadn't given up.

He opened his mouth wide, stretching his jaw. It was still tender, but not nearly as painful as when he'd come in. Even his ribs and his arm felt merely bruised, not shattered as they had at first. If his energy held out, he would be able to walk.

He wanted nothing more than to rest his wounds and his soul...but he knew now was the time. The previous group of Irons to go up against Yerin had come back defeated, and the next batch wouldn't leave until the morning. He had tonight, and only tonight, to find her.

Lindon staggered onto unsteady legs, using the corner of his bed as a crutch. The air was even colder than he expected, so he snagged an outer robe from another sleeping patient; the disciple wouldn't miss it.

He hobbled home as fast as he could, gaining strength slowly as he moved. The pale light cast everything in a strange hue, especially the rainstone buildings, which now looked as though they had been dipped in milk. Samara's ring was as thick as his arm in the sky, stretching from horizon to horizon like a river of light. Being up here, under the ring, surrounded by constructs of gleaming white... he was once again struck by the majesty of the Heaven's Glory School. It really was like living among a village in the heavens.

I wonder what they do to traitors in the heavens, Lindon thought as he reached his room, quickly ducking inside to grab his pack with the formation banners within. *Cast them back down, probably.* After a moment's thought, he brought along his second set of disciple robes as well.

If they had the same punishment here, "casting him down" would likely involve tossing him off the mountain.

The easiest way to avoid that was to avoid getting caught, so Lindon tucked his wooden badge inside his clothes. He couldn't leave it behind in case he had to prove his identity, but wearing it openly would be as good as painting his name on his clothes. There was only one Unsouled in the school.

With a last, longing glance back at his rigid bed, Lindon set out into the frigid night, hitching his pack up onto his shoulders.

The patches of snow became more frequent as he made his way up the mountain and to the north. The scraggly trees grew closer together, and he even caught glimpses of a few Remnants—a flash of glowing antlers, or a flicker of vivid green scales.

Most of the Remnants up here carried aspects of light, which was why they were attracted to Samara's ring. His mother had taught him that when he was a child. They drank from it as humans did from a river, but as a result, the Heaven's Glory territory wasn't safe at night. Wild Remnants wouldn't necessarily attack him...but it was impossible to predict what wild Remnants would do. They might shred him to pieces, ignore him, bite him once and run off, shine a light in his eyes, drag him back to a cave and imprison him, or swear eternal loyalty to him on sight. If you didn't know a Remnant, you had to treat it as though it were capable of anything.

Lindon wished desperately for a drudge. There had been a low-grade drudge in the Lesser Treasure Hall, and he had passed it up *only* because he wasn't a Soulsmith. But here, it would have made his entire journey simple. Not only could he have set the drudge to follow sword madra, it would have warned him away from especially dangerous Remnants and given him some options to defend himself if he were attacked.

As it was now, he had to risk it. The possibility kept him dancing on the edge of a knife, scanning every shadow and freezing at the sight of every spirit. If they looked even slightly aggressive, he would have to run for his life, dropping a crystal flask as a distraction.

As the night stretched on, his vigilance scraped his nerves clean, until his eyes felt frozen wide and his ears seemed to tremble at every sound. He didn't know how many hours he'd spent out here alone in the cold and wind, but it felt like days, and as he staggered forward with every step he lost a little more feeling in his legs.

Finally, on the jagged slope overlooking a natural chasm, he stopped. He'd been wandering around on vague instructions the whole night, every once in a while calling out Yerin's name and hoping she heard it before a Remnant did. He knew how unlikely it was to work, and had long since resigned himself to as many nights of this as he could physically survive.

But now, new breath filled his lungs as he realized: he recognized this place. This was where he'd seen Yerin in the first place, in Suriel's vision. The chasm was only about twenty feet deep, with a flat bottom covered in snow. The girl in black and red had been backed up against the end of the chasm, defending herself from Heaven's Glory disciples.

Looking around, he saw some evidence of the battle—a discarded sword, partially revealed beneath a pile of snow, gleaming where it had fallen. A bloody cloth wrapped around a tree's branch. A mirror-smooth stretch of rock where a stone had been sliced clean through.

It felt strange to see this in person. He had never really doubted Suriel's visions, but without confirmation they remained unreal, like particularly vivid dreams. Now he had proof in front of his own eyes.

The sight strengthened his flagging spirit, and he scanned for a way down. It wasn't easy, unless he meant to backtrack almost a half a mile to check and see if there was a smoother entrance. He certainly wasn't going to jump twenty feet down onto ground covered in snow; as far as he knew, there were jagged weapons coating the ground down there, and he would land right on a rusty spearhead.

He finally decided to climb down, but before he did, he called as loud as he dared into the chasm. *"Yerin."*

No one answered him. There wasn't any room down there for anyone to hide anyway, not unless she had buried herself in the snow, but he had to look. Maybe he would find...something. Just finding this place had been a major encouragement, so even a piece of her robe would be welcome.

He gripped cold stone in both hands and climbed down slowly and gingerly, favoring his ribs. When he finally reached the bottom, he discovered...nothing. The chasm was even smaller than it had looked from above, and he could see the whole thing in one glance. It did cut the wind nicely, and he spent a moment huddled in his own arms, enjoying the relative warmth.

Yerin clearly wasn't here, and he had wasted most of the night already. On top of which, he was now faced with a twenty-foot climb back up.

Well, although Suriel had promised him great opportunities outside of Sacred Valley, she had never said they would be easy. *A great sacred artist wouldn't complain about something like this,* he reminded himself, and steeled his body for the climb.

A cold point pressed against the underside of his chin, and he dropped his pack onto the snow. "I'd bet my soul against a rat's tail that I never told you my name," a girl said.

He'd never heard an accent like hers before, which was further proof that she was really from beyond Sacred Valley. Though he had a sword at his throat, Lindon still felt relief. He'd actually found her. "Yerin?"

"Your elders never asked my name, and I'd contend that you and I never crossed eyes before now. How do you know me?"

Lindon had considered several lies on the way here, but he needed Yerin to guide him voluntarily. He needed her on his side. Which meant he had to rely on the truth, such as it was.

"The heavens showed me," he said.

The wind whistled over the chasm until the quiet became painful. Finally, she leaned around to get a peek at his face, though he couldn't see much of an expression through her black hair.

"...you chipped in the head?"

"It sounds like I'm spinning you a story, I understand that. We don't know each other, you've never met me. You don't trust me, and that's wise. Why should you?"

He took a risk and started to turn, but stopped when the point stuck deeper into his skin. Lindon swallowed. Nothing like a sword to the neck to keep a man honest. "Let me tell you *why* you should. How else did I know you? How did I know you were here? If I were trying to kill you, would I come out here shouting your name? A name the school elders don't even *know,* so how would I get it? It's impossible."

She didn't say anything and she didn't kill him, so he took that as encouragement. "An immortal descended from heaven and told me your name, showed me this place. You were backed up against the wall, fighting a group of Heaven's Glory Irons."

Yerin's sword ran lightly down his throat to the silk around his neck. It tugged upwards, drawing his badge out of his clothes. "So you were with the last bunch that tracked me down. That's a pill I can swallow. They never made it to this place, but there was a group of Strikers in the back that I never..."

The badge emerged, but instead of an iron arrow, it displayed a single character carved in wood.

"*Unsouled*?"

"See? Not a Striker." Lindon took a moment to slide away from the sword, which was now pointed at his chest.

"Did you whittle a fake badge just to pull this trick on me?" She didn't sound convinced, and Lindon took the risk of letting out a small laugh.

"I tried to carve a fake badge once. It's harder than you think. I cut my thumb so deep they had to stitch it closed."

The sword moved away from his chest, and Lindon slowly turned around. For the second time that night, he was hit with the cold-water shock of coming face-to-face with something that Suriel had shown him.

Yerin was just as he'd seen her in the vision—a ragged warrior with shredded black robes and blade-straight hair. This close, he could see the hair-thin scars crossing her face, the threads in the blood-red rope tied around her waist like a thick belt. She held a long sword as though she'd forgotten it was in her hand.

All the details were the same, but she looked like a girl on the edge of death. Her eyes were wide and bloodshot, her lips cracked, her cheeks purpled with bruises, her robes caked with dirt. Her sword was steady, but her knuckles were white on the hilt, as though she strained with her entire being to keep from dropping it.

She looked, in short, like a young woman who had spent the last weeks on the run in the wilderness. He should have expected it, but she had seemed healthy in the vision, and nothing in her voice had led him to expect *this*.

Something in his gaze must have given him away, because she tilted her sword up. "I'm not so weak I can't kill a man on his own, even if you are a Jade."

Lindon spread his palms, showing them empty. "You could be fast asleep and kill me. I have no strength to hide."

He glanced up at the sky over the chasm, where Samara's ring had begun to fade. "They'll be sending more disciples after you today, and this time I think they're finally done underestimating you. Let's work together."

Her expression darkened as she looked at his disciple's robes, and she held the sword so steady that it unnerved him. "I don't hold deals with the Heaven's Glory School."

Lindon hurried to clarify. "I've only made some arrangements with them myself, I wouldn't call them *deals*. Maybe *dealings*. But that's over now, I'm done, I've gotten what I can out of them. Time to leave them behind."

She squinted at him, her weapon wavering.

"Let me paint this scene for you: I need to get out of Sacred Valley, and you need to get away from Heaven's Glory. We can help each other get what we want."

She sheathed the sword in one smooth motion, but kept her hand resting on the hilt. "First off, tell me straight. Are you a disciple of the Heaven's Glory School?"

"I tricked my way in," he said. "It's only been two days, and they've tried to kick me out at least three times."

"What about the badge?"

"It's real. Too real. I only wanted in this school to find you. The...celestial messenger...said that you had a way out." He felt a little foolish saying it out loud like that, but it *was* the truth.

She drummed her fingers on her sword, then added, "I'll be cutting through Heaven's Glory until I get what I want or they've run out of blood. That bother you any?"

"Do you have a grudge against the Wei clan?"

"Who?"

He gave her a friendly smile, hoping it looked sincere. "Then we have no grudges between us. I owe Heaven's Glory nothing. Burn them down and scrub the mountain clean, it has nothing to do with me." She looked into his eyes for what felt like a long time, and then she relaxed.

Rather than *relaxed*, it was as though every muscle in her body gave up at the same moment. She slumped down onto a patch of snow, leaning up against the chasm wall. The dark bruises on her face stood out in stark contrast to the mesh of silken scars. "It's plain you're lying, but I don't know how or why. This would be the worst possible trap Heaven's Glory could set."

"Apologies, but let me reassure you that this is not a trap. I want us to work together, and I wouldn't start a bond like that with a lie."

With her eyes closed, she stuck out a hand. Even that was covered in a network of scars, from wrist to fingertips.

"Swear on your soul."

He froze as though the hand itself were a trap. "I'm sorry?"

"We both swear on our souls, and we can trust each other. Maybe you're lying and maybe you're not, but once we both swear, then we're hitched to the same wagon."

Lindon wasn't clear about what would happen if he violated an oath on his soul, because no one spoke about it. He'd only heard rumors of sacred artists swearing such vows, and normally only in legends. Still, the rumors agreed on one thing: the more powerful your spirit, the more binding the oath. At the Foundation level, he might escape with only minor damage to his core.

As an Iron—actually, he wasn't sure what level she'd reached, since she wasn't wearing a badge—as an Iron or a Jade, her oath would be much more serious. She was taking the bigger risk, and he *was* dealing in good faith, so there was no reason to refuse.

Still, he hesitated. His parents hadn't even sworn to each other on their souls when they were married.

Yerin cracked one eye open to look at him, and at last he took her hand, gripping her wrist firmly. She gripped his in the same way...only much, much harder. It was all he could do not to wince.

He was starting to sweat in spite of the cold, and he still hoped she'd call it off once he demonstrated his willingness to swear. "We might want to consider this a little longer before we—" he began, but she cut him off.

"You try your hardest to get me away from Heaven's Glory, and I swear on my soul that I'll take you out of Sacred Valley and keep you safe until you're stable and settled outside."

A bit of her madra slid through his hand and slipped into his veins. It felt sharp, like a knife lightly dragged across his skin. He followed her lead, clumsily forcing his madra to follow hers back into her hand. "I, Wei Shi Lindon, hereby swear on my soul that I will do my best to help Yerin, the disciple of the Sword Sage, escape from the pursuit of the Heaven's Glory School. In return, I expect guidance away from Sacred Valley and into the lands beyond, as well as reasonable protection during that time."

The heavens didn't descend, and he didn't feel his spirit tighten. His soul did not change. He waited to see if there was any other effect, but Yerin pulled her hand free. "You were all shiny and polished about it, but you didn't have to be. Say what you want to say, and your soul will do the rest."

Lindon looked at his hand uncertainly, as though he expected to see the oath etched in his palm. "Did it work?"

"It's not a sacred technique, it's a promise. It worked." She leaned her head back against the stone and sighed. "Now that we're tied tight as string on a bow, you can tell me the truth. You were bait, true?"

Lindon didn't have much honor to offend, but her repeated doubts in his given word were beginning to wound his pride. "I'll swear on my soul again, if that would convince you. A genuine immortal messenger descended from heaven."

She squinted at him. "Bleed me like a pig. You're not joking."

"I'm not joking, and I'm not lying. She brought me back from the dead."

"And she...she wanted you to save me?" This time Yerin didn't sound doubtful, but confused. Maybe a touch hopeful.

Lindon didn't want to correct her, but he'd been honest so far. "I'm sure she had many purposes in sending me here. But I do know she wanted *you* to save *me.*" He thought about hauling her to her feet, but another look at her sword convinced him otherwise. "I'd like to get started on that if we can. How far is the road out?"

She hesitated. "So you know, I thought you were with them."

"You believe me now, though, don't you?" If a soul-oath wasn't enough to convince her of his honesty, he didn't know what was.

"I do. There's a chance you're chipped, and there's a chance you're a prophet. One way or the other, I don't contend that you're lying. But now I regret I didn't warn you about the seven armed fighters heading our way."

CHAPTER SEVENTEEN

Lindon's gaze snapped up to the top of the chasm. "Where? How do you know? When will they get here?"

She spun her finger in a circle. "I wrapped this place tight in formation banners. It's not a powerful boundary, it doesn't take much energy, but I'll sense anyone who steps across. It's about half a mile out in every direction."

The bigger the boundary, the more complex the formation and the more madra it took to operate. An alarm boundary would be among the simplest and easiest types, but he still wouldn't be able to activate one a mile across.

He scanned the entire chasm quickly, trying to take stock of their options. "You hid from me earlier, so you have to have a hiding place here somewhere. We can wait this out."

She pointed to the back of the chasm, where she'd fought off the Irons in his vision. "Crack is right there, presuming you can see it, and it leads to a shallow cave. It's tighter than the skin on a lizard, so you probably won't fit. Found it during that last fight, and I squeeze in there every night to try and chase down some sleep."

So hiding was no good. He could always walk out and pretend he'd gone looking for the Sword Sage's disciple on his own. He was wearing Heaven's Glory clothes, so they might believe him. But if anything went wrong, Yerin would have to face seven sacred artists on her own.

"All right," he said, "consider this. You hide in the cave. I'll go up there and talk to them, and I'll see if I can lead them in the wrong direction. Where are they now?"

Yerin slowly stood, but she didn't head for the cave. Her eyes were on the sky, and her hand on her sword. "First thing my master taught me about the sacred arts: when the time's right, you shed blood. There's no getting around it."

Her words were so cool and matter-of-fact that they sent a chill through Lindon's bones.

"The time isn't right," Lindon said desperately. He pulled the pile of purple banners out of his pack, rushing around the edges of the chasm to plant them in snow. "I have a boundary formation of my own. We can dig under the snow, hide there, and when they come down..."

Yerin took one unsteady step toward the wall, her weakness apparent. The wind snatched at the dangling shreds of her robes, and even that much force seemed likely to knock her to the ground. Lindon didn't see how she could even remain standing, much less fight off seven attackers. He almost said so.

Then she leaped out of the chasm.

It looked effortless, as though she had simply begun a step at the bottom of a twenty-foot rock wall and finished the step at the top. He saw her from behind, her hair and her tattered robes blowing in the wind. Her red rope-belt stayed utterly motionless, which attracted his attention until she drew her sword.

Hurriedly he finished planting the seven banners and hiding them in snow. If she'd brought her weapon out, that meant...

A high, young voice rose above the wind, sending Lindon's spirits even lower. He knew that voice.

"Your master would be proud of your courage, I can acknowledge that," Elder Whitehall said. "And your skill is outstanding for someone of your age. Truly outstanding."

"You sure you want to talk about age?" Yerin retorted. He could see her from below, and now he understood why she cut her hair so straight: no matter how the wind whipped or pulled it, not a strand covered her eyes. "The Heaven's Glory School is lower than I suspected. Even dogs don't send their pups to fight."

Whitehall's voice turned cold. "I'm not trading insults with a disciple. I'm not doing it. I've already lowered myself to come here personally, and even a blind man could see your path ends here. You can hardly stand, you clearly haven't had a whole night's sleep in weeks, and your robes are ruined. You must be freezing. But I'm here because I respect talent, I really do, and so does Heaven's Glory."

They need her, Lindon realized, and a range of new options opened before him. He had assumed they were only trying to eliminate Yerin, which left her with only two choices: run or fight. But they wanted her, which meant she had something to trade. She had leverage.

A head popped over the chasm as someone glanced down. Just an idle glance, but it was enough to doom Lindon.

Kazan Ma Deret looked down on him with a face first confused, and then drenched in self-satisfaction. "The Unsouled is with her," he called back to Whitehall.

Lindon rubbed his aching jaw. Maybe meeting a messenger from the heavens had used up all the good luck in his life, because since his visit from Suriel, his fortunes seemed to have gone sour.

"...Wei Shi Lindon?" Whitehall said blankly. "What... why? How did he get here?"

"He's with the Sage's disciple," Deret responded, without taking his eyes from Lindon. "This one humbly requests permission to treat him as an enemy."

"Permission? I don't care what happens to one or two Unsouled. If there were a hundred of him, I still wouldn't care. Kill him, leave him there, carry him back on your shoulders, just don't bother me while I'm working."

Yerin tilted her scarred face toward him, though she kept staring off at what must be Whitehall. "Can you bury him alone?" she asked, which sunk his heart into his stomach even further. He could have pretended he wasn't with her, or that she had kidnapped him. Now, he only had one option.

Lindon smiled up at Deret. "I don't need any help putting down a dog."

Red-brown bricks, Forged out of solid madra, condensed in the air behind the Kazan disciple. They fanned out like a bird's tail as he hopped down into the chasm, landing lightly on his feet.

"Start begging now," Deret said, "while you can."

Lindon let out a breath of deep relief and moved his hand down to the wooden ward key in his belt. It had been even easier than he'd hoped.

The strings of a zither filled the air with haunting music, and a transparent avalanche fell from the cliff above. It was clearly fake to Lindon's eyes, like a portrait overlaid on reality, but Deret screamed and covered his face with his arm.

"You forgot already?" Lindon said, and Deret turned toward the sound of his voice. The White Fox boundary distorted his senses, and the Iron hurled a Forged brick straight at the wall. "It's only been *one day,* and I win again with the same trick. Don't they say that even a dog remembers a beating?"

Deret roared, flinging another brick at the wall, once again missing Lindon wildly.

Above, the sky turned gold for an instant as a beam of destructive white-gold light flashed into existence. Elder Whitehall shouted to his disciples, and someone screamed. Seconds later, a thin line of blood trickled down into the chasm.

The white-gold light blasted past again, and this time Lindon felt the wave of heat on his face. Another man's bloody shriek told him that Yerin was holding her own.

A nearby thunderclap drew his attention back to Kazan Ma Deret. The image inside the boundary wasn't entirely clear to Lindon, and he certainly wasn't going to drop the ward key for a more detailed look, but it seemed as though the Iron was contending with an army of razor-clawed crabs. He screamed and scratched at his face as though the illusions were drawing blood...

But he wasn't using his bricks against the crabs. He may have fallen for the same trick a second time, but it wasn't as though he'd forgotten. He knew it was a dream, and he only flung Forged madra in the hopes of hitting Lindon or destroying the formation.

What do I do with him? Lindon wondered.

Setting up the White Fox boundary had been a last-minute act of desperation, and Lindon hadn't had time to come up with a real plan. Now that he was face-to-face with an enraged Iron, he realized that he didn't know what to do.

Last time, he'd only needed to defeat Deret in front of Elder Rahm. Immobilizing him in the boundary was just as good as beating him senseless. Now...

Lindon couldn't leave him here. The formation was fueled by vital aura, but even that would run out eventually. Before that, Deret had good odds of hitting one of the seven banners with his randomly thrown bricks. Besides leaving him, what else was there?

When the time's right, you shed blood.

Like lightning striking inches away, a Forged brick smashed into the rock wall beside his head with all the force an Iron could muster. Chips stung Lindon's face, and he flinched away so wildly that he fell to the ground. His ear rang like a struck gong.

Any closer, and he would have died. For a second time.

Deret still roared in the illusion, with no idea how close he'd come to victory. But that brick caused the reality of Lindon's situation to come crashing down.

He had almost died. His story had come within an *inch* of ending here. The heavens had already intervened once, a celestial messenger had reversed death and caused even time to flow backwards...and none of that would have mattered.

For reasons he didn't understand, he reached into his pocket for Suriel's glass marble. It was warm to the touch, and he rolled it in his fingers as he thought.

One thing was perfectly clear: with Deret sharing this chasm with him, Lindon was in mortal danger. And he couldn't trust heaven to save him a second time.

His gaze was drawn to a spear, abandoned from Yerin's last fight, half-buried in the snow. He kept low to avoid any potential flying bricks, crawling over to the weapon and cradling it in both hands.

You shed blood.

Before he had a chance to inspect the spear, he ran out of time. A brick struck the banner, and the field instantly blew away like mist on the wind. To Lindon, it really was like watching a cloud drift through the air, but Deret actually staggered as he was jerked from one reality to another. The banner itself wasn't broken, but it had been knocked out of alignment with the rest of the formation. The boundary was gone. In less than a breath, Deret would regain his bearings and turn around, ready to kill.

Lindon gathered himself. No matter how he reasoned, there was only one thing to do here. He gripped cold, slick wood in shaking hands.

Then he stabbed Deret.

There was less to it than he'd expected. The first stab was basically like sinking a blade into the earth; he jammed it into Deret's back, then quickly withdrew. The Kazan didn't react until Lindon pulled the spear out, and then he jerked forward as though something had stung him. He didn't look wounded at all.

Lindon panicked. Deret would turn and hurl a brick through Lindon's head at any second, and that would be the end. So he followed the other man forward, stabbing him again and again, expecting any second to end with a missile of Forged madra through the skull.

With no art, with no skill, Lindon stabbed Kazan Ma Deret until a bleeding body fell onto the snow-covered ground. He fell with it, swallowing air as though he couldn't get enough, still clutching the spear.

And a Remnant rose before him, and he choked back bitter tears.

Made of Mountain's Heart power, this Remnant was like the outline of an ogre painted in dirt. It stumbled around for a while, flailing at the air with heavy hands, but it was weak and barely coherent. Lindon held his eyes open until they watered, afraid to blink, but the Remnant never gave any indication that it saw him. It pressed into the wall and oozed away, squeezing into tiny cracks like soft mud.

Lindon dropped his weapon as the spirit vanished, panting, his stomach churning. He thought he might be sick.

He'd always accepted the fact that he would kill someone someday. Combat was a part of the sacred arts, and the clans were encouraged to kill one another within reason.

He knew his parents had killed people in their younger days, though they rarely talked about it.

But there was supposed to be more to it. He'd imagined standing in triumph over a blood enemy, veins pumping with the thrill of battle, proving his superiority in a final show-down. Not huddling in the cold, stabbing a blinded man.

Deret had given him no choice, and besides, the Wei elders would have given him a reward for killing a Kazan Iron. No one would blame him. If he had hesitated, even for another second, he would have certainly died.

Even so, he kept his eyes off the body. Despite what he'd been told as a child, there was nothing to celebrate here.

Another flash of gold light, this time sweeping in a hor-izontal arc, and Elder Whitehall shouted, "Stop her! Hold her down!" A black-and-red blur flashed over the chasm as Yerin leaped past.

Lindon snapped himself back to reality, rushing to collect his formation banners. He didn't look forward to killing anyone else, but leaving an ally to fight alone was the act of a coward. He had to at least try something, even if he was too weak to contribute much.

Once he'd gathered up all the banners, he slipped them inside his outer robe and steadied his grip on the jagged stone wall. His vision was swimming; the day of cycling, the night without sleep, the strain on his madra, and the burden of his emotions were all getting to be too much for him.

One more stretch, he said, focusing on the climb in front of him. He forced himself to forget the march out of Sacred Valley. *Just this one last thing, and then I can sleep.*

Inch by inch, he hauled himself up.

At the top, the patchy snow had been sprayed pink. Heaven's Glory disciples lay here and there, mostly wound-ed, a few probably dead. One held pressure on a deep gash in his arm, his face pale. He stared straight at Lindon, but seemed to see nothing, only rocking back and forth.

Elder Whitehall landed in a crouch at the bottom of a tree, snow flying away from him in a ring. He whipped a line of golden light forward, and the beam slashed through a tree in front of him, dividing it into two charred and smoking halves. It creaked as it toppled, sending splinters spraying into the air. The attack left deep, blackened gouges in the other trees nearby, but none of them collapsed.

Yerin slipped out from behind one of those trunks, her sword flashing. A thin wave of distortion blew outward from her weapon, like the edge of a gleaming sickle. Elder Whitehall ducked, and the sword-madra sliced deep into a boulder behind him. He gathered light to a point in his hand, but she had already disappeared.

Lindon prepared to jump back into the chasm. He'd only ever had personal experience with one Path, and while the elders of his clan could do some astonishing things with illusions, they'd never displayed anything like *this*. This was a true battle between Jades, and he would be safer if he hid until it was over.

...then again, Suriel had suggested that by leaving the valley, he could gain power even beyond Gold. The very idea beggared his imagination, but that only meant his imagination was too limited. He hadn't seen enough, hadn't experienced enough. If he wanted to travel his own path to its end, he had to do so with eyes wide open.

At that moment, Elder Whitehall spotted him.

The elder snarled, whipping a scorching stream of light Lindon's way. Lindon released the stone, letting himself fall, hoping it would be fast enough...and as he did, he glimpsed a slender figure in black robes leaping up behind the childlike elder, sword bared.

He landed heavily on his back, wind knocked from his lungs. Even as he gasped for breath, he was grateful for the snow and his pack cushioning his fall, but he hoped he hadn't broken anything. Especially his ribs. Even the thorngrass pill had started acting up, tingling in the most unpleasant way around his injuries.

When he finally caught his breath again, the world outside the chasm was silent. Samara's ring had all but vanished, and the sun had slipped a peek over the mountain. Only the wind continued, an unending and invisible stream.

With agonizing care, Lindon prodded his flagging body into yet another climb.

Yerin stood at the top of the chasm, loose hair flying in her face, panting heavily and leaning on her sheathed sword as a walking stick. Lindon glanced hurriedly around for Elder Whitehall.

"Where did he go?"

She evened her breathing before responding. "Deeper in. Other side of the mountain. He's bleeding like a butchered hog, but he'll be coming back."

Lindon hauled himself out of the chasm, hoping he didn't look as bad as she did, but knowing that he was probably worse. "You really drove off an elder and six Iron disciples? By yourself?"

She shot a sidelong glance at him. "Five, I did."

Deret was still lying in the bottom of the chasm, body littering the ground far from his home. Lindon cleared his throat. "You're incredible. Your master must have been an expert without peer."

"He was," Yerin said, her voice distant. She stared into the dawn in silence.

But Lindon was in no mood to wait around. He slipped the extra disciple robes out of his pack, holding them out to her. He was glad he'd brought them; there were plenty of other sets nearby, but the bloodstains would make them somewhat obvious.

"You should put these on," he said. "If the heavens are kind, there won't be any other disciples in the woods, but let's assume there are. Unless they've seen your face before, they won't recognize you in these. I don't have a badge for you, but..." He looked around at the bleeding disciples. Only one of them was dead, he realized, though the others weren't far away. The dead boy's Remnant peeled itself away from his corpse, like a yellow sketch of a skeleton. It glanced back in Lindon's direction only once before scampering off into the woods.

"I'm sure you can find one," he finished.

Without a word of protest, Yerin took the clothes and wrapped them around her tattered black robes. His clothes were large enough that she still had room to spare. Once again, his attention was drawn to the thick red coil wrapped around her waist; she didn't untie it, but it still ended up outside the clothes of the Heaven's Glory disciple. As though the belt had melted through her clothes.

She slipped an Iron Striker badge over her neck and gestured to herself. "Anything missing?"

Her clothes were too big, she was carrying a sword, and she looked like she'd been living in the woods for two weeks. But from a distance, she'd pass.

"As long as we don't run into Elder Whitehall on the way out, you'll make it." He was more worried about the elder than anything else, as Whitehall had fled in the opposite direction of the valley. If their luck was bad, they might run into him on the road out.

He reached into his big, brown pack, checking that he had everything important: his boundary flags, Suriel's warm marble, a few other bits and pieces. He wasn't bringing much, but nothing else would help him on his journey beyond the valley. He was ready. It was time to go.

Lindon's heart actually lifted at the thought. He was absolutely exhausted, every resource in his body and spirit expended, but he'd made it. He'd won. On the other side of this snow-capped mountain waited a dangerous and infinite world.

Yerin took a deep breath and straightened. "All right," she said. "Lead the way."

Lindon had already turned to face the range of mountains past Samara, but he stopped. Turned back. "I know it's this way, but beyond that, you'll have to lead us out."

"Out? I've still got a bone to grind with the Heaven's Glory School." She gave him a grim smile. "They took my master's body, and his sword, and his Remnant. If I was soft enough to leave him here, I'd have walked away from this viper's nest weeks ago. No, I've got a few chores left here, and the chief one is you leading me back."

It was like a bag had tightened over Lindon's head. Compared to the freedom he'd tasted just a second before, he felt like choking. Like the prison door had been slowly creaking open, only to slam shut. He couldn't accept it.

"No. No! You *swore*." He didn't know how punishing the oath would be to him, but for someone of Yerin's power, it would weigh heavily. She might even cripple her future

232 • WILL WIGHT

potential by breaking a vow like this.

Yerin raised one finger. "I said I'd shepherd you on the path out, and I will. Once we're free and clear. But I'm not popping the lid off this barrel yet."

While he searched for words, she patted him on the shoulder.

"If it eases you any, I'm starting to trust you," she said. "A little."

Nervously, Lindon had thrown together an appropriate story to explain why he was hobbling in to the school in the early morning with a battered sister disciple, but no one asked for an explanation. One man cursed at the Unsouled for getting in his way, a few passersby expressed sympathy, and a girl reassured them kindly that the Sword Disciple would "see heaven's punishment come soon."

No one questioned them further than that. These days, coming home wounded was more common than not.

When Lindon reached his room, he knew he couldn't stay long, but he was overwhelmed with the desire to simply collapse on the floor. "When Elder Whitehall comes back, this is the first place he'll check," Lindon said. His jaw had begun to ache again, and every word sent itchy needles dancing inside his face. "We should be gone before that happens, if that's agreeable to you. I have an idea where..."

He trailed off as Yerin stumbled past him, clumsily tugging off one shoe as she made her way toward his bed. "We're not drawing swords in this state," she said. "We'll die. Need rest."

Halfway through taking off the second shoe, she slumped face-first onto the bed. In seconds, she was snoring.

At first, Lindon wondered how she could possibly sleep with the threat of death hanging over them. And she had taken *his* bed. He slipped off his pack, leaving it next to the door, and reached for her shoe. He had intended to pull it off and put it next to the other, but that was the last thing he remembered.

When he came to, Samara's ring was in the sky again, and his neck ached from a night spent in an impossible position. He had collapsed on his side, his head jammed up against the side of his bed, Yerin's fingers dangling in his face.

For a few seconds, he tried to remember how they had gotten here. He recognized Yerin from Suriel's vision, but the events of the previous day were a blurry haze in his mind.

When the fog cleared and he recalled where he was, fear shot him bolt upright. He had aided an enemy of the Heaven's Glory School. He'd fought an elder, *killed* an Iron disciple. Even the Patriarch of the Wei clan would have to pay with his life for such an offense, and here Lindon was sleeping in his room as though nothing had happened. He needed to *move.* He'd staggered to his feet before he stopped again.

Move where?

He couldn't leave the valley without Yerin, and he couldn't go home. His clan would turn him over to Heaven's Glory for a bent halfsilver chip.

He calmed himself, gathering his thoughts, taking a long look at his situation. Given that Heaven's Glory would hunt him as soon as Whitehall returned, then Lindon had to treat this place like enemy territory. He and Yerin had stayed here too long already.

But she had her own conditions, and may she rot in the Netherworld for them. She wouldn't leave the valley until she got what she wanted, and he couldn't leave without her. He needed her guidance to escape Sacred Valley, and her strength to survive whatever waited outside. Even a Heaven's Glory elder had been crippled with only a few hours outside of the school's territory, so an Unsouled would be lucky to last ten seconds. He needed her.

She lay on his bed, her stolen white robes bulky, the blood-red rope tied at her waist looking tight and uncomfortable. She was defenseless, scars all over her skin, some of them fresh.

Though it burned him, he put away thoughts of abandoning her or tricking her into guiding him out. She cared enough about her master's legacy to stay on the mountain with an entire school hunting her; nothing he could say would change her mind. He wasn't happy about it, but he could respect resolve like that.

Lindon slid the door open a crack, peeking out. Samara's ring lit empty gardens and iced rainstone buildings. No one watched his door, at least as far as he could tell.

Whitehall must not have made it back yet, or else he hadn't spread the word about Lindon. So Lindon still had time to use his identity as a Heaven's Glory disciple. At the least, he should be able to find out where the Sword Sage's body was.

He reached for his pack.

"Where you going?" Yerin asked. Her voice was vague and bleary, as though she hadn't bothered to wake up before speaking.

Lindon glanced back. She was adjusting her sword-belt, moving the hilt around from where it had been poking her in the ribs. "Give me two seconds, and I'll find out where they're keeping your master. Until Whitehall comes back, I'm still a disciple."

He looked like he'd just returned from a fight on behalf of the school—his white disciple's clothes were stained with blood and dirt, he was scraped and bruised from his head down to the soles of his feet, and his spirit had only just started to recover. The elder should believe any story he spun, if they swallowed the idea that someone at the Foundation level had been allowed to fight the Sword Disciple.

She squinted at him, rubbing the side of her head with one hand. "Don't bother yourself. I know where he is."

Lindon froze in his doorway, his frustration returning. "Then why are we *here?* Let's pick up your master and leave."

"Need to harvest his Remnant," she said, stretching. "I was aiming to steal the gear from the school, but they kept me too busy. This is two steps closer than I ever got before."

Lindon stared at her. *Harvest his Remnant.*

"Are you a Gold?" Everyone knew the final step into Gold was harvesting a Remnant and binding it to your physical body, which made you more than mortal. That was why Gold was the pinnacle, a qualitative leap beyond Jade.

Of course, according to Suriel, Gold was just the beginning.

"Not yet," Yerin answered him. "Taking in the Remnant is the difference between what you all call Jade and what you call Gold. It's like an heirloom, passed from master to disciple."

A brief stricken look passed across Yerin's face, and Lindon reminded himself that she had just lost her master. For some, that could be a bond even closer than blood.

Lindon stepped back and let the door close, and she straightened in apparent surprise. "Thought you were leaving."

"If we know where we're going, there's no need. Now, how about a plan. I'm guessing the gear you need is a spirit-seal?"

Yerin's eyes moved between him and the door. "Well, that's pleasing. I thought you'd make an excuse to leave, go warn the elders."

Lindon wrestled down his irritation. She had forced him into helping, and now she *still* doubted him?

"We're both traitors. They won't treat me any better than you."

"Crack the door, but don't walk out. Just peek."

If Lindon had to play more of her games, he might try to strike out on his own after all. "Why?"

She didn't answer, waiting for him to open the door. With a sigh, he did. The night still reigned.

"No one's there," he said.

"Drop a knee," she responded.

Feeling like a fool, Lindon knelt in his own doorway. Then he saw what had been invisible to him head-on: a flat shimmer in the air, floating at eye height, like a sword hammered out of pure force. His throat caught. Earlier, if he had taken more than a single step out, it would have sheared through his skull.

He managed to fake some level of calm as he asked, "Are you a Forger, then?"

"Born a Ruler, but I did Forge that." That wasn't too interesting of a statement in itself. The First Elder of the Wei clan was rumored to know both the Forger technique and the Ruler technique of the White Fox Path, though of course he was more gifted in one than the other.

"When?" Lindon asked, still staring at the blade that had almost killed him.

"Right before I shut my eyes. We did swear an oath, but we also only met tonight. Didn't trust you then."

She'd Forged that hours ago, and it had remained steady and solid. Having grown up around his mother, he knew how much skill that took. If she only dabbled in Forging, she would never have been able to do it.

He couldn't stop imagining an invisible blade passing through his eyes, slicing his brain into two pieces, but he forced himself past it. "Does that mean I can trust you not to lay anymore lethal traps for me?"

She considered a moment, then nodded. "Not lethal ones."

"I'm pleased to hear that." He'd take whatever he could get. "Now, we need a spirit-seal?"

Yerin loosened her shoulders, swinging her feet around to the other side of the bed. She braced her sword in one hand, and she looked more like the formidable sacred artist she was. "You know where they're kept?"

"The Lesser Treasure Hall. A Jade Forger lives over the hall, and there are script-activated security constructs hidden in the floors."

Her eyes gleamed and she leaned in closer. "That's more than nothing but less than something. Now, this Treasure Hall...they keep more than *just* seals, true?"

Suddenly, it occurred to Lindon that something good might actually come of staying in Sacred Valley. "You wouldn't believe everything they've got in there."

"That's pleasing to hear. Now, what did the Wei clan teach you about stealing from your enemies?"

"I'll bring my pack."

CHAPTER EIGHTEEN

Elder Whitehall had never felt so miserable in his life. He'd long since closed the bleeding sword wound on his shoulder—such injuries were only minor irritations to anyone with Jade madra and an Iron body—but his spirit was exhausted, and an eight-year-old's legs were not suited to trudging through snow. He felt as though his knees would buckle with every step, and the few scraps of madra he could scrape up were spent melting his way forward with beams of hot gold.

Especially grating was the knowledge that he could have been back at the school by now, a hot mug of tea in his hand and hundreds of disciples rushing out to find Wei Shi Lindon and the sword girl. He would have reached the Heaven's Glory School long ago.

But that wasn't where he'd decided to go, and he clung to that decision with dogged resolve. He was heading to the Ancestor's Tomb.

The Tomb was actually closer than the school, but the way was anything but clear. There were no roads out here; he had to scale rock faces and push his way through snow. With no madra. In a child's body. If he'd known, he would have brought a Thousand-Mile Cloud.

With every agonizing step, he was tempted to turn back, but he never did. The Sword Disciple had been making her way closer to the Tomb for the better part of two weeks now, and now that she had help from that Unsouled, he had every reason to believe that they'd head straight for her master's body.

He could bring in help, give away the credit, and never see a single one of the Sword Sage's fantastic treasures. Or...

Samara's ring was a bright line in the sky when he reached the Ancestor's Tomb. The Tomb predated their school by unknown centuries, a titanic monument to an age long past perched at the edge of the mountainside. Behind it was a sheer thousand-foot drop and a picturesque view of distant snowy peaks. The building itself was bigger than anything in Heaven's Glory, a square mausoleum that stood proudly on vast pillars. Far above Whitehall's head, a mural of four gigantic beasts locked in battle rose over the entrance.

A man and a woman in Heaven's Glory colors waited on the steps at the bottom, huddled behind the pillars against the wind. They wore purple sashes, only a step away from Whitehall's gold, and their badges were jade.

Every elder was a Jade, but not every Jade was an elder. These two had no problems in their mastery of the sacred arts, but they were too young to actually administrate the school, so Whitehall outranked them both. He'd counted on that.

Once he knew they'd seen him, he allowed himself to pitch forward and fall into a patch of snow. It didn't require much acting.

Footsteps crunched rapidly through the snow, and the male guard shouted something to his partner. Seconds later, a pair of hands scooped up Whitehall's whole body and carried him to the steps.

Ordinarily he would resent the indignity of being treated like a child, but his relief outweighed any irritation. At last, he was off his feet.

"Elder Whitehall?" the woman asked anxiously. "Are you wounded? We'll send for healers now."

Whitehall reached out blindly and seized her hand. "No!" He wasn't pleased by how young and weak his voice sounded. "Please. I will recover soon, and my pride could not stand the blow."

Through half-closed lids, Whitehall saw the Jade guards exchange glances. "Of course we will shelter you, elder. If I may ask, why did you come to us? Why not return to the school?"

Whitehall struggled up to a sitting position, grimacing in pain that was only half-feigned. "It was my shame that I was wounded by the Sword Disciple before I could defeat her. How could I show my face as an elder if I returned without victory? I couldn't. I will rest here for a night or two, and when I am recovered, I will show her the wrath of Heaven's Glory."

The guards bowed to him. "Your words are wise, elder," the woman said. "We have a hut just to the side of the Tomb. It is nothing much, but you are welcome to it."

Whitehall returned a seated bow. "When the Sword Disciple is dead, I will remember this favor." They brightened; if Whitehall killed the Sage's disciple, he would instantly gain status in the school, and a favor from him would become that much more valuable.

A screech like a razor sliding along rock echoed from the Ancestor's Tomb, ringing in the air and stabbing his ears. The guards winced and backed up together, turning to face the Tomb. The sound faded a second later, but Whitehall already wondered if his ears were bleeding.

"Is that the Remnant?" Whitehall asked.

The male guard kept a hand on his weapon. It was a club, Whitehall noted, not the sword he would have expected. "The Sage has been quiet for over a week, but last night he started up again. Elder, when you return to the school, I humbly request that you send reinforcements to us before our shift is up. If he escapes, we will not be enough to contain him."

Whitehall rapped his knuckles against the man's wrist, as he would discipline a student. "Cowardice is not fitting for warriors of Heaven's Glory. That is not the Sword Sage, it is only a Remnant."

"I do not mean to contradict the elder," the woman said, "but last night the Remnant did *that.*" She pointed to the top of the Tomb, just above and to the side of the beast mural.

In the harsh light of Samara's halo, colors were muted and edges sharp. He squinted at the corner of the building, along the side of the roof, trying to distinguish between the folds of shadow.

Finally, he saw it, and he took in a breath of freezing air. Between the roof and the wall, there was a crack. It was difficult to see if you weren't looking for it, but now that he stared directly at the spot, he could see it: a slice of deeper shadow where the Tomb's ancient walls had been split open. It looked as though a massive blade had slipped into the top of the wall, opening a wound.

"That's..." he began, but he had no words. The Ancestor's Tomb was set with deep, ancient scripts that had gathered vital aura into those walls for centuries. They should be next to indestructible by now.

A *Remnant* had done that?

"The elder knows best," the male guard said, without a trace of mockery in his tone. "But I thought he should be made aware."

"After I recover, I will return here with reinforcements," Whitehall promised. He actually meant it.

He let them guide him back to their hut on the edge of the cliff, drape a snowfox pelt around his shoulders, and heat fish soup for him. If he understood the Sword Disciple's character correctly, she would be here tomorrow, or a day later at the most. And if he grasped the scope of her power, she would tear through these two Jades.

He hoped they would survive—they had been kind to him, after all—but death in combat was the most honorable end for a sacred artist. If they died for their weakness, he would not be to blame.

And once the girl opened the Ancestor's Tomb, she would have to face the Remnant of her formidable master. Either it would kill her unassisted, or Whitehall would take advantage of her distraction to kill her himself.

After that, there was no losing scenario for him. A Remnant of the sword aspect was powerful in combat but weak in pursuit, so he would be able to escape. Either he would retrieve the treasures on the Sword Sage's body, or he would return to the school with the Sword Disciple's head.

In that case, he would have rendered such merits to the Heaven's Glory School that he should end up with some prizes regardless.

As for the Unsouled, if he knew what was good for him, he would never show up here. There was nothing he could do but die.

With his pack on, Lindon crouched in the shadow of the Lesser Treasure Hall as it glistened in the pure white light. There were no guards on the porch this time, just a locked door with security scripts and deadly constructs behind it.

He glanced over at Yerin, who stood openly in the street. He'd already explained the security measures to her, but he wasn't sure she'd heard him. "The script will trigger if we break in," he reminded her.

She adjusted the blood-red ropes at her waist, which stood out in stark contrast to her white Heaven's Glory clothes. "And the script's in the doorframe?" She didn't whisper.

Lindon nodded.

With a sigh of steel, she drew her sword. It shone in the white light, steady and straight. He thought she was going to explain her plan, but without even opening her mouth, she whipped her blade forward.

Colorless light rippled out of her sword, as though her cut moved forward of its own volition through the air. It was so thin it was practically invisible, like a half-loop of fishing line sliding forward.

It sank into the middle of the door and vanished with no apparent effect.

Yerin's sword was already sheathed, though Lindon hadn't seen it, and she strode forward. "I've seen these scripts before. You break them before they trigger and they don't bother you."

With that, she pushed on the door. The left half swung inward, having been split cleanly down the middle by her sword madra. The side with the lock was still attached, but the side with the hinges was now separated. It slid open easily and soundlessly. As Lindon followed her inside, he looked down at the script on the floor. One of the runes was cracked in two just as the door had been.

Unless the rune was broken *instantly*, breaking this type of script would trigger it. He couldn't imagine the sort of speed, the degree of control, it would take to do something like this to a script six inches away, much less from a distance.

He hungered for such skill. If Suriel's promise held true, he would have the opportunity to learn sacred arts like this. Power even the Wei Patriarch had never imagined.

"Is that something you can teach me?" he asked.

He assumed she would laugh at him, but she turned to face him properly without the trace of a smile. "A disciple is not worthy to take a disciple."

If she was only a student, how could anyone call themselves a master? "You're stronger than anyone I've ever seen. If you stayed here, you could open a fifth school."

This time Yerin did laugh, but not at him. "Sacred Valley is too soft. Only storms turn fish into dragons, and there are no storms here." She turned to the treasures behind their display cases before adding, "If you didn't know that yourself, you wouldn't be leaving."

That was true enough.

"Fill your eyes with *this!*" Yerin exclaimed, moving past him. "Bud of a Starlotus! It's a miracle before Copper, but it'll do wonders for anybody's madra base. Where's your pack?"

She stared at the spirit-fruit with a hungry look, holding a hand over it as though she wanted to reach straight through the Forged glass. Just as Lindon had done before. He was going to politely offer her his pack, but she'd already moved to another display.

"A Sylvan Riverseed? That's a gem and a half. Even if we can't use it, we can sell it." She put a hand on her sword.

Lindon considered warning her, but he'd told her about

the security measures before. Rahm had Forged these cases himself, and he would have countermeasures in case one was broken. But he'd told her that already, and he had to trust she knew what she was doing.

In one smooth motion, Yerin drew her sword and sheathed it again. The case split in half.

A gong sounded, filling the Lesser Treasure Hall in echoing alarms. Runes in the corners flared ominously red. Two constructs rose through the floor, head-sized eggs of shining gold. Plates on the bottom rotated, spilling blue light, keeping the constructs aloft. Those would be made out of different types of madra, but everything else would be Heaven's Glory, serving as both power source and physical material.

Light coalesced on the tip of the eggs, and Yerin shot him a sheepish look. "Sorry."

"I warned you!"

"Yeah, this one's on my account."

"I said there would be an alarm on the cases. 'Don't break the cases,' I said!"

"Next time, I'll give you a shout first."

The constructs were focused on Yerin, so Lindon was backing away, glancing from case to case in search of something that might save them. "Why would there be a next time?"

A door in the back swung open, revealing a shadowed set of stairs, and Elder Rahm entered the room. They must have disturbed his sleep, because he wore only a shapeless white robe. He didn't even have on a badge. His hunched, aged figure leaned on a cane in one hand and held a slender sword in the other. The sword didn't tremble at all.

"If you think you're getting another chance, you've underestimated me," Rahm said. He shot Lindon a glance. "I thought I told you not to steal from me."

"This one regrets it already, honored elder," Lindon said, pressing his fists together in a salute. Manners couldn't save him now, but they couldn't hurt.

"He'll have friends coming," Yerin said, one hand on her sword and her eyes on the constructs. She hadn't even looked at Elder Rahm. "Grab the prize, then stuff your pockets while I bury the old man."

"You don't have to *bury* him," Lindon hedged. "He's treated me well."

She didn't loosen the grip on her sword. "If he lives, I won't finish him off. That's the best I can promise you, 'cause I'm not leaving without a fight."

The constructs still hadn't attacked, which meant they were primarily designed to contain thieves until Rahm could deal with them personally. But they wouldn't remain so passive if Rahm gave the order to attack, or if Yerin showed herself as a threat.

Lindon looked from the constructs to Yerin. "You *want* to fight?"

"I want to clean this place out." Her razor-straight hair shook as she turned to look at him, punctuating her words with a grave look. "Sacred arts cost a bundle. Go now."

Lindon didn't need to be told again.

The priority was the spirit-seal, of course, but how could he pass up a room full of sacred artifacts? Yerin obviously agreed, because when the first construct blasted out a stream of golden light, she reflected it with her sword into another case, shearing the top off the glass without touching the artifact inside. The second construct fired, and she moved so that it wouldn't pierce the case behind her.

She was fighting a Heaven's Glory elder and his two security constructs, and she intended to do so without damaging any of the treasures around her. And judging by her words, she had complete confidence.

One day, Lindon hoped to be more like Yerin.

A plane of glass condensed from light behind her, boxing her in, as Elder Rahm joined the fight. Lindon left them to it. He couldn't fight, so the least he could do was focus on his task.

It was hard to concentrate with the sounds of battle behind him, but he knew he had only seconds until someone arrived to back Rahm up. He had to work smart. He needed something to break the cases as fast as possible, and something to speed up their escape later.

First, to break the glass. He ran to the racks at the side of the room, where halfsilver weapons were displayed on open shelves. They were comparatively less valuable than the other artifacts in the room, so they didn't rate a case.

Lindon snatched a halfsilver dagger away. It looked like ordinary silver, but veins of some brighter mineral shimmered beneath the surface, as though the blade contained a constellation. It would shear through madra faster than through half-melted butter.

Still, he didn't rush straight for the spirit-seals. He ran to the back of the room, where Rahm had shown him a rust-colored cloud.

The Thousand-Mile Cloud filled its case like a bloody mist, and Lindon's halfsilver dagger worked even better than he'd hoped. It shattered the glass directly, which released a wave of heat—the glass had golden edges, and it must be crystallized Heaven's Glory madra. The Striker technique released a lance of focused golden light, so their Forgers must create this glass with burning shards. That seemed useless, except perhaps in constructs.

Out of confinement, the cloud inflated to its full size. It was round and fairly large, about three feet in diameter, and dense enough that he couldn't see through it. It didn't look solid enough to support solid matter, but he'd grown up with a mattress stuffed with cloud madra. He pressed on it, and it was like pushing on a pillow. It only gave to a certain point, and then it was solid.

This would be their getaway.

A deadly gold beam flashed by his head for an instant, five feet away but still close enough that he could feel the heat, and he dropped into a crouch. Madra trickled from him into the Thousand-Mile Cloud, and it drifted forward according to his direction.

He vaguely remembered where the spirit-seals were, the collection of paper seals painted with scripts that would help bind and manipulate Remnants. He half-crawled through the aisles, circling around the outside of the room to avoid the slashing sword-force and the deadly light flashing overhead.

As he did, he helped himself to the treasures of Heaven's Glory. Even the danger of the fight around him couldn't mute that thrill. In his most daring daydreams, he would never have imagined that he could one day choose freely from the vaults of a prestigious school of sacred arts. A smile crept onto his face as lethal madra flashed over his head.

With resources like these, even an Unsouled could rise.

He glanced at everything he grabbed before he stuffed it into his pack. First, he snatched the folded white Starlotus Bud and the tank containing the Sylvan Riverseed. The little blue spirit inside darted around its tree, standing on top of its tiny hill to glance at him curiously. The parasite ring went into his pocket, as he wanted to keep that on his person in case he had to abandon everything else. Only then did he reach the spirit-seals.

The dagger destroyed the glass with ease, and Lindon reached up to snatch a heavy sheaf of palm-sized paper seals, stacked like a deck of cards and tied at the top. Each seal was covered in layers of profound brush-strokes, forming scripts according to principles he couldn't begin to grasp.

He slid over to the display containing the flying sword, which had caught his eye before. Once he reached Iron, he could use it, and now that he would be traveling with Yerin it was even more valuable. A sword artist like her would be able to work miracles with such a weapon.

No sooner had he broken the case than Yerin came sliding down the aisle on her back as though tossed there by a heavy blow. Her sword was still held in front of her, and the edge of her hair was smoking.

"This is taking a *notch* longer than I'd thought," she said.

Lindon risked a glance outside. Sure enough, a small crowd of disciples had gathered at the bottom of the steps. They were murmuring among themselves at the moment, but they could rush forward to assist Elder Rahm at any second.

He looked down the aisle at the dozens of cases he hadn't broken and spoke through gritted teeth. "Let's... just...take what we have." It grated on him to leave so many riches behind, but they'd die if they stayed.

She grimaced and rolled to the side, narrowly avoiding another beam. "Once I ease him on his way, we can go."

While she struck out at the construct with another ripple of sword-madra, he stared at her. "We don't need to fight him at all. Get on the cloud and let's go."

"The strong don't run," she said.

The elder himself stepped into view at that moment, waving his sword. Madra followed the motion, and transparent madra walls bloomed to either side of them. They were trapped in a column, one row of artifacts with Rahm and his two constructs on one side and Yerin and Lindon at the other. Behind them, a group of enemy disciples waited out the open door.

The old man pointed his blade at them. He must have given the constructs an instruction, because they were both silent as he spoke. "We want you alive. Swear yourself to my keeping, give us answers, and we won't kill you. We'll allow you to take your own life."

"Can you keep me alive?" Lindon asked, voice low. "Because you might survive that crowd rushing in here, but I won't. And you swore to keep me safe."

She shuddered, expression flickering between anger and agony, but eventually she nodded.

Yerin knelt next to the case with the flying sword, her own blade pressed against the ground. She had lost her Heaven's Glory robes at some point, leaving her own tattered black clothes, though the stolen iron badge still hung around her neck. "Did your messenger tell you what Path I follow?"

Suriel's ghost had given him that information, but he couldn't remember. He shook his head.

"Grab that sword," she said, pointing at the case. "Then throw it at him."

Lindon glanced nervously at the battle-ready Jade. "Now?"

"Now."

The elder faced them impatiently, constructs hovering over each shoulder and weapon in hand. With as little movement as possible, Lindon slid the scripted blade off of its stand.

"Your answer," Rahm demanded.

Lindon hefted the blade.

Yerin took a deep breath. "This is the Path of the Endless Sword," she said.

Lindon threw.

As the sword tumbled end-over-end in the air, Yerin

tightened her grip on her own weapon. Her blade rang like a struck bell, and suddenly the air was filled with flying splinters as the floor tore itself to pieces. It was as though a thousand hatchets struck the same point at the same time.

The display of halfsilver weaponry echoed the sound weakly, and a few cuts appeared around their case, but they remained intact. Even the halfsilver dagger at Lindon's belt rang softly, and he jerked as light cuts appeared on his robe. Around the room, three bells rung louder, and three cases burst.

Another bell, and Elder Rahm screamed. His sword had rung in sympathy with the others, and his sleeve exploded in blood. His arm and the right side of his clothes had been slashed to tatters, and his weapon fell to the ground from a hand that no longer had the strength to hold it.

In the air, the flying sword rang as well. Barely visible lines of sword madra reflected from its edge as it flew between the Heaven's Glory constructs. They were still quiet, having been pacified by Elder Rahm, and so they did not protest as they were sliced to pieces that trailed golden smoke as they drifted to the ground. Only the blue circles on the bottoms remained floating, supporting nothing.

The sword finished its arc and clattered to the ground, nowhere close to Elder Rahm. The old man moaned as he fell to his knees, clutching his ruined arm.

Lindon stared.

Yerin pushed him toward the Thousand-Mile Cloud and the stuffed pack on top, still talking. "That's called resonance. Uses sword madra to rile up the aura in the air, which gathers around sharp weapons. Doesn't work so well with halfsilver."

For that, Lindon was grateful. Otherwise, he might have been split in two by his own dagger.

He sprawled onto the cloud, pushing down the pack full of loot with his body. She hopped on in front of him, feeding her spirit into the cloud construct. It was off like an arrow, shooting through the door and away before any of the stunned Heaven's Glory disciples outside could react.

"That's the heart of my Path," Yerin said. "All swords are one."

While she spoke, she steered the cloud down the street. It only hovered about three feet over the ground, but under the influence of Yerin's powerful spirit, it was faster than a galloping horse.

"I will do anything, *anything*, if you can teach me to do that."

Streaks of light blasted after them, scorching rainstone buildings, as Yerin navigated them away from the school. Her scarred face was tight with concentration.

"He's not dead," she said, ignoring his comment. "But I'd contend that I won." She nodded decisively. "Yeah, we'll mark that one up as a win."

They streaked toward the Ancestor's Tomb, leaving their pursuers far behind.

CHAPTER NINETEEN

As the sun rose, Lindon and Yerin flew over the rough terrain of Mount Samara. Yerin kept the rosy cloud skimming the rocks, scattering snow as they blasted north toward the Ancestor's Tomb.

Meanwhile, Lindon concentrated on not falling off.

Once he had found a position that he felt he could survive, he slowly began picking through his pack of stolen items. Once they landed, they might not have time to take full inventory.

The Thousand-Mile Cloud itself was probably their greatest prize, and Yerin insisted that even Lindon's madra was enough to power it. Though he would travel much more slowly. According to her, clouds like this were valuable transportation beyond the valley.

There were forty-eight spirit-seals in the stack, and they were prepared to use all of them on her master's Remnant. But if they had a few left over, the seals would be precious advantages against other Remnants in the future. Still, it was best not to count on that. The Sword Sage was their priority.

The Starlotus bud would help him break through to Copper almost immediately, and he had to remind himself more than a dozen times that it would be foolish to eat it now. The ancestral orus fruit had taken him days to digest, and the Starlotus should take even longer. The last thing he needed was something in his own core distracting him when he might need to fight. Even so, he longed to swallow at least one petal.

Instead, he occupied himself watching the Sylvan Riverseed, the little blue-flame spirit that danced around in its glass enclosure. The river that spun around the inside of the little tank had remained steady as they flew, neither spilling nor splashing, but the spirit had thrown itself against the glass walls to stare at the passing landscape.

Lindon had asked what the Riverseed could be used for, but Yerin herself was unclear. They were rare, she knew that, and you were supposed to raise them. Or maybe plant them. Either way, she was certain it was worth more money than anything else they'd snatched, including the cloud.

The parasite ring was like the Starlotus bud, in that it would eventually help Lindon overcome his deficiencies but wasn't of any immediate use. He added to that the halfsilver dagger—his parents had owned a few halfsilver weapons, but he'd never had one of his own—and the White Fox boundary flags as the least valuable treasures they'd stolen. The boundary was difficult to obtain, but it also took a long time to set up, and a powerful enough opponent would simply tear through it. He had been lucky to use it against Kazan Ma Deret.

Seven treasures. They were an unspeakable fortune to a Wei clan Unsouled, but looking at them like this, they were almost disappointing. When he compared them to what they *could* have gotten away with, had they been allowed just another minute in the Treasure Hall...

"Dragon fever," Yerin said from the front of the cloud.

Lindon jerked up, startled out of his daydreams. "Dragon?"

She laughed into the wind as they skipped off of a outcropping, floating down to land above the ground again. "That's what master would say. Sacred arts are expensive, and it takes a pile of pills and treasures to advance.

It's when you get lost in gold for it's own sake, that's the dragon fever."

Lindon's face heated. She'd seen through him without even looking at him. "I'm not trying to take your share. My contributions pale beside yours. But some of them, I think, might not suit someone of your strength."

"No, don't get me wrong. I'm burning up with the fever. I'm just boiling to turn around and scrape that Treasure Hall clean."

He exhaled, relieved. "This is a bigger fortune than I've ever seen, and for some reason I'm disappointed it isn't bigger."

"Dragon fever," she said decisively. "Helps to keep your eyes fixed on one thing. Grab whatever else you can, but don't go blind to what really matters. My master says—" She stopped. Wind whistled by. "My master used to say distraction kills more sacred artists than enemies ever do."

He couldn't ignore that pause. Having never been trained, he'd never had a master, but how would he feel if his parents had been taken from him?

Suriel's vision flashed through his head, Sacred Valley blasted out of existence, and he spoke with real sympathy. "He must have been a great man. Even in the outside world."

"The spine of the matter is, he only came to the valley for me," she said. He couldn't see her face, but suddenly he could barely hear her words over the wind. "Wouldn't have bothered coming on his own, it was just a safe place for me to train. But it doesn't matter how strong you are when you're poisoned in your sleep." By the end, her voice carried the ring of cold steel.

"I wish I could have met him," Lindon said. It was true, but it was also what he was supposed to say to a grieving relative.

"He might have taken you with us, had you asked him. He could be soft that way. But first, he'd have killed your clan elders for what they were teaching you."

Lindon leaned around her shoulder, trying to catch a glimpse of her expression. "Forgiveness, but...what did they teach me?"

He crashed into her back as the cloud came to a sudden halt. A massive square building loomed in the distance, set with huge columns and a stone mural of four beasts locked in battle. The whole edifice lurked on the edge of an enormous cliff as though it had done so since the beginning of time.

"The Ancestor's Tomb," Yerin said, and vaulted down from the cloud. "Master went to the Heaven's Glory in particular just for this. They say it leads down into some labyrinth where even my master couldn't step easy."

Her hand was on her sword, black sacred artist's robes trailing shredded edges in the wind. She pulled the stolen badge over her head and tossed it to one side. "They poisoned him and they stabbed him, so he tried to hide in the Tomb. Died two steps from the door."

She looked back at him, but her scarred face wasn't as cold as he'd imagined from someone seeking revenge. It was etched with grief. "Last thing he said to me, he told me to finish forming my Path. He didn't know he'd be leaving me his own Remnant, but...he did. Nobody else touches his spirit but me, and that's the fact of it."

Lindon surveyed the giant Tomb. Two guards had revealed themselves on the front steps, and they would certainly have seen the Thousand-Mile Cloud by now. One of them raised a hand, sending a flash of gold light streaking into the air. A signal.

"There's not much I can do in a straight fight," Lindon said honestly. "But I'll help you however I can."

Yerin patted him on the shoulder. "Yeah, I'm convinced that you will. You've got less choice than a tethered ox."

He cleared his throat. "I would have helped you without the oath."

"There's a chance you would, but now you won't give up midstream and beg for your life."

Lindon prickled at that. "There's no reason for that. I

may be weak, but I'm not a coward."

She rolled her arm in its socket, loosening it up for the fight, and she grinned at him over her shoulder. "Couldn't know that when I made you swear, could I? I trust you more now. A notch more."

At least she hadn't set another trap for him. He sighed and began sorting the Heaven's Glory artifacts into different pockets. He'd jammed them all into his pack without looking, but now he might need to draw them quickly.

One of the guards activated an egg-shaped golden construct that looked the same as the one Rahm had used, and the other was beginning to set up walls of gold-tinged glass.

"Now, Wei Shi Lindon, we live or die together." Yerin took off in an explosion of snow, blasting forward with a speed only an Iron body could achieve.

As she shattered the first wall of glass, sending a hot wind billowing out as the glass broke, Lindon took his time packing up the treasures. He couldn't help until the fight was over, and he wouldn't run headlong into death. If the heavens considered that a violation of his word, so be it.

The Thousand-Mile Cloud wouldn't compress, and he determined that it required a special case to fold up. Since he didn't have one, he fed it a trickle of his madra and dragged it along behind him as he picked his way across the frozen boulders and toward Yerin. It followed like an obedient bird.

Light burned a river of steam in the snow, and a wall of glass appeared to block Yerin's counterattack. She was steadily advancing, but the two guards and the construct were using every trick at their disposal to keep her at bay. When she flipped in midair to avoid two golden beams and then sliced a fifteen-foot glass wall from top to bottom with sword-madra, Lindon knew it was only a matter of time before she closed the gap. He knew what would happen when she did.

He kept an eye on the battle as he advanced, but by the time he reached the bottom step of the Ancestor's Tomb with his cloud in tow, Yerin was flanked by two bleeding bodies and fizzing golden plates that had once been a Heaven's Glory construct.

"Are they dead?" Lindon asked. He wasn't sure why. It didn't matter to him if Heaven's Glory lost two more fighters.

Yerin cleaned her blade on the snow and then wiped it dry on the corner of her robe. "Iron bodies are tougher than snake leather. The man's not long for breathing, but I didn't want to stare down more Remnants than I have to. The woman might hang on until her school gets here. She passed out from the pain."

He picked around the bloody snow, following Yerin up the stairs. "Sacred artists are supposed to be beyond pain."

"No one's beyond pain," she said, and then she stood before a tall door. It looked like wood, but it carried the eternal aura of solid rock. From within, a sound rang out like steel on stone. The note hung in the air, endless and pure.

"Seals?" she asked, adjusting her red rope-belt.

Lindon held up the stack.

"Let me hear your role," she ordered, but Lindon didn't take offense. She was stronger than any of the Jades in Sacred Valley; she had more right than anyone to order him around, even if she was barely older than he was.

"I'm putting these seals into a circle in front of the door," he said. "When you lure it out, I throw a seal directly at it and run while you fight it here, where the seals on the ground can help you. If that's not enough, I come back and seal it again."

She eyed him. "If you thought I told you to run, you heard wrong."

"I have to run to set these up," Lindon said, revealing an inch of purple banner. "I'm not even running, I'm providing *strategic support*. Now, you have your ward key?"

"Remnant will tear through that like a bull through a paper door."

"If he's tearing through this, he's not tearing through

you." The air of tension around her was lifting, which was a good thing as far as Lindon was concerned. She'd been talking like someone on her way to the grave, and if she died, he wouldn't be far behind. Now, he saw the distant shadow of a smile on her face, and she turned as though to respond.

The door tore in half with a sound like screaming metal. He registered nothing beyond sudden light and agonizing noise before something hit him in the chest and he tumbled backward down the steps, slamming onto his back at the bottom.

His body hadn't had a chance to recover since the *last* time he'd jammed his full pack into his spine, and he indulged in an instant of self-pity imagining his rare boundary flags snapping in half. Then the reality crashed in: that door had split in two from the inside. The impact on his chest was Yerin pushing him back faster than he could react, or he would be lying at the top of the steps in two pieces.

The Remnant of an expert beyond Gold, the spirit that they had assumed was sealed inside the ancient tomb, had cut through its restraints like an axe through a spiderweb. It hadn't been sealed.

It had been waiting.

He pushed his battered body to his feet, taking quick stock to make sure nothing was broken or bleeding. Then he saw the Remnant of the Sword Sage.

It was a mass of rippling liquid steel in the shape of a human, as though someone had poured a mirror over a man. Its face was featureless, blank, polished to a flawless reflection. It had no arms or legs, merely an uninterrupted sheet of metal, and it flowed over the ground like a snail.

The Remnant was far more solid, more *real*, than any Forged construction Lindon had ever seen. The only parts he recognized as madra at all were three hoops criss-crossing its chest: one a loop of vivid white color, one scarlet, and one inky black. The circles spun in rapid orbit around the sword-Remnant's chest as it surveyed the scene mirrored in its smooth face.

It reflected the two bodies and Lindon slowly edging backward before its gaze rested on Yerin. There it stopped.

The disciple faced her master's ghost with sword bare. She was a mundane echo of the Remnant; its red ring was her belt, its black ring her tattered robes, its white ring her pale scars, and its chrome her shining blade.

"Disciple greets her master," she said quietly. A student in her place would normally have saluted respectfully, but she kept her eyes on the spirit.

For a long breath, the Remnant remained quiet. Powerful enough spirits could speak, and there was no doubt that this was the most potent he'd ever seen. It would talk soon, and the reunion of master and disciple would give him time to set the boundary. The Remnant had crashed through the door before he could lay seals, but he'd watch for a chance to hit it directly with one.

Six limbs of liquid metal sprouted from the Remnant's back, flattening and sharpening until it stood under a halo of blades. It still didn't speak.

Without a word, it attacked.

The Remnant's main body stood like a statue, but its blades were invisible as they whispered forward. Yerin moved in response, and weapons crashed in an explosion that sent sharp ripples in every direction. The stairs under them cracked, shards of stone blasting into the air, and gashes appeared in the thick pillars. Snow split as though invisible giants hacked away at the ground with hatchets, and a nearby boulder slid into two pieces.

Lindon hopped onto the Thousand-Mile Cloud and fed it all the madra he could. He hadn't seen a single meeting of blades, but he heard them all, filling the mountainside in one seemingly constant note. Whatever Yerin might believe, he would never be able to approach the Remnant like this. He'd never see the cut that killed him. He could only hope that she would wound it badly enough that it would lose some of its substance. Without a supply of external energy, it wouldn't recover, so it should get weaker as the fight progressed. But then, so would Yerin.

A spray of blood told him that the unconscious Heaven's Glory guards hadn't made it after all. Two Remnants rose from the corpses, one a string-puppet of burning gold lines, and one a skeleton of yellow-tinged glass. They hadn't even straightened to their full height when more invisible blades minced them to chunks.

We don't have time for this, Lindon thought, as he fled as fast as his cloud would carry him. They needed to end this fight before Heaven's Glory showed themselves, but he couldn't get close enough to set up his barrier. She had already demonstrated her Endless Sword technique; with two experts using it, they might have been surrounded by hundreds of whirling invisible blades. To pass close enough to plant a flag would be to risk death, and if he reached the Remnant with a seal, he'd be shredded.

He glanced behind, in case the battle might have crept closer to him, and from farther back he could see something he hadn't noticed before. There was a small wooden hut sheltered in the shadow of the Tomb, and a child in white robes was peeking around the corner at the battle.

The child raised his arm, and golden light lanced toward the fight. Lindon's heart stopped.

Elder Whitehall.

Something deflected the beam, sending it arcing into the sky, but neither girl nor Remnant could spare the attention to deal with the intruder. He was the vulture, waiting for the wolf and the tiger to kill each other so it could feast on both corpses. He would never let Lindon approach with the seals.

The freezing mountaintop wind felt very close. Whitehall hadn't noticed him yet. He had a chance here, a chance to at least stall the elder and give Yerin a chance.

But he had no time. Whitehall could notice him any second. He had to act now.

He removed the glass ball with its azure flame, rolling it in his hand. If Suriel looked, what would she see in his fate now?

Before he could think himself away, Lindon leaped onto the red cloud and sped out in a wide arc. He couldn't move nearly as fast as Yerin could, but it was enough. He circled behind Elder Whitehall.

Then, still scraping the back of his brain for ideas, he charged.

In the eyes of a Jade, the fight between the girl and the Remnant was nothing short of spectacular. An ocean of silver sword-aura gathered around them, rolling like a sea in storm. Even to Whitehall, their blows moved at a speed that he could barely catch. The disciple in black gathered aura with every motion, which condensed around her blade in a steadily increasing silver glow. She leaped, ducked, slid, and dodged, her weapon never pausing, meeting every strike from the six-bladed Remnant with her own sword or a blast of razor-edged madra.

Whitehall knew some peers in the Golden Sword School that would have sacrificed three fingers for a glimpse at this fight. This was a sword-aspect Path taken beyond anything in Sacred Valley, beyond what anyone could conceive.

He drew Heaven's Glory energy from his core, focusing it according to the Heaven's Lance technique. The energy struck out in a line of light and heat, scoring the floor between the two fighters. The girl faltered, taking a narrow slash across the cheek as the glow around her sword flickered. Even the Remnant slid slightly to the left. Whitehall might not have been able to kill either of them on his own, but sparrows didn't bring down hawks by attacking head-on. They nipped and circled until the larger bird collapsed from exhaustion and fell from the sky.

Then the treasures of the Sword Sage, relics of a world beyond this valley, would be his. Not only might he restore his body, he could become the first Gold since the founding of the Heaven's Glory School.

He'd leveled another golden lance when something slammed into him from behind.

A thorn of pain blossomed in his shoulder as he pitched forward, and the lance of light flew wild, scorching the surface of the Ancestor's Tomb. But it didn't last as long as it should have, guttering out like a candle as the madra in Whitehall's body went wild.

He landed face-first in the snow, his insides twisting as though his intestines had tried to coil up and escape through his mouth. His spirit burned and writhed in chaos, searing him from the inside out, and he coughed a mouthful of blood onto the ground.

With one hand, he reached up and pulled the spike out of his shoulder. It glittered in the morning sunlight: a half-silver dagger.

Whitehall turned in a fury, bloody dagger in his hand. His body was still Iron and his spirit Jade; he would recover in minutes. His attacker had done nothing but earn a quick death.

Wei Shi Lindon loomed overhead, and though his spirit made him weak, he had the body of a strong man. Even the huge pack on his back lent an intimidating cast to his silhouette. Whitehall hesitated for a mere instant of purely instinctive fear, the gut reaction of a child facing down an angry adult. His mind was still that of an expert, but there was something primal about looking up to a human being twice his size.

During that half-second of vulnerability, Lindon pivoted and planted a fist in Whitehall's gut.

The impact didn't do much—despite his advantage in weight, Lindon still hadn't reached Iron, so Whitehall had the absolute lead in strength—but pure madra leaked into Whitehall's core from outside.

His training took over, and he cycled madra defensively, but he might as well have saved his effort. Nothing happened.

Whitehall couldn't deny a small measure of relief. The Unsouled might as well have tried to put out a forest fire with a splash of water. He grabbed the young man's wrist in an iron grip, locking him in place, and took a moment to savor the sudden look of fear on Lindon's face.

Then he struck back.

●

Lindon was actually grateful for his experience at the Seven-Year Festival. Without all that practice fighting eight-year-olds, he would never have been able to accurately strike Whitehall's core.

Not that it mattered, in the end.

He'd counted on the disruption from the halfsilver dagger lasting long enough to let him land an Empty Palm, which would have bought him enough time to run. Whitehall would have recovered in seconds and chased him, but he'd planned for that.

He *hadn't* planned for the elder grabbing him by the wrist. He tried to resist, but it was as though his arm had been planted in stone. Panic bloomed in his chest, and he had time for only one panicked thought. *Too fast.* He'd shaken off the halfsilver in an instant. Lindon had never had a chance.

Whitehall smiled, his lips bloody, and the expression looked demonic in a child's face. Then he turned around without releasing his grip.

At the last second, when Lindon realized what was about to happen, he slipped his free hand inside his outer robes and gripped the stack of spirit-seals. He didn't even have time for fear before he was launched into the air.

The elder hurled Lindon toward the fight.

As he tumbled forward, time came into absolute focus. Though the flight must have taken a second, it felt like minutes. The Remnant's six bladed limbs flashed, Yerin's sword wove a defensive tapestry, and around them stone was sliced to pieces.

With one clumsy effort, he flung the entire packet of spirit-seals into the Remnant's general direction. They would most likely be cut to pieces in midair, and even if they landed, they had a better chance of slapping harmlessly into the ground than touching the Remnant. He needed something else.

He could still feel his spirit's connection to the Thousand-Mile Cloud, so he poured madra into it desperately, clutching at anything that might save him. It would never reach him before he plunged into that deadly whirlwind, but he had to try.

When Yerin saw him, her eyes widened, then narrowed on the falling seals. She didn't hesitate. Her defensive stance collapsed, and blood instantly sprayed up from her body in five lines as she took the Remnant's attacks. Her sword gathered force like a heat haze, and as she sliced from bottom to top, a wave of colorless power tore out from her weapon. The madra struck the Remnant head-on, slashing a vertical gash in its pristine surface and knocking it back a few paces, into the falling seals. It shuddered as the scripted papers sank into its body, causing the Forged madra that made up its form to ripple like a slapped puddle.

The rest of Yerin's slash whipped through the open door of the Tomb, dragging a line of destruction across the tiles and blasting a man-sized tear in the interior wall. Stone crumbled away from the triangular hole the size of a doorway, and he caught a glimpse of the mountains behind the Tomb before his thoughts caught up.

They had won.

He fell anyway.

Instead of slamming into the edge of a sword or the ragged corner of torn stone, he fell into a red cloud hovering three feet above the ground. It caught him on the right side of his body, flipping him over, and yet again Lindon landed hard on his back. The impact to his skull sent stars shooting through darkness, and he was *sure* something in his pack must have broken this time.

But he lived.

The battle resumed overhead, blades of invisible force whistling as they sliced through the air over his face. Covered in blood, Yerin forced the Remnant back step by step. It was leaking silvery motes of essence now, and the battle slid steadily away from the door.

As it did, Lindon maintained his spirit's grip on the Thousand-Mile Cloud. Weakened or not, the Remnant's attacks were still enough to kill him, and he wanted to put as much space between them as he could. With one hand on the construct for support, he half-crawled, half-limped into the Ancestor's Tomb. There, he would be safe from the fight. There, he could think.

He'd just pulled his feet in past the doorway when a line of gold heat blasted after him, missing him by inches.

Part of his mind was still moving, taking stock of his options, but the rest of him was shivering terror. When Whitehall appeared in the doorway, a child in bloodstained white robes, Lindon whimpered.

The elder took a step inside, glancing from side to side as though checking to see what other trick Lindon had prepared. That sight was like dawn rising before Lindon's eyes.

Elder Whitehall, a Jade leader of the esteemed Heaven's Glory School, was wary of *him*.

Lindon straightened and rose to his feet, though he needed to lean on the Thousand-Mile Cloud to do so. Wind whistled between the open door and the gash in the side, whipping against his skin like ice, but he ostentatiously ignored Elder Whitehall and looked to the walls and ceiling as though checking on his traps.

The inside of the Ancestor's Tomb was vast and empty, set with as many pillars on the inside as there were on the outside, and the ceiling was covered in another mural of four beasts: a blue serpentine dragon on a thunderstorm, a crowned white tiger, a stone warrior with the shell of a tortoise, and a blazing red phoenix. In the back of the room was an ornate door, presumably leading to the actual *tomb*, because there were no bodies here. Or perhaps that was the entrance to the labyrinth Yerin had mentioned.

Whitehall brandished the halfsilver dagger in one hand. "I'm not a fool, never think that I am. I've caught on to you. You're no Unsouled."

Lindon focused on catching his breath, and tried not to betray himself.

"Unsouled don't have the madra to use a Thousand-Mile Cloud."

Without the ancestral orus fruit, he would never have been able to activate the cloud. Or the White Fox boundary. Now that he thought of it, that fruit had saved his life more than once.

"Unsouled don't win tournaments, not even among children."

Without the Empty Palm, he never would have.

"Unsouled don't beat Irons, with or without tricks."

Whitehall had actually *seen* the hornet Remnants defeat Amon. All Lindon had needed was the strength to open a scripted jar, and the elder had to know that.

The Jade in the boy's body toyed with the halfsilver dagger, studying him. "I believed you must have cheated to pass the Trial of Glorious Ascension, but now I understand. Anyone can put on a wooden badge. What are you really? Iron? You're not Copper, a Copper body would have died by now. And a Jade wouldn't throw away his pride."

"Apologies, elder," Lindon said respectfully. "This one is honored by the attention, but the elder surely has bigger problems than this humble disciple."

Whitehall nodded slowly. "I will soon. Dropping seals on a Remnant in midair while calling a cloud? Those are not the reflexes of a Copper."

This time, Lindon did allow himself a small smile. He was proud of that one.

"Whoever you are, you're traveling a fool's path." Then Whitehall did something that Lindon hadn't predicted: he flipped the halfsilver dagger around, offering Lindon the hilt. "Work with me."

CHAPTER TWENTY

"I have no grudge against you," Whitehall said, the expression on his face far colder than anything a child should have produced. "I don't even need the girl dead. I want the treasures of the Sword Sage, and nothing more. Here and now, with the heavens as my witness, I'll swear an oath on my soul to leave you both alive. Furthermore, I will take you as my personal disciple. Whatever you are, you're not a Jade yet, and in my care you will be." He held the dagger out in a steady hand, waiting for Lindon to take the hilt.

To win, all Lindon had to do was delay while Yerin harvested her master's Remnant. "Forgiveness, elder, but it seems as though..." He considered saying 'this one,' but it didn't seem like time for humble speech. "...I have no reason to accept. If the Remnant is sealed, and I mean no disrespect, but Yerin will destroy you."

"She's more powerful than any Jade in Sacred Valley," Whitehall said frankly. "But the battle has weakened her. I give myself even odds of defeating her, but whether I do or not, I hereby swear on my soul that I will first destroy your core. Unsouled or not, you will be truly crippled then."

Lindon shivered, though he covered it by adjusting his robe against the cold. Unsouled were considered cripples, but they could still use basic madra. With his core destroyed, it would be as though he truly had no spirit—he couldn't work with scripts or Remnants, and no elixir would save him. Some sacred artists spoke of losing their core as worse than death.

He still needed time.

"Yerin promised to take me beyond the valley," he said slowly. "I've been weak for too long, and I won't settle for the mediocre strength we have here."

Whitehall's eyes lit up, and his grip on the dagger tightened. *"Exactly right.* That is the heart a sacred artist should have." He waved his hand around them. "Even this place is built on foundations deeper than we've ever explored. Our elders stay Jade because they're too afraid to risk what they have and dig deeper. I am not."

From outside, there came a crash, and the sound of metal bent past breaking. Whitehall's expression hardened. "Choose now. Join me and rise, we'll leave together, or else I'll cripple you and take my chances against the Sword Disciple."

Lindon prided himself on thinking through his options. He had sworn an oath to Yerin, but he wasn't even Copper. Whatever oath the heavens extracted, it wouldn't destroy his core.

But though he remained at the Foundation stage, there was some iron in him that would not bend.

He was not a coward. He would not abandon Yerin to captivity. And, more than anything...

"This is my second life," Lindon said. He pushed off from the cloud, balancing on his own exhausted feet. Whitehall's eyebrows drew in, but Lindon didn't care to convince him. "It was a gift from the heavens, and I'd rather die than waste it." He shrugged. "At least I'll die trying."

He stood proudly before Whitehall, tired and weak, his empty hand bared. He had no cards left, no tricks left to play. There was a certain peace to it.

Whitehall's face twisted in disgust, and he tossed the stolen dagger to the floor. "Trash." That was all he said.

He covered the distance between them in a single step, his palm striking Lindon just below the navel.

And in the last instant, in that knife's edge of time during the elder's attack, Lindon remembered that he did have one more card after all.

The Heart of Twin Stars cycling technique had been preparing his core for months now, but he'd always stopped before that final step. Now, as Elder Whitehall injected his burning madra into Lindon's core, Lindon activated the technique.

He tore his core in half.

The agony was unspeakable, beyond physical, and his scream shook every corner of the Ancestor's Tomb. Whitehall's energy flooded into his body. The Empty Palm was only remarkable as a technique because it allowed a sacred artist to affect an enemy on the same level. A Jade did not need a technique to destroy the spirit of an Unsouled; he would simply overwhelm the weaker core with power and let it burst under pressure.

But if Lindon's core exploded, he didn't feel it. The agony of tearing it in two blanked everything, washing his world in white. He collapsed to the stone floor, and he welcomed the pain in his body.

When he came to, Whitehall had only taken one step to the door. The skin of Lindon's stomach was scorched where the palm had struck him, and his spirit cycled rapidly on its own, trying to rid itself of the foreign Heaven's Glory madra. His veins felt like they were on fire, but even that was a relief next to tearing apart his core.

And when he thought of the core...

His spiritual sense dipped down to the center of his spirit, where two dim balls of light floated inside him like blue-white stars. Weak, but whole and unharmed.

After only a blink of thought, he understood why: when the cores split, they had *moved*. Where once he had one in the center of his body, now he had one a half-inch to the left and one a half-inch to the right. Whitehall had missed. Heaven's Glory had entered his body, but it had only burned him. He wasn't a cripple. At least, no more than before.

He wasn't any stronger with two cores, of course, and in fact cycling would likely become twice as difficult in the future. But he had one crucial advantage: Whitehall wasn't watching.

And no matter how strong his Jade spirit made him, he was still in the body of an eight-year-old boy.

Summoning strength from the depth of his spirit, scrounging for every scrap of madra, Lindon rose to his feet and lunged. Before Whitehall could react, Lindon had wrapped both hands around a small waist.

Then he lifted Elder Whitehall into the air.

The elder screamed incoherently as Lindon staggered over to the wall. A shoe caught him in the nose with a crunch, sending blood streaming into his mouth. Lances of Heaven's Glory struck the painted ceiling, the pillars, the walls, but none reached Lindon. A flailing fist hit him in the side of the head, and the world around him spun. He limped forward, hoping he was going in the right direction.

When the floor fell out from under him, he knew that he'd chosen well.

They pitched out the hole in the side of the wall that Yerin had accidentally opened. Whitehall tumbled away from him, grasping at air with one hand as golden light shot from the other. His eyes met Lindon's, and he looked pitifully like a confused, terrified boy.

While Lindon couldn't deny some anxiety, he'd fallen too many times in the last few days. He'd learned to expect it. This time, he'd planned ahead.

He caught himself on the edge of a floating red cloud.

It had taken him the very last drop of strength to drag the Thousand-Mile Cloud along behind him, and when he hauled himself up to its surface, he collapsed in utter weakness. This time, finally, he had absolutely nothing left. No madra, no strength. Even his eyes were covered by tears, his nose and mouth filled with blood, his ears deafened by rushing wind. He drifted as if in a dream, feeling nothing but pain and gratitude for life.

Unguided by his spirit, the cloud drifted slowly toward the ground.

Hundreds of feet beneath him, Elder Whitehall's body hit the rocks. He swiped tears from his eyes for a better look, horrified that the elder might survive, but then a golden Remnant wrenched itself free of the boy's corpse. It was a twisted dwarf, a deformed imp drawn in shining yellow lines.

It would be poetic, Lindon reflected, *if I killed a Jade just to die at the hands of his Remnant.*

Not all Remnants were malicious, but Lindon had the suspicion that Whitehall's likely would be. It didn't drift away, but sat on its haunches like a frog, watching Lindon's cloud descend.

Here he was, with no options left, waiting to slowly slide into inevitable death. It was not how he had imagined dying, but he hoped the story would make it back to his family. They would be shocked at how far he'd made it.

A weight slammed into the Thousand-Mile Cloud, bringing a veil of darkness over Lindon's eyes, and then the same weight settled on him, pushing his pack into his bruised back. A choked gurgle escaped from his mouth as his breath was forced out under the pressure.

Yerin pulled her outer robe away from his eyes, leaning down to look at him upside-down. She looked...horrifying. He'd thought she looked halfway dead before, but with the fresh blood on her face, she looked as though she'd crawled out of her own grave.

"Don't fall," she said, and Lindon took her advice, hugging the cloud to his body.

Her madra filled the construct, and it lurched back into the air. It didn't seem to want to rise, but she forced it up, jumping it back to the cliff in a series of awkward jerks. Finally, it slid through the gap in the Tomb wall and they both spilled out onto solid ground.

"Gratitude," Lindon said between breaths.

She raised a hand in acknowledgement...and a steel limb lifted along with it. It looked exactly like one of the six blades on the back of the Sword Sage's Remnant, and now it dangled from Yerin's back like the single leg of a spider.

"Is that what Gold looks like?" he asked.

Yerin began to fumble around in her robes, searching pockets. "If my memory's true, master left me..." An instant later, her hand emerged with a badge of solid gold. In the center, there was a simple picture of a sword. She slipped the ribbon over her neck and held the badge, examining it.

He collapsed onto his back, wallowing in pleasant relief. He hadn't wasted his life yet. And now he had a Gold on his side.

"Do you trust me now?" he asked.

"More than none," she responded. She heaved herself into a seated position, and the new limb on her back bobbed with her. "Real test hasn't even arrived yet."

Lindon craned his neck, looking out the door, and he almost cried. Three other rusty clouds had come to a stop, carrying men and women in white robes. "Oh look," he said. "There it is now."

Yerin didn't seem to hear him. She was kneeling in the corner of the Tomb, next to something he hadn't noticed before: the body of a man in black robes. The stone around him was charred in a long, black line, and a sword lay bare beside him. Its blade seemed unnaturally white.

She bowed so deep that her forehead touched the ground. Three times she bowed, as the first man from Heaven's Glory ran through the door. His hands were glowing golden, and his Jade badge marked him as an Enforcer. Enraged eyes fell first on Lindon.

"Disciple, report!" he demanded.

Then Yerin rose from beside her master's body. She had left her own sword with him, and was sliding the white-bladed one into a sheath at her side. The silver blade on her back rose like a scorpion's tail, and she turned her scarred face toward the Heaven's Glory elder. A gold badge dangled from her neck.

The Jade scrambled backward so fast that it looked like someone had kicked him. He screamed for the others to stop, to back up, to surround the tomb.

Lindon had discovered that he could only stay tense and afraid for so long before his body just grew numb. Yerin could frighten Heaven's Glory away from the Tomb on her own, and if she couldn't, it wasn't as though he would be a great help.

So he was free to pursue an idle theory that had bothered him for some time.

From his pack, he withdrew the Starlotus bud. It was pale white with streaks of pink, the sort of pure color that he normally associated with Remnants, and its petals were curled into a half-bloom, as though it had frozen in the act of opening completely. It was a natural work of art.

He bit it in half.

It tasted like sweet grass with a slightly bitter undercurrent, but it dissolved like sugar on his tongue. He swallowed it in seconds, crossing his legs and straightening his back into a cycling position.

"They have to pull the tiger's tail, don't they?" Yerin said. "If they want their share sooner rather than later, I'll... what are you doing?"

The energy of the spirit-fruit—was it still a spirit-fruit if it was an edible flower? He assumed so—showed in his mind's eye as a bright pink-tinged white. It dispersed in his stomach, flowing around his spiritual veins in a river of lights that tickled as they traveled. When they had traveled around his body, they tried to enter his core.

Or rather, his cores.

When he had first read the Heart of Twin Stars, he'd theorized a few uses for the technique besides defense. He hadn't been able to test them without ripping his core in half, but now he had his chance.

While keeping one core tightly closed, he directed the

Starlotus madra into the other.

The right-hand core grew brighter, stronger, immediately nourished by the spirit-fruit. It had a small effect immediately, but many of the pale pink dots stayed in the core, tickling him from the inside out. They would be digested over the next days and weeks.

When he'd finished gathering the Starlotus energy into one core, he inspected the other. It was totally clear.

He emerged from cycling with a bright smile on his face. Yerin laughed at him. "You look like you just tore that elder apart with your teeth."

He rubbed at his front teeth, and his finger came back sticky with blood. He spat out a mouthful, but his enthusiasm was undimmed. "I took half the Starlotus."

A lance of gold shot through the door, and she dodged to one side, baring the white blade in her hand. "You thought *now* was the opportune moment to fuzz up your core?"

Lindon climbed onto the Thousand-Mile Cloud, beckoning her to join him. "We're not fighting, and I wanted to test a theory."

"If Heaven's Glory wants me to spill some more blood, I'm not telling them no." Yerin strode over to the open door, her master's pale blade to one side.

Even to Lindon's numb heart, some feeling returned. Panic. "We have to leave *now.* They won't follow us outside the valley." She wasn't listening to him, so he added, "What would your master say about throwing your life away here?"

She deflected another lance of light, but she didn't leave the Tomb. "He'd say if I killed one of them for each of my fingers, I could die proud."

Of course he would.

Lindon considered a number of approaches. His first instinct was to shout at her, reminding her of her oath. He considered begging, bargaining, even leaving her and taking his chances outside the valley.

Quietly, he said, "Please don't leave me to die."

She flinched visibly, even as a trio of Heaven's Glory enforcers came up the stairs, their hands shining gold. The grip on her sword shifted. She leaned forward, then back.

With a growl, Yerin swept her white blade across the doorway to the Tomb. The colorless sword energy hung in the air at neck-height, frozen in place even as she turned and ran toward him.

"You can go rot," she said, shoving him to the back of the cloud and hopping in front herself. "But bleed me if I'm leaving anybody. Not even you."

On their way out, Yerin sliced another pillar. The Ancestor's Tomb groaned, cracked, slowly crumbling under a lack of support. As they flew out the hole in the wall, the ceiling tilted and collapsed into a landslide of rubble, delaying Heaven's Glory.

And interring the Sword Sage forever in his killer's tomb.

They slid down the other side of Mount Samara on the Thousand-Mile Cloud, and as Yerin steered them down the slopes, Lindon kept his eyes on the scenery at the bottom. It was a rolling ocean of green, and every once in a while something stuck its head up over the treetops like a fish breaking the water's surface.

He drank in the sight, because it was one no one in the Wei clan had ever seen. This was the land beyond Sacred Valley.

"If you're through with the other half of that flower," Yerin called back, "I'll give it a home myself. It'll do anybody's spirit some good."

"Apologies, but I still need it. The other half only went to one of my cores."

"...you've got two short breaths to explain that before I push you off and let you roll down."

So Lindon explained the Heart of Twin Stars. It turned into something of a winding story, as he had to explain the orus spirit-fruit, his fight with the Mon family, the Empty Palm technique, and eventually the Seven-Year Festival.

"As soon as I found this manual, I had an idea. If I could separate two different types of madra into different cores, then maybe I could learn *two* Paths!"

"Two Paths," Yerin repeated. She didn't sound nearly as excited about it as he was. "That'll cost you twice the work. You're having enough trouble with one Path as it is, I wouldn't scrape yourself too thin trying for two."

"I'm sorry, you must have misunderstood. I'm not on a Path. They wouldn't teach me. I'd be open to learning a sword Path, if you had some extra time..."

She turned to him, her scarred face still streaked with blood. "This is why my master would have killed your clan elders."

"Because they didn't teach me a Path?"

"I'll feed it to you in small pieces. You saw me stick solid sword-madra in the doorway, true?"

"Right," he said. "Uh, true."

"What kind of a technique do you contend that is?"

"It's a Forger technique," he said.

"And when I throw madra out of my sword?"

"Striker."

"And when I call up aura from every sword in the room?"

That was a Ruler technique, and he saw where she was heading. "I know about all that. Some of the elders in my clan can use techniques outside their discipline."

She nodded along. "Since you know, then answer me this: if anybody can do anything, what does your spirit matter?"

"*Anybody* can't," he said. "Most people can only learn a technique if their spirit has an affinity for it."

"Is that true? That's a mind-bender for me, then, because Heart of Twin Stars sounds like a classic Enforcer technique."

He paused, because he wasn't sure. Enforcers could use their madra to make themselves stronger, and their techniques had to do with strengthening the body...but the core was part of the body.

"Here's another riddle for you. That Empty Palm you worked out? Looks to me like a Striker move."

"It only reaches a few inches."

"It's a rotten Striker move, then, but a runty cub is still a tiger. See, your test everyone in Sacred Valley loves? That bowl of liquid madra? It's a rotting trap of a test, and it's filled you all up with lies."

Lindon's breaths were coming more and more quickly until it felt like he couldn't breathe.

"That test doesn't show you what you *are.* It shows you what you're best at. Shows where you start, not where you end up. You start as a Forger, well cheers and celebration for you, that means you'll have to work extra hard as an Enforcer. Outside of the valley, you don't get to call yourself a sacred artist until you've at least learned the basics of all four disciplines *and* harvested a Remnant. To my eyes, every one of your elders is still in training."

"So then...how could I be..."

"Unsouled?" She shrugged. "Never heard that word before coming here. You just started two steps behind, that's the spine of it. Nothing worth crying about. Some of them polished families can take a squalling baby from Foundation to Jade in two and a half pills. It's practicing your Path that's hard, and it sounds to me like you're halfway through with yours."

For a long time, Lindon couldn't say a word. The truth blasted through him, leaving him numb. He didn't need to find a Path of his own.

He was already on it.

The wind pressed icy needles against eyes covered in

tears, and suddenly he was scrambling through the pack on his back, digging out the Heart of Twin Stars manual. It was only halfway complete; the rest of the pages were blank. While Yerin asked him what he was doing and if he was crying, he juggled the manual, a brush, and a jar of ink. Anyone who founded a Path was expected to take careful notes, to pass their knowledge on to future generations.

With careful hands, he wrote at the top of the page:

The Path of Twin Stars.

EPILOGUE

INFORMATION REQUESTED: CURRENT STATUS OF WEI SHI LINDON.

BEGINNING REPORT...

Wei Shi Lindon and Yerin, Disciple of the Sword Sage, leave Sacred Valley on the back of their constructed cloud. They plan to hide and rest before moving into the forest. Sacred beasts the size of buildings prowl in the shadows beneath the leaves, and even Yerin has no confidence in her power to protect them both. She knows that only if they are stealthy and quick will they survive, and then only if nothing goes wrong.

She is not aware that the Transcendent Ruin has risen in the heart of the forest, for the first time in eight hundred years. Its promise calls to sacred artists for thousands of kilometers around...and to the other, older, darker things that wait in the surrounding wilds.

DIVERGENCE DETECTED: THE DESOLATE WILDS, TRANSCENDENT RUIN. CONTINUE?

DIVERGENCE ACCEPTED, CONTINUING REPORT...

On the peak of Mount Samara, a crippled Heaven's Glory elder named Anses picks through the ruins of what he calls the Ancestor's Tomb. His pride is trampled, the power of his school has been questioned, and now it seems that they have created for themselves a powerful enemy. The Sword Sage's disciple will return, he knows, with greater force and with vengeance.

But despite his certainty, he has a deep-seated fear of the wilderness outside Sacred Valley. He could not survive it, and therefore he believes no one could. In his judgment, the Sage's disciple must have doubled back. Where will she go if not to the home of her ally, the Unsouled Wei Shi Lindon?

He crafts a message to his fellow elders, urging them to march with all their flagging strength on the Wei clan.

DIVERGENCE DETECTED: THE DESTRUCTION OF THE WEI CLAN. CONTINUE?

DIVERGENCE ACCEPTED, CONTINUING REPORT...

As the members of the Heaven's Glory School excavate their ancient tomb, a five-tailed snowfox the size of a man waits nearby. He is soundless, scentless, his presence masked to both sight and spirit. He is an ancient sacred beast, one of the original inhabitants of this valley, and he is only seen when he wishes to be.

He has followed the Unsouled Lindon since the intervention of Suriel, the Phoenix, Sixth Judge of the Abidan Court. Though he does not remember the events prior to her temporal reversion, he has noticed the effects of her involvement and believes that Lindon is favored by heaven. He watches the two young sacred artists leave the valley, and for the first time in centuries, he experiences hope. Maybe these children, blessed by the heavens, will save the valley from the Dreadgods' return.

DIVERGENCE DETECTED: return of the Dread-gods. Continue?

⬡

ITERATION 217: HARROW

[Divergence report denied,] Suriel's Presence said. [Report complete.]

The reports came to her in a mix of words, images, and impressions, retrieved by her Presence and transmitted to her in an instant. She'd looked into Lindon's past, his surroundings, his upbringing, even his future. He was an interesting distraction.

Her Presence told her he had a seventeen percent chance of surviving the Desolate Wilds, a four percent chance of making it past Gold, and a zero-point-three percent chance of ascending beyond Cradle.

But in every world, in all the thousands of variations on humanity the universe spun out, people always loved to bet on the underdog.

She would return to the reports later, but although they took virtually no time, they did take her attention. She needed to focus now, to treat the situation with the gravity it deserved.

Makiel was coming. And the First Judge of the Abidan Court demanded all of her concentration.

Her hair had been restored to its radiant emerald shine, her eyes to vivid purple. She drifted in high atmosphere, waiting, as fiery chunks flew out from the planet and past her into space.

This world was beyond healing.

A glimpse of rolling, textured blue, and someone stepped into reality. Not Makiel, as she had expected. This man was young and compact, with dark blue skin and rows of tightly packed horns instead of hair. Gadrael, Second Judge and Makiel's loyal right hand.

He was dressed as she was, in the seamless white armor of any Abidan on active duty. The Mantle of Gadrael streamed from his shoulders like a furiously burning cape of pure starfire, just as the Mantle of Suriel hung from her own. Instead of her correlation lines, which trailed from her fingers like ribbons of gray smoke and connected to the back of her neck, he carried a black circle strapped to his forearm like a medieval buckler.

He'd brought his weapon, primed and ready for use. She summoned her own, the meter-thick bar of blue, but he held up a hand. "Peace, under the Way."

She clipped the weapon to her waist without banishing it. He wouldn't violate a truce, but he'd been too quick to offer one. "Tell Makiel I haven't found him. My Presence can give him a full report."

"He knows. He's looking himself, since you remain unmotivated."

The barb didn't disturb her, but the content of his message did. She'd been sent to hunt for Ozriel because she was the only one of the Seven capable of finding him without being killed on sight. If she tracked him down, Ozriel would talk to her.

If Makiel found him, they would kill each other.

Gadrael waited for the reality to settle on her. "He thought that would convince you to search. If that wasn't enough..." he turned to the burning planet. "...this might be."

The planet beneath them fuzzed and flickered with visual static, even as it burned. Continents appeared in the ocean, vanished, appeared again. Water plumed kilometers in the air, calmed, shot up again. A city rose from the ocean in ruins, and then was drowned.

When one world crashed into another, this was the result. Time, space, and reality itself bent and warped while the Way tried to force order out of the collision's pure chaos.

"Which one is it?" Suriel asked quietly. She could have asked her Presence, but she wanted Gadrael to hear the question.

"Iteration two-sixteen, Limit. It was scheduled for demolition no later than two standard months ago, its adept population already evacuated."

But they had no one to remove it, with Ozriel gone, so now Limit had dragged Harrow with it into the void.

"Quarantine protocols?" she asked.

"Effective. I implemented the walls myself." So no other worlds would be drawn in to this disaster. "It only escalates from here. If we don't recover Ozriel, or at least the Scythe, we could lose it all."

He wasn't wrong. This was Sector Twenty-One, but if it was happening out here, it was potentially only days away anywhere. Sector Thirteen, where she was born. Sector Six, with its rich history and gorgeous natural art. Even Sector Eleven, with one-one-zero. Cradle.

Important worlds like Cradle, Haven, Sanctum, and Asylum would be protected. Even in the event of total system collapse, the Abidan would collect and quarantine these worlds, their last bastion against the infinite chaos.

But in times like this, anything could go wrong. Cradle might be safer than anywhere else, but it wasn't safe.

"Acknowledged," Suriel said. "Designation zero-zero-six, Suriel, formally accepts the charge to locate and withdraw zero-zero-eight, Ozriel, under censure."

Gadrael nodded, his expression firm as granite. It always was. The Way would crumble to dust before he smiled.

She accessed the Way, drawing flows of pure order around her as she prepared to exit Harrow, but the other Judge didn't follow. He stood on nothing with his arms crossed, black buckler facing the dying world.

"What is your mission here?" Suriel asked.

"Mercy," Gadrael said.

She stopped. The tendrils of layered blue returned to the Way. She had faced patients in the past that were too far gone, where the only comfort she could offer them was a painless end. She had gained her power, in a large part, so that she never had to face that again. Now even death was no barrier to her healing.

And it still wasn't enough.

"A shield is meant to protect," she said. "It's not an appropriate tool for this." She drew her weapon.

Gadrael nodded, his arms still crossed. She wondered if this had been Makiel's plan all along, to make her face the reality of the situation by dirtying her own hands. It wouldn't change anything either way. This was still her duty.

Heart aching, she activated her sword.

THE END
of Cradle: Volume One
Unsouled

LINDON'S STORY CONTINUES IN

SOULSMITH
CRADLE : VOLUME TWO

AND

BLACKFLAME
CRADLE : VOLUME THREE

WILL WIGHT lives in Florida, among the citrus fruits and slithering sea creatures. He's the author of the Amazon best-selling *Traveler's Gate Trilogy*, *The Elder Empire* (which cleverly offers twice the fun and twice the work), and his new series of
mythical martial arts magic: *Cradle*.

He graduated from the University of Central Florida in 2013, earning a Master's of Fine Arts in Creative Writing and a flute of dragon's bone. He is also, apparently, invisible to cameras.

He also claims that *www.WillWight.com* is the best source for book updates, new stories, fresh coriander, and miracle cures for all your aches and pains!

Printed in Great Britain
by Amazon

71298547R00169